Mayhem

ISBN 978-1-79487-717-7

90000

9 781794 877177

Prologue

Sam

I was on my way home from work when I met him, same road, same rain, same old, same old. There was a man sitting on the guardrail of a bridge. He didn't have a coat on and his scrawny frame was shivering in the wind. I considered driving past him. Whatever he's doing there was none of my business; it shouldn't be of my concern. I still couldn't leave him there. I pull onto the shoulder of the road and call to him.

"Why are you out in the rain?" *Great start, Sam. You know why he's here.*
"I have nowhere else to go." He says and glances at me. His eyes look so hollow.
"Well, then at least take this," I hand him my windbreaker, "What's your name?"
"Matthew Lin. Look, I appreciate what you're trying to do here, but I would like to remind you that this isn't your problem. Hell, I don't know a thing about you. If I want to do this, I will. Just leave me alone." His voice is nearly gone, cracked and desperate.
"My name is Sam O'Henry. I'm an accountant. My sister, Krista, is a world-class chef. She makes bank off of *my recipes.* I don't care who went to culinary school, half of the papers in her restaurant are in my handwriting. Now that you know a little bit about me, can I give you a ride somewhere?"
"Fine," Matthew stands and walks towards me, shaking, "I'm tired, I'm cold, I'm soaked to the bone, and I still want to jump. But you win."
"How exactly did I win? If that's how you feel?"
"You won because I'm not going to do it. I just want to go *home*," He sniffs, "But it's not exactly like I have one."

He starts crying, shielding his face from me. Honest, burning tears start to mix with the rain. His broken sobs and pleading eyes make me very glad I decided to pull over. *I'm going to help him, I didn't come this far to give up now.*

"You can stay at my apartment for a while, as long as you need."

Chapter One

Sam

It's been five months since we first met. Matthew is healing. He didn't want to tell me what had happened to him, he said he "shouldn't have let it get to him." When he started talking, the floodgates opened. He told me everything. That night on the bridge, he had escaped an abusive... I don't think I can bring myself to call that scum his ex-boyfriend. His name is Nick Garcia. Things had apparently started really well between him and Matt. Matthew fell in love with the sweetened persona Nick showed. But he was manipulative, until love became fear and *I never want to leave you,* became *I'm terrified to leave.*

"Sam? I think I broke the T.V."

We're roommates. How Mattie puts up with me I can't comprehend, but I'm not about to complain.

"What did you-?"
"I don't know! I'm telling you, I'm cursed. Technology hates me."
"You are not 'cursed.' Just... *challenged* by anything with wires."
"Shut up and fix it..." He pouts and flops onto the couch.

I set about solving the mystery of the cable box while Matthew sings to himself in the background. He's an incredible musician and the lead singer of a band called Mayhem. It's still underground, especially since the lead guitarist got married and had kids. He's quote unquote "no fun." The band has a gig at *The Rusty Moose.* They've been performing again lately despite having only three members. I don't know how they do it, but *damn* they do it well.

"Fixed it!"
"How did you fix it so fast?"
"It just needed to be plugged into the wall outlet. You know, so it has electricity?"
"No need to rub it in. Gadgets are not my forte." He pauses, looking slightly horrified. "I mean, I just said the word 'gadget,' all I need is a cane and some meddling kids to yell at for being on my property. I feel old."
"You are 24. You are not allowed to feel old until you are 30. Understood?"
"Yes, Sir!" He mock-salutes and looks through a stack of DVDs. "Kids' movie or something with actual plot?"
"It's Friday, I'm tired, let's just watch some mind numbing nostalgia."
"Fine by me."

---

3 hours and many tissue boxes later, ("The Fox and the Hound" is sad as shit!) Matthew is barely able to keep his eyes open. He yawns before tipping over and crashing onto my chest. *What do I do now?* He sighs contentedly and relaxes in my arms. *So he's just going to stay here?* Eventually, my eyes grow tired, but even then

it's tough to fall asleep. *They say find something you love and let it kill you. Matthew Lin, you will be the death of me.*

I wake with a jolt. Matthew is still leaning on me, but he has his head in his hands.

"I'm right here. You're okay, you're safe. It was just a dream, it wasn't real. He can't hurt you."
"Sam... you haven't been able to do anything since I moved in," He takes a shaky breath, "Your friend, Jackson, has been begging you to go clubbing with him, not to mention that your girlfriend dumped you because of me."

I open my mouth to protest, but he cuts me off.

"Don't even try to argue with me, Sammy. She said it's 'him or me,' and now she's gone. Please, Sam, do something for yourself once in awhile."

I stare at him, dumbfounded. Mattie just woke up from a night terror that haunts and jeers him, why is he thinking about me?

"I guess I feel like a burden. You're probably a little too nice, Sam. You do everything for everyone other than yourself."
"Matthew James Lin. For the thousandth time, you are not a burden. I want you here, Mattie. I want you to be happy, to be loved. You deserve to be loved, Mattie. What Nick did to you was despicable. You are a human being. I want you to live, not just survive."

Matthew nods, already mostly asleep.

"G'night, Mattie-Bird. Sweet dreams."

I wake the next morning with Matthew clinging to my shirt collar. My arms are around him, and I smile. He's *adorable.* He's got a few freckles on his nose, his lips in a near constant pout, and he looks calm. Mattie starts to stir, blinking as if he's trying to throw the sleep from his eyes.

"Morning, Mattie. How'd you sleep?"
"Better than usual. What about you, Sammy?"
"I slept well, I guess. You want to eat breakfast yet?"
"No. You're warm and I don't wanna get up."
"Okay, Mattie-Bird. Go back to sleep if you want."

He hums in response and presses his face into my shoulder. I don't know if I'm enjoying this too much or not enough. It's like I'm being torn in half. A part of me is screaming every time he calls me "Sammy." It's just a nickname, there's nothing else there. Nothing to analyze. That does not stop my mind from playing through every situation where it *could* mean something. My mind just loves clinging to false hope, and then being inevitably heart broken. There's probably some twisted, masochistic tendency locked up in there. *And that's where it will stay.* I still can't control my racing heart when Matthew even just looks at me.

I wish it wasn't so easy to fall in love.

A little while later Matthew opens his eyes and looks at me. Without a word he stands up and walks towards the kitchen. He turns when he reaches the doorway.

"We agreed to have breakfast later. Make waffles or we're both going to be forced to eat the leftovers of the barbecue pizza." He says flatly.
"We still have that?"
"Yep. Why wouldn't we?"
"Because you should have maliciously burned it with the yard waste!"
"Well, we still have some lawn clippings-"
"I'll get the lighter fluid."
"Not until after we have waffles, right?"
"I suppose."
"Please?" He whines and puts on those big puppy dog eyes I just can't resist.
"Fine. I'll make you waffles."
"Yes!"
I grin. "Was the fist pump really necessary?"
"Would you rather I'd ripped my shirt off and swing it over my head like a frat boy at a bowl game?"

Matthew puts down the waffle recipe and smirks and me. He looks me in the eyes over the tops of his wire-framed glasses.

"Well?"
"'Well' what?"
"Would the frat-style celebration have been more appropriate?"
"Appropriate? No. Amusing? Yes."
"I don't know, Sammy. Waffles are a pretty big deal." And he *winked.*

Is this flirting or you just being you?

"I suppose so..." My vocal chords crumble under my overarching awkwardness.

"Well, then I 'suppose' you should make some waffles." He does the most dramatic air quotes I have ever seen on the word "suppose."

I start in on the waffle batter and Matthew retreats to the couch.

"You seem to be in an awfully good mood today."

"Yeah, guess so."

Mattie's smirking at his phone by the time I bring out the waffles.

"Tumblr?"

"Not this time. The official Mayhem Twitter seems to indicate that we might have a decent crowd at the *Moose* tonight."

"What about lead guitar? That's kind of important, Mattie."

"Well..." He's using the *I-need-a-favor-and-please-help-me-this-is-important* tone. "You play guitar, and you've helped me practice for stuff before so if you don't mind...?"

"You want *me* to play lead *right* when you're doing well?"

"Yeah, that sounds about right."

Matthew pouts and whines and I, being a doormat, agree to play the gig.

"When do I have to be ready?"

"Chris will swing by and 6:30 tonight to get us. He's got the van because he plays the drums, and biggest instruments are hardest to load."

"So this really is tonight?" A bit of panic seeps into my voice.

"Yup! I'll get you the tab for the solos!"

"Sounds great." I hitch a smile in place and begin to self-destruct.

What did I just get myself into?

It's song after song, riff after riff, note after note, for hours. Matthew heads out for a bit and comes back bearing sandwiches from the deli down the street. Ten minutes to eat, then right back to work.

At around 4:30, Matthew starts tearing up the apartment looking for "stage-worthy" apparel. Nice, but not fancy, not flashy, and *absolutely no fringe.* Chris is knocking at the door by the time I'm wearing anything other than pajamas.

"Good evening, ladies and gents. Lovely to see you here tonight..."

Matthew is schmoozing the crowd, smiling sweetly, but the smudged black eyeliner and gaudy stance make him look less boy band and more... *something.*

He's hot as hell.

I walk stiffly onto the small stage. The bar is packed, there's some chatter here and there, but most people are quiet.

"Ahem…" Matthew speaks into the mic this time, and all remaining conversations cease. "Okay, lovelies, you may have noticed our new lead. His name is Sam O'Henry, we're roommates-"

A few hollers come up from the crowd.

"Yeah, yeah… I'm allowed a personal life." He's blushing and looking all-too-smug. "Hit it, Sammy!"

The night goes great. News cameras from all over Chicago start pouring in, and Matthew still seems right at home on that stage. The last chord rings out and he wanders off to talk to some reporters.

He's a new breed of confident.

Ricky

"Dude! My bro Mattie's on the news!"
"We talked about this, Ricky. Do not call me 'dude' within fifteen minutes of having your tongue in my mouth. We've been married for *two years.*"

What a romantic…

"I know, I know! But Timmy…" I've nearly perfected a whine that is both annoying and cute.
"Who's on the news?" He walks over to the couch and flops back.
"Matthew, my best friend since we were kids, my adopted brother?"
"I know who Matthew is. Why is he on the news?"

"He's been lead of that old punk band 'Mayhem' since high school. I guess he finally caught a break, and maybe a recording contract."

"Call him. He's probably waiting by the phone for his big-shot older brother to give him some tips." Timmy gives a cheeky grin and heads into the kitchen. "I bought a ton of potatoes for some reason... There will be potatoes in every meal for like 3 weeks."

"Okay? Why are you telling me this now?"

"Just as a warning. I can almost guarantee you'll be sick of potatoes by the end of this."

"Why do we even have 3 weeks worth of potatoes?" I am mildly concerned.

"Typo in an online order. I typed '30' pounds instead of '3.'"

"Yay..."

"I don't need your sarcasm, thank you very much!"

I laugh and turn back to the T.V., where Matt's laughing in an interview, and one of the guitarists looks petrified in the background. He must be new.

"Hey, Matt, my man! You're on the news, bro."

"I know. I'm super excited, man." I can hear his smile through the phone. "I don't think Sam's too happy, though. Poor thing's been in the shower for like an hour. I should probably make sure he didn't have a heart attack and then drown."

"That would totally suck. Wait, was he the guitarist?"

"Yeah! He did great, don't you think? Especially on such short notice..."

"Eh, he was okay." *Yeah, I'm lying. He was great. What does it matter to you, anyway?*

"We've known each other since we were in diapers, Ricky. I can tell when you're lying. Now tell me! What did you think?"

"Y'all did amazing, even your new guitarist. By the way, he was totally checking you out."

"Ricky! He was not!"

"So naive. He was looking at you like he wanted to wine and dine you and then take you home and fuck your brains out."

"*Ricky Black Kenfeld.* This is your last warning to *shut up* or, so help me God, I will drive to your house just to punch you in the dick."

"Alright, jeez! But you never shut up about him, Mattie. Have you taken a bit of a liking to your roommate?"

"Ricky, you assjerk! Maybe I have, it's not like I'm going to make a move on him. He probably has no *feelings* feelings for me."

"You have got to be kidding me! He had a Mayhem poster! Before you even moved in!"

"And he hid it in the closet."

"With the rest of his feelings, Matthew!"

He huffs a sigh. "Sam's just a fan, Ricky."

You oblivious bastard. "He looks at you like you're heaven on earth. He's smitten with you."

"If you're thinking of *that* conversation, we were drunk and talking about Metallica."

"You could've been drinking strawberry goat's milk and talking about the stock market. I *guarantee* he still would've been clinging to your every word."

Another sigh, this time directly into the mic on his phone. I have to lean away as not to shudder in disgust.

"You know I hate that. I can almost feel you breathing on me. It's gross."

"That's why I do it, Ricky."

"Ass."

"Oh, c'mon. You love me."

"True, but you're still an ass."

Matt laughs like I haven't heard in years. "You crack me up, Ricky."
"I do my best. Have a nice night, Mattie."
"You too, Ricky."

I hang up. Matt sounded so happy. I haven't heard him talk like that in years. He was always such a ball of sunshine, like the golden retriever of people. That happiness faded and went out right in front of me. Matt always forced a grin when I asked how things were. *"That looks like a nasty bruise, Matt." "Oh, ha, it's nothing."*

It wasn't nothing. It was Nick, and there were so many signs. A million reasons to be concerned and I did nothing. What kind of brother am I?

Matthew

"Sam!" My voice is panicked, despite the great news I'm intending to give.
"What? Is everything okay?" Sam nearly breaks his ankle running into the room.
"We just got a recording contract. So, uh, everything is glorious."
"Wow. Just... 'we?' You're the one who earned this, Mattie."
"But you'll stick around, right? Like, stay in the band?" *This could be so, so bad. If he doesn't want to stay, we don't have a band. I don't have anything.*
"Of course! Wouldn't trade this for the world, Matt." He grins that wide, dazzling smile, the kind that lights up his eyes. Sam's lovely when he smiles.

Maybe I have "taken a liking" to him.

"Hey. Earth to Matthew. Hello?"

"Sorry, spaced out." *Liar liar pants on fire.* "What'd you say?"

"I didn't say anything. You were staring at me, though."

"Really?" *I know I was.*

"Yup. Is there something on my face?"

"No, I was just, uh, trying to figure out what color your eyes are." *And thinking that you would look great in old school punk eyeliner, from the era where everybody wore black collared shirts with red ties and-*

"Birdie? Are you feeling okay? You're really spacey. Do you have a fever?"

"I'm fine, Sammy. I guess I'm still in shock about the whole fame thing."

"Okay. You should relax, Mattie-Bird, watch a movie, eat cake, just celebrate a little."

A tiny, tender smile crosses my face briefly. "Sure thing, Sammy."

I walk into the living room, not quite sure of my steps. Sam's a sweetie, albeit a tad shy. He's also someone I can't afford to lose. I guess I'm stuck with pathetic pining and sidelong glances for a while.

"Hey, Mattie?" Sam has to shout to be heard, so he's probably in the kitchen. *Is that the human equivalent of echolocation? Figuring out where somebody is by how loud they are and how far away they sound?*

"Yeah?"

"I was serious about the cake. I mean, I was serious about everything, relax and celebrate and all that jazz but you know I bake when I'm stressed and you took a 5 hour nap so things got a little out of hand."

I pry myself off the couch and plod into the kitchen. I'm greeted with a bashful Sam and about 2 dozen different pastry products.

"Why." It's not a question, it's an accusation.

"Because I thought you'd wake up sooner than 6 p.m.!" Sam drags a hand down his face. "Also, 5 hours is not a nap, that's a full 30 winks, at least!"

"Did you just-"

"I did! I did just say '30 winks' because if a full night's sleep is 40 winks, you got at least 30. So. Not a nap."

"Alright, Sam. Maybe *you* need to 'relax and celebrate.' Have your cake and eat it too, literally."

"Fine. Only if you help me eat some of this, though. I can only pawn off so much food to that little old lady down that hall who adopted us as her grandkids. She thinks we're married, by the way."

"Rosa thinks we're *married?*" I sputter.

"Yeah. She seemed so pleased about it too. She was all, 'how are you and your husband?' And I just didn't want to break her poor old heart."

"That explains the toaster oven that says 'congratulations!'"

"No, that was Jackson. He's a total doofus, I have no idea why I'm friends with him. 'You're famous, here's a toaster!' He doesn't make any sense."

"But about the Rosa situation. She really thinks we're married?"

"Yes! Is that an issue? I mean, she's an old lady who uses us as pseudo-grandkids, do you think she could cause any harm?"

"No, but I'm just confused as to why she thinks we're married."

"I don't know! I guess I usually sling an arm around you and you're just a touchy-feely type person so I guess she thought-? I don't know, maybe she just thought we'd be cute together or something!"

"What?" I didn't even know my voice could go that high, "Do we really act that much like a couple?"

"Probably. It's not a bad thing, though. I'm pleasantly surprised anyone would think I have half a chance with you."

You've got a good chance with me!

Some kind of strangled groan of exasperation finds its way out of me. I snatch an eclair and chomp down on it.

"Hey now, you can't do your 'I'm flustered so I'm going to eat pastries until I collapse' thing with the eclairs! I only made 6!"

I shamefully lower my hand that had been reaching toward the tray.

"The rest are fair game. C'mere, Birdie, you wanna watch that show with all the suitors and the girl and-"

"*The Bachelorette* is on? Why didn't you tell me! I'll get snacks, you get the T.V. turned on!"

"Is this your guilty pleasure show?"

"It's better than yours, Mr. Jersey-Shore-At-Two-AM!"

"Shut up..."

Smirking, I venture back to the kitchen and load up with all the sweets I can carry. Sam is curled up on the couch when I return. He smiles broadly and pats the cushion next to him.

"Hey Birdie. This show is total bull, but it's so cringy it's actually pretty good."

"Told you."

An hour of petty drama later, I've somehow migrated onto Sam's shoulder. He's warm and comforting and that's nice, especially after plowing through an ungodly amount of sugar.

"You do realize I'm trying to *lose* weight, not gain 30 pounds because of this, right?"
"You're dieting? Why? You only get one life, Mattie, eat as many cookies as you want."
"Alright, that *is* hard to argue with, but I'm kinda fat, Sam."
"Yeah, so? You're fine health-wise, right? You're just a little fluffy, no problem."
"More than a little, Sammy."
"That's *fine*, Mattie-Bird. You worry too much. Just relax and here," Sam rustles around in his pocket, pulling out his phone. "Watch this video of a duckling cuddling an old dog. Smiles guaranteed."
"You're a dork."
"You're smiling."
"Of course I am. It's an adorable video."

Of course I am. It's you.

Sam

Matthew is snuffling and sighing in his sleep. He leans into my chest, his arms slung over my shoulders. We end up sleeping like this a lot. Mattie hates being alone, he needs company. He told me that it makes him feel safe. He said he's terrified of getting close but needs somebody to help him out. He's hurting after all Nick did. I'm nearly asleep myself, Matthew snoring in my arms. I start to doze off and my final thought before I drift into dreams is *I love you, Birdie.*

I dream and I dream and I dream. I dream of being able to hold Matthew, cuddle him, call him mine. I know I'm in way too deep. I'm so soft for this guy. He's a sweetheart, a lover, he's funny, witty, and snarky. And he's so cute! He's warm, cuddly, absolutely precious. It hurts my poor, pining heart when Mattie talks down on himself, calling himself fat, saying he needs to change. He's chubby, and not in the way the tabloids say anyone without washboard abs is "fat." Mattie's actually, real-world chubby and it's not a problem. It's actually quite charming. He's softer around the middle, plushy hips with stretch marks that show when his t-shirt rides up. He's a real person. I like Mattie how he is now, as compared to when I first met him. He was tiny and thin and frail, hadn't had real food in weeks. He was quite literally starved. I'm relieved he filled out. Better to be a little heavy but healthy and happy than stick thin and sickly. I love this man to death, but all the reassurance in the world won't change his perception of himself.

I wake early the next morning, Matthew's arms firmly around my shoulders. I start to push him off and get up. Mattie makes a small, discontented whimper and clings closer to me. Sighing, I sit back down and turn on the TV. There's never anything good to watch on at 7 a.m. on a Thursday. I guess *The Notebook* will have to do. I'll finally know what all the hype is about, at least.

I'm crying into my hands when Mattie wakes up.

"Sammy? Are you alright?"
"Stupid movie made me cry…" I try to sound tough, but little hiccupping sobs ruin it.

"You're watching *The Notebook?* Really? And crying? Cute."
"No, not cute! Puppies are cute! I am strong and resilient."
"No, you're cute, plain and simple. You're blushing up to your ears 'cuz I called you cute."

I just grumble at him.

"My sweet little Sammy, crying over a movie. Deny it all you want, pretty boy, but you're adorable." His tone is teasing, but fond.
"Fine, I'm cute. Why don't you get up and we go to that pancake hut?"
"Yes! I'll, like, brush my teeth and stuff. Let's celebrate your new job, huh?"
"Not a boring accountant anymore."

Matthew grins and trots off to the bathroom. "One of my old high school friends works at the pancake place, so be prepared for an onslaught of questions." He yells.

Oh boy.

Matthew

We end up having to call an Uber to get to the restaurant. Sam's ancient Honda wasn't having it this morning. The Uber driver isn't the worst I've had, but not the best. She smiles and unlocks the doors, a nice, normal thing to do. What isn't nice *or* normal is how she bats her lashes at Sam and giggles at literally nothing. It's weird! *Teehee, you're a cutie, let me flip my hair and flutter my eyes at you.* On some level, I know I'm jealous in a weird *only I can pine over him* kind of way. It's sad, really.

"Oh, Sam…" She swoons.

"Yeah, Jess. I'm cool now."

Hold on, *they know each other?*

"You are *so cool.*"

"Mhmm. All thanks to Mattie-Bird, here."

"No more beige suits for you, Sammy." *Smooth, Matt. Real smooth.*

Sam's nose wrinkles adorably as he laughs. "The beige was pretty off-putting, wasn't it?"

"It was awful, Sam," I snicker, "You're lucky to have me as your own personal fashion police."

"Where would I be without you?"

"You'd be an accountant."

"It was a rhetorical question, Matthew!"

The car is quiet for a minute before the girl, Jess, asks Sam something.

"How have you been since the breakup, Sam? I'm sorry I made you pick between your community service project and me. I'm sure he was great."

"I've been amazing, actually. I got a new job, with a much better dress code, I've been baking again, movies on the couch… it's pretty fantastic."

"I'm not a 'project!' I pay half the rent and I'm the one who got him that new job!"

"So I've been thinking," Jess ignores me entirely, "Maybe we could get back together?"

"No, are you kidding? You called Birdie a 'project,' which is just such a *you* thing to do, by the way, and dating you was exhausting. I had to answer the phone by the second ring or you'd get mad.

You were controlling and I don't really want to go back to that!"
Sam sits back and sighs at the end of his little rant.

The rest of the ride is uncomfortably quiet. When we finally get
out of the car, Sam turns and apologizes.

"No."
"What do you mean 'no?' It was an apology, not a question."
"You were fine. You stood your ground, didn't let her push you
around. You even stayed calm through the whole thing! I'm fucking
proud of you, not mad."

Sam smiles sweetly at me.

"Let's get pancakes and meet that friend of yours."

The scent of pancakes and honey hits me like a wall the moment I
open the door to the diner. I walk in, Sam trying to hide behind me.
It's not working out so well for him.

"If you're trying to hide, you might want to crouch. I'm shorter and
fatter than you."

Sam whips around to stand in front of me.

"Don't fight me on this, pretty boy. It's a *fact*, not an insult."
"Mattie!" I'm suddenly tackle-hugged by none other than-
"Lindsey! Still running the family business, I see!"
"Yup! Oh my God, Matt, it's been too long! How have you been? I
saw you on the news. Who's hiding behind you? Are you on a date?
Booth or table?"
"Wow, okay. That was a lot. I've been good. You remember
'Mayhem,' right? Yeah, that's why I was on the news. This is Sam," I

grab Sam's hoodie sleeve and yank him forward, "And we're not on a date. Booth, please."

"Not yet, you're not." Lindsey winks and snatches two menus.

"You weren't kidding about the questions." Sam whispers. I chuckle.

"What's so funny?" Lindsey points to a booth and we sit. "The whispering, giggling, I can see it from a mile away. You're smitten with each other."

Sam's phone rings before she can go on.

"Hey, Krista." He turns to me and makes a face like he smelled moldy cheese. "I'm kind of busy. What? No! Why would you- well yes, he's here but- it's not even close to-! Krista!"

Right on cue, Ricky texts about Sam's car. He'd gone over to check it out and it's apparently pretty bad.

"Why'd you call, dude? Didn't the text make sense?"

"No, Ricky. Not everyone is as well-versed in car speak as you."

"It's really super dead, dude. Like, just get a new one."

"Really?"

"Yup. So how's smatt doing?"

"What in the living hell is 'smatt?'"

"It's your ship name! Sam and Matt. Smatt."

"Okay, but why?"

"It's an internet thing. When word got out that Timmy and I were together, some fucking *genius* came up with 'tricky!' Isn't it great?" For claiming to be such a tough guy, Ricky sure does squeal a lot.

"Sure, Rick. It's great."

"Don't be all passive-aggressive monotone at me..."

"Okay, back to the car. We really just need to get a new one?"

"It'd be more expensive to fix the old one than to buy a nice little V6."
"Alright, I'll tell Sam."
"Good luck!"

Why would I need luck? Why does it scare me that I might need luck?

We order food, and I figure when he's munching on French toast is as good a time as any to break the news.

"Sam."
He looks up, wide-eyed with syrup on his nose. I didn't know that was even possible.
"Your car isn't able to be fixed. Ricky said it'd be cheaper to buy a new one."
"That was my first car," He pouts, "I had been saving up since I was 12. I was 18 when I finally had the money. It lasted me 7 years. I'm gonna miss that hunk of junk."
"Hey, I know. I'd miss it too. Sammy, are you crying?"
Sam fervently shakes his head, but his shoulders sag out his usual perfect posture. He sighs and nods once. I stand and gesture for him to scoot over. He does and I sit gingerly next to him. Sam leans over until we're touching from thigh to shoulder. I wrap an arm around him, pulling him close. I desperately want to be closer still, tell Sammy that it's okay to cry, kiss him and hug him until everything's alright.

But I don't. It's not the right time. I can almost feel Lindsey's eyes burning a hole into my back, urging me to do *something,* but I don't. She's never been the friend I go to for good advice. I just sit still and let time pass. I'll know if there's ever a time to start moving.

Sam

I cried over my car. Pathetic, right? Matthew is wrapped around my shoulder, nevertheless. It's like he doesn't mind the way I'm mourning my car like a love lost. He's tracing the back of my hand with his thumb, pressed up against me.

"You're gonna be okay, Sammy. I know that you cared about your steel horse. You saved up for so long, pretty boy. Now we have all that money coming in, just waiting for the album to come out in a week. Then we get paid and you can get a nice car. A fancy-schmancy caddy, or something."

I sniff and pull Mattie closer, smushing my face into his hair. He holds me tight in one of those sweet, warm hugs. Mattie is precious. The only real way to describe him is *soft*. He's wearing an AC/DC shirt that's a little too big and almost see-through from use. I think it might be *my hoodie* wrapped around him, he's nearly in my lap and I'm starting to wonder what the real odds of spontaneous combustion are. If anyone is ever going to just burst into flames, it's going to be me, right here, right now. My face is already feels like it's on fire.

"Let's go home, Sammy," I glance down at Matt to see his eyebrows knit together, looking at me worriedly, "I'll get another Uber. Hopefully not your ex this time, although it was fun to watch you get a little mad at her. You're even cuter when you try to be all protective."

Matthew smiles and stands up. "C'mon, pretty boy. Let's get you home."

Matthew

A car pulls up outside the diner. The driver waves our way and I open the door for Sam. I slide in next to him and curl up against his side. A sandpaper voice grits its way into the backseat.

"Where to?" *This cannot be happening. I'm trapped in a car with him.*
Sam gives him our address and the driver laughs.
"What are two guys like you doing *here?* You're from the 'good Chicago,' the one on billboards. Hey, do I know you?"

Nick glances at me in the rear view mirror.

"I think I do," He snarls, "Moved on so soon, Lin?" I can hear his sneer, nearly feel his hands on me. My throat is closing.
"And who are you?" Sam pulls me in a little closer.
"Yes, where are my manners? I'm Nick Garcia. Matthew and I are well acquainted, right Lin?"
"We were." My voice is weak. Sam's got an arm around me, but my head is swimming too much to know if he's being protective or just feeling handsy. It's nice either way.
"I'm sorry, we '*were?'* Oh, Lin, we never really broke up, did we?" Nick's voice drops lower still until he's almost growling.
"No, but-"
"But you thought running away with *him* would make you happy. Isn't that right?"
"I ran away by myself! Sam found me right before I was going to jump off a bridge. I was miserable with you. Anything would've been better than one more day with you. You're a monster."

Nick is silent. *Nick is never, ever silent.* He grumbles something under his breath. There's only six blocks until we're back at Sam's - our- apartment.

"I'm not a monster, Matthew," *Only six blocks,* "I always wanted the best for you. I *loved* you." His words would be sweet if they came from anyone else's lips but they're so tainted, so *sick.* Nick never loved me, he said that he did, he said it all the time. He never meant it. Not once. My ears are ringing and my cheeks are wet but I can't stop it. Sam is tugging me out of the car, hauling me into the elevator. I bury my face in Sam's shoulder. *Why can't I stop shaking?* My breathing is labored and my legs give out under me. I crash into Sam as we're leaving the elevator.

"Easy, Birdie," *He's marvelous. Too kind, sweet,* "We're almost home. I got you, whatever you need."
"Can you carry me? I think I'm gonna pass out."

Sam nods and scoops me up bridal style. "Everything's gonna be okay, Mattie-Bird. I promise, no matter what else happens, I'll even watch that idiotic movie you wanted to see. Things will go back to normal, Mattie, just you wait." Sam stops outside our door, just staring at it.
"Sammy, you dingus, open the door."
"Yes, let me just grow a third hand and I'll be right on that."

I laugh, embarrassed, and hop down to the floor. Sam opens the door and gravitates to couch. He pats the cushion next to him and I sit, slumping into chest.

"Hey, Sam? Do you think I'll ever actually, like, heal?"

"Of course you will, Birdie. You are the greatest, strongest, toughest person I have ever met. I mean it. You can do anything, you could change the world with your hands tied." Sam says each word like it's the easiest thing he's ever done, like he really, truly believes what he's saying. I believe him, he's too good to lie.

"Thanks, angel."

Sam hums a nonsense tune and pulls me in close. He's been really touchy-feely today, not that I'm complaining. It's just odd.

"You're awfully cuddly today, Sammy."
"Do you want me to stop? Sorry, jeez, I feel like such an ass-"
"It's fine, Sam," I laugh, "You are really just too sweet. It's nice, actually. I love it when you're snuggly and handsy with me." I flush, face heating up at the candor of that last bit.
"Alright, Birdie," Sam yawns and stretches languidly, "Let's watch that movie."

I pull up Netflix and scroll until I find the movie that Sam thinks is *so dumb* even though he's *never seen it.*

"I don't understand your infatuation with this. I mean, nobody's house can just float away on a bunch of balloons! It's simple physics!"
"Shush. That's not the point, it's the friends to lovers growing old, and running out of time. It's about cracking through the rough exterior of an old man to find youth. Just watch."
"It's a one word title, too. Not even 3 letters."
"Hush! It's starting."
I don't have to look behind me to know Sam is rolling his eyes.

"How is this a kid's movie?" Sam sniffles, "It's so sad!"

"I know. I told you that you'd like it, Mr. Notebook."
"Oh, shut up!" Sam lets out an indignant, wet sob.

The movie drones on, there are talking dogs, squirrels, a mama bird named Kevin, and a happy ending. Sam folds his arms in front of my chest once the credits start rolling. *Why can't you put your hands literally anywhere else? Alright, not anywhere, but I'm sure Sam can feel my heart start pounding on my ribs like it's trying to escape.*

"I'm gonna fall asleep here, Mattie-Bird."
"Okay. Your point?" I take pride in my vocal steadiness.
"It's kinda rude to anchor you to the couch."
"I'm not really anchored-"
"Oh, yes you are! I used to share beds a lot because of swimming and according to my sister, I was the cuddler. I used to latch onto people with my lanky eighth-grader limbs and not let go. I'm like a venus flytrap. There's no escape."

That is the most adorable thing I've ever heard in my *entire life* and I was Ricky's go-to for "cutesy calls" where all he said was "oh my God, Mattie, he's precious" and squealed incoherently.

"You're a dork." *You're so pure I can't handle this.*
"I'm a sleepy dork," Sam yawns through his words, "So this is your last chance to get up."
"I think I'll make it a co-op nap, if you don't mind."

Sam hums and leans back against the sofa. I nestle into his side and close my eyes. I realize I'm willing to drop my guard when I'm around Sam. I feel safe. If I'm being honest with myself, any walls I had didn't stand a chance of holding. I am so, so gone for this guy.

My conscious thinking fades into dreams, walls barring me from letting myself be happy start crumbling while I sleep.

Sam

Matthew must've fallen asleep with his glasses on. They're sliding down his nose in a way that cannot possibly be pleasant. I reach over and pull off his glasses, being careful not to wake him. He yawns and flops into my chest. Matthew is a sleep-cuddler, wanting to be held and loved. It's sweet how tactile he is. I love him. It's as simple as that, but I can't have him. He's fresh out of an abusive relationship; I'm not going to push it. Mattie starts to stir and looks up at me.

"Why can't I see?"
"I took your glasses off, they were poking your face." I grab Matt's glasses off the coffee table.
"Thanks, Sammy. I'm going to go to the grocery store and get gummy worms."
"Okay? May I ask why?"
"Because I want gummy worms! I never had them as a kid; we were poor. I want gummy worms and dammit I'm gonna get them!"
"Alright. I'll make lasagna while you're gone."
"Please limit yourself to lasagna. Don't open a bakery, please," He smirks and tugs on a jacket, "Bone app the teeth, Sammy."
"That's not-"
"I know. I say that to annoy you, my little Gordon Ramsay."

Just like that, he's out the door, tapping on his phone. I sigh and preheat the oven. *Please be alright, my songbird.*

Matthew

My song is on the radio. The Uber driver cranks it for the chorus.

"Hope you like Mayhem." He says.

You have no idea.

I get out of the car and practically skip into the store. Gummy worms and maybe some of those molasses old people candies that Sam loves so much. For such a sweet thing, his taste in candy is awful. See what I did there? No matter, I head down the candy aisle and grab yummy gummies and gross molasses things. Several children look at me enviously. I feel their pain. I toss my haul onto the checkout counter. A cheery store clerk rings me up and I walk back outside and open the Uber app. A man walks up behind me, trying not to be seen. I whip around, and he's gone. Alright, I'm officially losing my mind. Great. I turn back around and the man is *right there.*

"Hello, Lin." Same sinister smile.
"Hello, Nick. What brings you here, other than grocery shopping?" I steel my nerves and refuse to let my voice shake.
"You left me, Matthew. Do you really think anyone could do more for you?"
"Yes, I do. I have my roommate, I have Ricky, my entire family-! You are nothing to me." I can see his nostrils flare. Nick grabs my wrist and drags me into his car.
"You will regret that, Lin."

Panicked, I slump into the seat and wait to wake up. Nick drives and drives until we're so far from anything I know. He gets out of the car, slamming the door behind him. Nick pounces on me and I am completely powerless. Fight or flight, my ass. I'm frozen, forced to bend at Nick's will.

Sam

It does not take hours to get gummy worms.

There's a rapid knocking on the door.

"CPD, open up!" Then more knocking.
"I'm coming, just let me put the lasagna down to cool."

I throw the door open, two officers in uniform look at me. I duck my head and let them inside.

"Sorry about the mess and the apron. What can I do for you, officers?" The leopard-print apron is... it's a look.
"Is this the residence of Matthew Lin?"
"Yes, ma'am. He went to the store a few hours ago."
"We know. We received a 9-1-1 call. We found Matthew and he's in the hospital. Wants Sam O'Henry there. Where can we find him?"
"That's me! I'm Sam O'Henry. Oh God, what happened? Is Mattie okay?"
"I can't tell you much, but he's expected to be alright. We can give you a ride in the cruiser, Matthew said your car is broken."
"Yes, please. Oh Mattie-Bird, what happened?"

I'm escorted on shaky legs to the cruiser. The drive is silent, tense, and terrifying. I still have no idea what happened, but I have a pretty good guess. That might scare me most of all. I burst through the doors to the hospital.

"Mattie! Birdie, are you alright? Are you in pain?"
"Sam..." *He sounds so hurt.*
"You're safe now, Mattie. My sweet songbird, it's going to be alright. You'll be fine..." I sit in one of those terribly uncomfortable hospital chairs.
"Sammy, it hurt and he-" A full-bodied sob cuts him off, "He was- touched m- I hated it. I couldn't- I can't- I'm sorry, Sam. Hurts so bad, Sammy."

Sometimes I hate being right. I'd rather be here because Mattie got hit by one of those wild CTA buses than have this happen again. At least those injuries are only physical.
"Hey, don't apologize. You're innocent here. Did you get the gummy worms, at least?"
"In the bag by your feet."

I pick up the bag and inside, there are gummies and the molasses chews that I love.

"But you hate molasses!"
"I got them for you."
"Aww, Mattie, thanks. You're so *sweet*." I wink. "Pun very much intended."
He laughs. "Ow, oh my ribs. I haven't gotten the X-ray back but they're broken."
"Have you gotten pain meds?" I frown.
"Not yet. The doc has to read my drug test before they pump me full of morphine."

"Fair enough."

The doctor comes in a few minutes later, followed by a whole herd of nurses.

"Two of your ribs are broken-"
"Told ya!"
"-a few others are bruised, and we can give you pain meds now."
"Oh thank lord. Breathing hurts."
"You're probably going to feel very sleepy. Don't fight it, just sleep. Take it easy the next couple weeks, too."

Mattie nods. A nurse pushes some kind of IV. Not even a minute later, Matt yawns and smiles dopily.

"'M sleepy." He rocks back and forth. "It's like that time in high school with Lucifer..."

I'm going to ask about that one later...

"Go to sleep, Birdie. Tell me all about Lucifer when you wake up." *I really need to look into this. It's intriguing, at the very least.*

One last yawn and he's *out*. He looks so peaceful and precious, but seriously. *Who in the hell is Lucifer?*

Matthew

When I open my eyes, I immediately regret it. Everything is way too bright and my ribs still ache. Sam's slumped forward, falling halfway out of his chair and sprawling across my chest. I kind of thought he would've gone home by now. I can't say I mind that he stayed. He's a nice guy. I don't want to wake him, not when he looks so serene. He twitches slightly and- *fucking hell!*

"Sam! My ribs! Get off, ow fucking shit, get off me!"
"What is it, Mattie?" He notices my writhing and gently rolls off my ribs. "I'm so sorry, Birdie. Are you alright?"
"I'm fine, Sammy."

He smiles that blazing smile and helps me up.

"You've been released," He says, "I just wanted to let you sleep off the drugs, you know?"
"I know."

Sam wraps an arm around my middle and pulls me close. He keeps me steady enough to stumble out of the ER. When we get to the parking lot, a horn honks obnoxiously. Sam informs me that Jackson Christopher is going to drive us home.

"Wait, Jackson Christopher? As in, your old friend who's just a little bit nuts?"
"Yup. He's a good driver, though!"

I don't exactly believe him, but I get in the car. Sam wraps his arm around me in the backseat.

"How are you doing, man!" Jackson cackles, "Are you two shacking up yet?"
"Jay!" Sam balks at the sheer notion of it, "*No*, we are not."
"Well, I didn't know. The arm around the shoulders, calling your buddy to drive you home... I just thought you were probably doing some hardcore banging."

"Not everyone fucks anybody within a five foot radius, *Jackson.*"

"Okay, harsh," A pause, "I'm not that bad, right?"

"I still need a ride home so I'm going to decline to answer that."

"I feel like you just did, Sam," I laugh, "Is this the guy that set you up with Jess?"

"Yeah! I did that. She dumped you so hard bro. Dumb reasoning, right? I mean, she was super controlling. You couldn't even see me! I'm your best bro, it was totally uncool!"

"Hate being tied down like that," Sam sighs, "Anyway, how's Claire been?"

"Who's that?" I am more than a little out of the loop with Sam and Jackson's "bro-a-palooza."

"Claire was our neighbor growing up. She's a badass-"

"Krista loved her."

"-and Krista loved her, yeah. She's been great, works at that upscale taco joint. She's proud of you."

"Oh yeah?"

"She's so happy you got out of that accounting gig."

"So am I. No more beige!"

I love this dork. "No more beige. Also, turn here Jackson, this is our street."

"Right on, dude."

Sam and I get out of the car, Sam first so he can keep me and my busted ribs from falling. The elevator is out of order, of course. The one day I need it, it's out of order. Sam glares at the sign plastered on the doors. He sighs and starts taking me towards the stairs.

"Sammy, I don't think I can-"

"I will carry you if I have to. I know you're tired, Birdie. I'll get you upstairs so you can rest, alright?"

"Okay." I mumble, heat crawling up my neck at the thought of Sam carrying me up six flights of stairs. "I'm probably be too heavy for you, though. I mean, you'd have to carry more than your own body weight up a helluva lot of stairs."

"No, I'd be fine. Come here, let's go upstairs."

Sam opens the door to the stairs and helps me limp my way up the first couple flights. By the time we reach the third floor landing, however, my broken ribs are throbbing and legs are about to give out.

"Sam, wait."

"Need help?" He sounds so earnest and non judgemental. I nod shamefully at him. I've always hated being dependant.

"It's alright, Mattie-Bird. Do you think you can walk or should I carry you?"

"Sorry, I don't think I can walk. Can you carry me? I'm sorry, I really would walk but-"

"It's really no trouble. I'll take care of you, don't worry. Now c'mere."

I take a few steps towards Sam, he looks at me before holding out his arms. He lifts me up, moving his arms to support the backs of my thighs. I loop my arms around Sam's shoulders, cheek resting against the nape of his neck. Surprisingly enough, Sam *is* able to carry a full-grown man up several flights of stairs. When we get into the apartment, Sam sets me on the couch. He settles in next to me, wrapping his arms around me. I lean heavily into his chest and snuggle him. I'm pulled in closer, and Sam traces my bruised sides with gentle fingers. We sit in comfortable silence for a while.

"Do you have bruises or scrapes anywhere other than your ribs?" Sam grimaces just after he says it, "That was super blunt. I just don't wanna hug you too hard, or squeeze your shoulder if it hurts. I don't want to hurt you."

"It's just the ribs. My shoulders and back are really tense, but that's about it."

"Can I do anything to help?"

"You don't have to."

"I know, but is there anything you'd like? I want to help you, Mattie. Bad things happened to you. I want you to feel better. Do what you can, you know?"

"Well, if you'd massage my shoulders, that'd be nice."

Sam beams and moves to sit behind me. He puts his hands on my shoulders and rubs carefully, avoiding my ribs. I sigh and unconsciously shift back, pressing into Sam. He laughs quietly, which I feel more than I hear, and works the stressed muscles in my neck.

"Thank you, Sammy." I slur my words more than I expect.

Sam curls around me after a half hour or so. He runs a hand through my hair and places the other gently on my thigh. It's cozy.

"I should probably shower. As comfy as this is, I stink." I say flatly.

"Sure thing, Mattie," He smiles, "Careful with the ribs."

"Of course. They're attached to me, I think I'll remember to be careful."

I turn and walk into the closet, grabbing a change of clothes, then into the bathroom. Looking in the mirror is not a pretty sight today. My ribs are black and blue, there are half a dozen hickeys on my chest, and handprint bruises on my hips. It's disgusting. Not only did he kidnap and assault me, he marked me. He begged to have me back, he said I was pathetic and miserable, but he wanted me back. It *hurt*. It hurt my body -*Nick hurt me.* He hurt my body, my heart, he fucked with my head. He would taunt me, if he saw me like this. He'd say I'm too fat, that nobody but him would want me. I look in the mirror, my reflection stares back at me, all sad eyes and tear streaks. I stagger back, away from the mirror, before crashing forward and gripping the vanity. I swallow a sob, knuckles turning white from holding on to the edge. My head starts spinning and I can't breathe- can't move. A harsh sob shakes me, rattling my ribs and making it hurt *that much worse.* I'm having a flashback in my boxers, in the bathroom. *Could this be any worse?*

"Mattie? Mattie-Bird, are you alright? I'm worried about you. Open the door." A long pause, then some shuffling. "I'm coming in."

Famous last words.

"N-no, I'm fine." The whole sobbing thing depreciates the value of my words.
"Like hell you are," The door swings open, "Birdie! Oh, my songbird, c'mere."

I stay put, clutching the vanity even tighter. Sam puts a tentative hand on my shoulder. I straighten up and try to smile at him. The facade crumbles and I'm crying more than I was before. Sam leans back against the vanity and sighs. He waits for me to relax before looking me over.

"More than the ribs." He whispers.

I don't move, just keep my gaze focused on the obnoxiously pink shower curtain. It was cheap.

"He did... all of this?" Sam says softly, eyes sad.

I nod.

"Fuck."

I smile, albeit humorlessly. "Yeah. Wasn't good."

"You don't have to sugarcoat it, Birdie. I am sorry, I am so, so sorry this happened to you. This should never happen to anyone ever."

And I'm crying again.

"You're alright now, Mattie. Safe, you're safe, okay? I'm here, Birdie, right here."

"Thanks, angel. 'M sorry you had bust in here and, like, see me all naked."

"It's alright, Birdie."

Sam turns and leaves, leaving me to wonder why heaven didn't keep its angel.

Chapter Two

Sam

My phone lights up with an unknown caller. I let it go to voicemail.

"Hello, son. It's been a while and we didn't part ways on the best of terms. Krista gave me your number, by the way. Please call back, Samuel."

My mother hasn't called me in eight years and now here she is, speaking as though we're still remotely civil. No one has called me "Samuel" since I was six, though I'm not surprised she forgot about that. I call back, nevertheless. I'd be lying if I said I hated her. For all the shit the whole family's been through, I can't blame her for much of anything.

"Mom?"
"Samuel! Oh my boy, how have you been?"
"It's Sam, Mom. I've been great, thanks. I just quit my accounting job when my friend's punk band really took off. I'll make a lot of money, get famous and stuff."
"That's amazing! I'm proud of you. Did you go to college? Do you have a nice girl yet?"

That's the mother I remember.

"Yes, Mom, I went to college," *No thanks to you,* "And no, I'm not seeing anyone." *And they wouldn't necessarily be a girl!*
"How'd you get the money for tuition? Your father was not the most understanding of... you."
"I had to work two jobs for minimum wage, live with *Jackson,* but most of my savings came from a less than ideal source."
"Did you sell drugs?"
"No! I got a job as a stripper, Mom. It was humiliating."
The line is silent for a few painful seconds.

"Well, if it paid for your schooling..." She doesn't sound angry, more like she regrets landing me in that situation in the first place. *Although, she is still not entirely to blame.*
"How's Dad been? Is he still an abusive alcoholic with no sense of empathy?"
"Sam. You know that's not true, that it's never been true. I don't know why you and your sister started making these wild accusations. He doesn't have a drinking problem and he's never been abusive!"

"Like you would know anything! You worked nonstop," I take a breath, "He drank my college fund. I dislocated my shoulder hopping a fence while trying to get away from him! That's why I didn't compete in the scholarship dive. Krista hated him so much, she punched him right in the kisser when we were real little. I don't blame her. You always wondered why Krista was getting in fights every other day? Maybe it's because she was fighting *everyday* to keep her weak little brother safe. She never got a scratch in a fistfight with kids her own age."

"Sammy?"

I turn around, hoping he didn't hear anything, but based on the worried pout on his face, he heard *everything.*

"I'll call you back sometime. Maybe tomorrow, maybe not." I hang up, not really needing a goodbye. "Hey, Mattie-Bird. Feeling any better?"

"Nuh-uh, don't you 'Mattie-Bird' me. I'm doing fine, Sam. How are *you?*" He takes a few steps closer to me, grabbing my arm and leading me to my bedroom.

"I'm alright, Mattie, it was just an unpleasant call."

"Sam, I heard the whole thing." He points at the bed. "Now lay down, I'll get you some tea."

He walks out, already hellbent on taking care of me. When Mattie reenters the room, he looks me over and shakes his head.

"What?" I say, mildly offended.

"Nothing, pretty boy. I just hate seeing you stressed, that's all."

He hands over a mug of vanilla chamomile, keeping one for himself, and produces a book seemingly out of thin air.

"Ta-da!" He says, beaming like the adorable little dork he is, "This was my favorite book as a kid, and so now I read it whenever I'm stressed or sad or something. Thought you could use a little TLC, Sammy."

This guy. I am so frickin' lucky. Even if all I ever get is platonic, I'm still so, so lucky.

"Thanks, Birdie."
"Yup! Now scoot over, today's been pretty tough. I'll just stay for the reading," *He sounds like he's convincing himself...* "And then I'll leave you be. Is that alright with you?"
"Perfect. Now c'mere and hold me so that I don't have to think about that stuff."
"Angel," Matthew cups my cheeks so I'm forced to look at him. "I don't know everything about you, but from what I've heard and seen, you're a survivor. Krista's a badass, by the way. You had to fight to stay safe. You took in an abused stray and made him better. You went to fucking college *all by yourself.* You're not alone anymore, though, Sammy. I swear, you've got to be a saint or an angel or something."

Mattie lets go of my face and pulls me into his chest. He runs his hands through my hair before slipping away to grab his book.

"Ah, thanks Mattie," I sniffle a bit, "I have never been a saint, but thank you."
"Fine, then. An angel."
"No, not that either."
"Well, why not?"
"My parents, er, my dad kicked me out when I was seventeen. Because he found out- someone told him I was dating a boy in my class. That's not really the worst thing he did-" Matthew sits up

and loops a comforting arm around my chest, "He told me I was a sin, that I was disgusting, and I didn't want to believe him but I-"

I break down, bawling my eyes out on Mattie's shoulder. He shushes me, and just like I asked, he holds me so I don't have to think about that stuff. It takes a few minutes for my breathing to stabilize. I lift my head from Matthew's shoulder and *oh God.* I wish I could just look at that stupidly handsome face *all day.* But I can't.

"I'll read to you," Matthew says softly, grabbing the book again. "This was my absolute *favorite* Seuss book, I really hope you like it."

I nod and lean back into the thick stack of pillows. Matthew curls into my side and begins to read.

"'They still talk about it in the Kingdom of Didd as The-Year-the-King-Got-Angry-with-the-Sky'..." Mattie's reading voice is so relaxing. "'...oh, bring down oobleck on us all!'"

I vaguely remember Matthew saying goodnight and getting up, but I must've fallen asleep shortly after. I couldn't help it! His reading voice is almost as smooth as his singing voice. Almost.

"Sammy?"

I wake up to Matthew lingering in the doorframe, voice hushed and eyes red. His pillow is tucked under his arm, blue plaid pajama pants bunched at the ankles. *Are they too long for him?* It's cute no matter what.

"Yeah? What is it, Birdie?" I yawn.

"Bad dream," *That usually means something related to Nick,* "Can I sleep here? I could be on the floor or something. I brought my pillow so I won't be in your way."

"Yes, but you are not sleeping on the floor. I'll get you a sleeping bag, or you can just sleep with me. Not like, *sleep with me,* but. You know. I don't want you to sleep on the floor. It's November in Chicago, that floor's probably freezing."

"Thank you, Sammy. I just didn't want to be alone in my head tonight."

"Anytime you need something like that, just come on in. Door's always open, Mattie-Bird."

He lays heavily next to me, face smushed into the side of my chest. His soft stomach is pressed up against my hip, his arm around my waist. I place a cautious hand on Mattie's shoulder before pulling him into me.

"Keep you safe." I whisper.

He doesn't answer, just rests his head on my chest and smiles.

Matthew

I have no idea how this happened.

I went to Sam (just like always), asked for company (how I always do), and now I'm waking up in his arms (like I always wanted). He always used to be one taking care of me, so the reading and the tea just felt *right.* Something I should do, just on principle. He's a fucking saint, I don't care what anyone says. *My guardian angel,* which, yes, is sappy as all hell. I don't care.

Sam shifts around behind me, before flinging an arm across my middle and tucking me into his chest. He really is a venus flytrap. I sigh and fold my hands over his. *May as well enjoy this while it lasts...*

My phone pings with the alert for "check cleared, pay your damn bills, and/or urgent business matter." The alert is just a recording of me saying "go be adult-ish" three times. It's awesome. It does mean, however, that I'm going to have to squirm out of Sam's vice grip.

Four minutes of wiggling and twisting and *how are you not waking up goddamn* later, I manage to make it to my phone.

Mr. Matthew J. Lin,

I believe the payment for your new album has been cleared. You will receive royalties weekly.

Sincerely,
Mrs. Mary May Jones.

Holy shit. The album came out at midnight.

"Sam! Sam, album payment midnight look phone! I can't believe-! Sam, wake up and look at money, please!"
"Matthew, it's way too early for this-"
"Look!" I shove my phone in his face.
"Have any sold yet?"
"Yes, because I know my dad bought one."
"Well, look on the online thing! The thing, Matthew!"
"That narrows it down so much, Sam."

Eventually, I do find the *thing* that Sam was talking about.

"Holy flying crap that's a lot of copies." Sam says.

I was too busy fainting to say much of anything.

"You scared me," Sam grouses, "You can't just faint like that!"
"Sorry, Sammy. Did you see the royalties figure?"
Sam looks at the screen then back at me. "We're rich!"
"Even without the payment upfront for signing."
"How much was that?" Sam looks awestruck.
"A lot." I say, and show the check receipt to him from my phone.
"Wow... I've been poor my whole life, what do people even buy
with this kind of money?"
"You could get a new car. Like an actual *new* car, from the
dealership. A cadillac, even."
"Yeah! I could get a new leather jacket-"
"-that you don't have to sew the sleeves back on once a month!"
"From a *mall*."
"Not goodwill. Although goodwill is still fun," I grin, "This is
awesome, Sam. We should go to that fancy-shmancy mall
downtown. I could get new boots, ones that the sole isn't falling
out."
"Those are halfway to heaven, Mattie," Sam says, then cracks up at
his own stupid joke, "Get it?"
"Yes, Sam, I got it. Sole versus soul, a very basic pun," I glare him
down. Puns: I love to hate them, "Car shopping or mall?"
"Both?"
"Both is good."

Sam

I walk back through the glorious doors of the car dealership. Mattie and I bought a cadillac! A brand new car that doesn't clank when it starts, or rumble ominously whenever I drive on the highway. It's a miracle. I haven't driven a car like this in... well, ever. Now I'm in the front seat with a rockstar talking my ear off.

"We should go to that high end mall today," Mattie says, "Or maybe just hit the boulevard, old Hollywood style. Looking all fancy, rolling up in a caddy, paparazzi snapping photos, posing for the limelight..."

I roll my eyes at him at the next red light.

"Yeah, you're right. Let's go to that fancy mall. I can annoy posh old ladies with my sweats."
"Sounds good. Wait, what about your sweats?"
"They're the kind with writing on the ass. I've got 'NOPE' in big, bold letters."

How in the fresh hell did I not notice that?

"Where do you even buy those?" *My voice did* not *crack, thank you.*
"Some store. I think they were supposed to be for women, but the cashier saw me try them on. She said I wore 'em better anyway."
"You don't have to explain yourself, Mattie. Whatever makes you happy."
"Thanks, Sammy," I don't have to look over to see that he's beaming, "Let's buy all the stuff we wanted as kids."

Matthew has to stand and stare for a second when we walk in. There are glass storefronts filled with ostentatious clothing and jewelry. Matthew looks around in awe at things that are ridiculously overpriced for their materials, but people only care about the brands.

"Sammy, let's go in here!"

Matt pulls me into a prim little store that seems to house mainly fine jewelry. He scans the displays and follow; the shopkeep eyes us dubiously. Mattie seems to find whatever it is he's looking for. He pauses at a case of brooches and pins, before asking the store clerk if he has anything else.

"Do you have any pins that I could put on a leather jacket?" Mattie asks, "I want, like, a signature piece. That would be wicked cool."
"Are there any specific requirements? Any theme for the pin, perhaps?" The clerk looks confused and miffed.
"Maybe a bird? A bluebird. Those symbolize happiness and enjoyment of the little things."

He's so precious! I think I'm going to explode.

"I have one in the back of the shop. I'll be right back with it." The shopkeeper unlocks a door and disappears through it.

Matthew grins and sways along to the Frank Sinatra drifting around the room. He dances alone, twisting with an odd sort of grace. Of all the ways to pass time, I think this is the best. While the grumpy manager is gone, my Birdie dances. I say that as if I have any claim to him. I don't, no one does. Even if some beautiful twist of fate brings us together, I have no *claim* to him. Matthew is his own person. He is not *mine.* He floats across the tiles, humming the melody to a song lost in time. The shopkeep gets back then, and Mattie stops dancing. A sad scene, indeed.

"I have a little bird with your name on it, sir." He says, and Matthew's face lights up. The man opens his palm to reveal a tiny bluebird.

"It's *perfect.* I love it," Mattie gasps, "How much is it?"

The man discusses pricing with Matthew, who urges me to go ahead and shop. I leave the jeweler and enter a department store. I walk in circles aimlessly. There's a rack of jackets that are so incredibly expensive I barely give them a second glance. I wander to another few hangers, but nothing catches my eye. Having money is more boring than I thought it'd be. Soon enough, Mattie comes bouncing into the store. He's still wearing those sweatpants, (now that I've noticed, I can't *un-notice* the writing on his ass), and looks comically out of place in this store.

"Find anything yet, Sammy?" He smiles sweetly at me.

"Not really. Let's go to another store."

"Sure! Can we get fitted for suits? I mean, fame comes with the expectation that your suit actually fits. Mine most certainly does not, at least not after the months I've lived with you and your compulsive baking."

"Okay, ouch," I feign offense, and Matthew laughs, "But yeah, we could do that."

We start walking towards the tailor we saw on the way in. An old lady with a thick Italian accent greets us at the door. She whisks Matthew inside, muttering something about young people and their clothing. I'm taken away by another lady. She's much younger, maybe late twenties at the oldest.

"I'm sorry about my grandmother. She can be quite pushy."

"He'll be fine." I say, and it's true. If there's one thing Matt's good at, it's socializing with cranky old people.

"She is probably mad about his pants, if I'm honest. She doesn't understand the youth."

"Matthew would be pleased to hear that. He wore those for the sole purpose of annoying people."

"He sounds fun. You two are super cute together." She says and takes me into a fitting room.

"We're not dating." I murmur, face burning.

"Really? You're giving each other heart eyes every other second!"

I shrug as she takes some measurements. She makes decent small talk, picks a suit, and practically throws it at me. She says it'll be very flattering. She looks thrilled, says I was almost built for this. I look in the mirror and it becomes apparent that this lady knows her stuff. It's a classic black without any bells and whistles, slim fit, and I look *fine as hell.* I decide to step outside the little dressing room and take a look in the three-way mirror. I'm too late, though, because Matthew is already there, twisting at the waist and admiring himself.

"I gotta hand it to you, Cheryl," He says, "This really *does* make my ass and thighs look fan-freaking-tastic."

"I told you! You have a glorious figure, so rich."

Matthew turns around and smiles at me. He looks me over, sauntering towards me. I tried not to stare, I really did, but *come on.* I can only take so much.

"Well, don't you look dashing?" He grins.

"I, uh, I guess so? You look amazing, Birdie. I've never seen someone look good in a tailcoat until now."

Matthew smirks, not saying any more, just turning and swaggering back to the fitting room. I get redressed, hanging the suit back on its hanger, and move to the checkout counter. I swipe my credit card, thank the ladies running the store, and leave. Mattie hugs me from behind as we're leaving. He latches on to my shoulders, smushing his form against mine. He's always been pretty tactile with me, from brief hand squeezes to laying across my lap for hours while watching TV. It's lovely.

"Isn't that your sister? It looks like she's hefting a frying pan."

The moment is ruined, but at least Krista hasn't seen us. I really want to go in that fancy cooking store... Dare I risk it?

"Yo! Little bro!" *I was only two feet in the store.*
"Hey, Krista."
"Okay, Mr. Grumpy Pants! How've you been? Where's your celebrity crush turn roomie?" Krista flashes a devilish smile, "Remember how you went to a Mayhem concert freshman year? You took a girl to the park, didn't speak to her all night, and stayed out too late to buy a poster *for yourself.* You guys walked home, and she told you to ask out the singer you'd been ogling all night. Hello, Matthew!"
I turn around so fast I get dizzy.
"Hey Krissy!" Matt smiles wolfishly, "Sam? Did you really ruin your own date because you were staring at a certain somebody?"
"That's not exac-"
"Don't even start, Sammy dear. He totally did, Matt. He used to have that poster in his apartment, but I think he took it down when said idol moved in." Krista wears her signature shit-eating grin.
"You're a dork, Sammy," Matthew says, "You wanted something from here, right? Pie weights or whatever?"

"You remembered what they're called!" I grin, "Will you stop calling them the 'oddly sexual food thing' now?"

"Never! You *know* what they look like. You're lucky I figured it out before-"

"Matthew! Shush!" I squeak.

"No, don't! Tell me more," Krista cackles, "Any story that embarrasses Sam this much is fine by me."

Before Matthew can continue talking about *improper* ways to use pie weights, I've already paid and I'm dragging him out the door. Matt laughs and slings an arm around around my waist.

"Sorry, Sammy," He giggles, "It's just so much fun to tease you."
Mind out of the gutter, oh my god.
"It's alright, Mattie-Bird. Besides, I walked into that one. Thanks for not violating my pie weights."

"I wouldn't get any pie if I did that!" He smiles.

"You're adorable, Mattie," *Then I yawn,* "No! It's only mid-afternoon. I don't wanna be tired, but my feet hurt and I really *am* tired."

"It's been a long day. Let's go home, pretty boy. I'm hungry, probably because we talked about pie..."

We trudge to the car, toss the suits in the back, and I rev the engine. The drive is quiet, mostly because Matthew is asleep. He doesn't snore, not really, but he makes these little breathy noises. It's hard to even stay on the road.

I pull into the parking lot of our apartment. Matthew is nearly impossible to wake up, I even tried pushing his face into odd expressions. After a minute or two (or ten) of making Mattie make a fish face, I resort to the big guns. No one can sleep through tickling, not even Matthew. He bats me away, and glares at me sleepily.

"Let me sleep..." He groans and throws himself dramatically against the car door.
"You can sleep upstairs, drama queen."

Despite his complaints, Matthew hauls himself up and out of the car. He plods upstairs and immediately flops onto my bed, mumbling something about how I have a TV.

"So you want to watch something?" *Laying next to me, in my bed-*
"Yeah," He murmurs, faces muffled in the pillows. "I wanna watch some horror movies, but I don't want to just be in my room alone on my laptop."
"Alright, but you're going to have to scoot over so I can lay down too."

Matthew obliges, rolling onto his back and sitting up enough to see the screen. He lets me pick the movie, as long as it's a horror. I don't usually watch anything with blood and guts because it's icky. I guess some suspense psycho flick will have to do.

"Sam, this is morbid."
"I know," My eyes are still fixed on the screen. Horror-fascination is a thing, after all. "I don't like horror movies with guts flying everywhere, but this might be even worse."
"You stubborn idiot," Matthew says, "Why didn't you tell me? Let's do something else, Sammy, if neither of us are enjoying this."

He turns off the movie, before leaning against my chest. Mattie relaxes visibly, his shoulders sinking back to a comfortable position. I loop an arm around his waist, tucking him just a little closer to me.

"You know, Sammy," He whispers, "I didn't think I'd ever let anyone near me again, after what happened with Nick. Remember how I used to flinch whenever somebody would just tap my shoulder to get my attention? Now, I'm letting myself trust people again. It's nice, not to feel so alone. You're a miracle worker, Sammy, I swear to god. What your dad said to you? Bullshit. Total bullshit. You dropped everything for a total stranger, let him interrupt your life, and let him in. If that doesn't get you into heaven, Sammy, I don't know what will. You're a saint, Sam."

Mattie doesn't even pause, just turns on a nature documentary that he claims is like a lullaby.

Matthew

I fall asleep watching a penguin propose with a shiny rock. I don't know why I said what I did to Sam. I meant it, of course, but why the hell did I think that when I'm *laying next to my only love interest* is the time to spill my guts? This isn't some cliche BL manga! We're not just going to just going to exchange a look and start making out. It's not that easy. (Sometimes, I wish it *were* that easy to get together with somebody, but that's beside the point.)

Sam's playing with my hair, one arm still anchored around my middle. I stretch, being careful not to hit Sam in the face.

"Morning, sunshine." He says muzzily.
"What time is it, anyway?"

"6 o'clock, about time for dinner."
"Good, I'm starved."

Sam laughs and pushes me off of him. *What a shame.*

"I'll make something," For some of Sam's cooking, I would sacrifice my cozy spot any day, "Is fried chicken okay?"
"That sounds wonderful, Sam!" *Wait a second,* "We don't have a deep fryer, though, do we?"
"No, but we have a pot, some oil, and a fire escape. Those are the fireproof part of the building."
"Just be careful, Sammy. No ER visits, please."
"I've been doing this since I was eight. It'll be fine." He waves me off.
"I'm… not sure how I feel about that."
"Eh, Krista was eleven. She supervised. We watched a few youtube videos, no one died, and the chicken was fantastic!"

I nod dubiously. Not dying seems to be a pretty low standard for cooking. Sam climbs onto the fire escape with a campfire stove, an enormous pot full of oil, lighter fluid, and a whole chicken. I'm not going to lie; this entire situation is very strange.

While Sam's off doing… *something,* I take to the 'net, see how the band's doing. I answer a few tweets, just because I can. "Why'd you name the band Mayhem?" "Idk? It sounded cool and we're a bit of a chaotic group, lol." So on and so forth, occasionally checking to see if Sam's set himself on fire yet.

"Look at me, I'm a yummy chicken!" Sam pitches his voice higher and and points at a, well, yummy-looking chicken.
"Sam, what the actual fuck are you doing."

"I thought it'd be funny." He pouts so sincerely that I genuinely feel bad.

"And it kind of was, in a 'what the fuck are you doing' way. I never thought I'd see a grown-ass man wave a cooked chicken around to make it talk. Not while he's sober, at least."

"I get it, the chicken-waving was dumb. Will you forgive me, if I offer you a piece of the offending bird?" Sam's laughing -no, giggling- so much I can barely understand him.

"Are you okay? Did the fumes from the lighter fluid get to you or-?" I laugh a bit, "You sound like you're high off your ass, Sammy."

"I'm not, I swear! I just made myself laugh at my own stupid joke, and now I can't stop even though it wasn't that funny-" He breaks off into another fit of sobbing laughter.

"You're such a dork, Sam."

After a wonderful meal, I wander to the sofa and collapse into the cushions. Sam nuzzles into my shoulder and yawns. He's such a cuddler, all wrapped around me like this. It doesn't mean anything, I know that, but *God* I wish it did. Sam trails one hand up and down my arm. It's so nice to be held. Sam pulls me into his side, TV humming in the background, resting his chin on my head. We don't move for a long while, Sam looping his arms around my middle. The characters on the television are laughing, but I'm not paying any attention.

"You're soft," Sam mumbles, "I like it. Warm and cozy, good to hold."

"Thank you? Should I take that as a compliment, or-?"

"It was a compliment, Birdie. You beautiful, sweet boy."

He's almost snoring against my shoulder and people say strange things when they're sleep deprived. I shouldn't read into it, I know I shouldn't, but it's so tempting. Sam is such a sweetheart, and I could have sworn he was checking me out at the mall. That, and

Krista told me about Sam's botched date. (She wasn't even trying to be sneaky; she was looking right at me.) I want this to be more than a "just friends" situation. I want *Sammy.* Not in that sexy way, I just want to be with him.

I hate having feelings.

Sam

I am *this close* to cracking. I know I've been too complimentary to be platonic, I know I've stared longer than is normal, but Matthew doesn't seem to notice. Besides, can you blame me? His face lights up so much when I say something nice. I've got a hundred crumpled love letters tossed in my drawer. Every single one has something too sappy or stupid or cheesy or something for me to show Matthew. I want to be with him. I don't want anything too physical or intense, not yet. I really like Mattie and I don't want to rush anything.

Matthew is asleep in my arms, still on the couch. He usually sleeps much later than I do, so I guess I'm not going anywhere for the time being. Well, unless I have a legitimate excuse to move, such as making breakfast. Good thing I can cook. I slip out from Mattie's grip and patter into the kitchen. He doesn't stir, just curls into a ball and starts snoring again.

I make chocolate hazelnut waffles, mainly because of the sweet smell that'll be in the house all day. Definitely not just because Mattie loves them. Speaking of Matthew, he's thrashing around on the couch. He's a restless sleeper, (he even threw me off the couch after a movie one time) but this seems different. He's mumbling, tossing and turning, grimacing; he looks miserable. Breakfast is ready anyway, so I decide to wake him up.

"Mattie?" I tap his shoulder gently, "It's time to wake up, songbird. I made waffles."
"I feel sick, Sammy..." He groans, "M'head hurts, chest hurts."

He coughs, and I mean *coughs.* Mattie's whole body shakes, and he gasps for breath when the coughing finally stops. I wrap an arm around his shoulders, touch his forehead, and he is *burning up.*

"My poor Birdie," I mumble, "You've got quite a fever. I'm going to take your temperature, so stay here. I'll be right back."

He nods and pulls the blanket tighter around himself. I fetch the thermometer, some cough syrup, and another blanket. Matthew grabs the blanket and wraps it around himself. I measure and pour the cough syrup, then stick the thermometer under Mattie's tongue. He glares pathetically and grumbles at me.

"I know you don't feel good, Mattie. I'll get you a cool cloth for your head, how 'bout that?"

He nods sluggishly. I come back a moment later, drape the washcloth on Matthew's forehead and check his temperature. *102.4°F.* No wonder he feels awful, that fever is so high.

"I'm taking you to the hospital, Birdie. You've got a fever of over 102. I think you've got pneumonia."
"'M so tired... can't get down, Sammy."
"Get down where, sweetheart?" *No pet names!* (Even if he's sick, and I want to take care of him...)
"Downstairs to the car."

"We can take the elevator, it's fixed."

He hums, then starts up with that hacking cough. I try to lift him up, pull him to the door, but *he's heavy* when he's just dead weight like this. I manage to get Matthew to the door, down the stairs, and into the car. The ride to the hospital is silent except for Matthew's coughing fits. It's disconcerting; Matthew never shuts his mouth.

"I'm so sick, Sammy." *He sounds like he's suffering.*
"I know," I whisper, "We're almost there."

I pull into the complimentary valet and toss the car keys to one of the hospital volunteers. She grabs a wheelchair and pushes it up to the passenger door. Matthew almost falls out of the car, collapsing into the chair and wrapping the blankets back around himself. I rush Matthew through the sliding glass doors and into the hospital.

"Here, put this on," I hand him one of those face mask things, "Because of the cough."
"M'kay, Sammy."

There's a check-in station. Mattie tries to tell the nurse about his symptoms, but breaks off into a coughing fit. I suppose that *did* tell her about his symptoms, though. Mattie's admitted to a room, but damn hospitals and their stupid rules! The nurse tries to turn me away, saying "family only, sir." Formalities are not going to help! Mattie is sick, I want to stay here and keep him company.

"Sam's my boyfriend," *What. The. Hell,* "So he can stay, right?"

The nurse nods, and Matthew -that cheeky fucker- actually winks at me. Once in the room, Matthew lays down on the cot, completely oblivious to the non-medical heart attack I just suffered.

Doctors are in and out constantly. They take blood, get x-rays, and stick one of those horrible cotton swabs down Mattie's throat. *Gross.* A nurse explains why antibiotics work on bacterial pneumonia and not viral pneumonia. He pushes some IV that'll make Mattie stop coughing, then an actual antibiotic. Just as quickly as it started, it stops. All the doctors leave in a group.

"Sammy?"
"Yeah, Matt?"
"I'm sorry if the whole 'boyfriend' thing made you uncomfortable. I just- I didn't want you to leave and I panicked."
"Like if I said I was pregnant to keep somebody around." *Where the fuck did that come from?*
"Oh my god, please tell me you've done that! And your girlfriend just laughs-" Mattie giggles.
"For your information, I have never done that. I read it online."
"You're adorable," He yawns, "But I'm gonna take a nice nap. Stay here until I wake up?"
"Sure thing, Birdie. I don't have a book or anything, though. Am I just supposed to watch you sleep, or...?"
"Or you could watch YouTube on your phone. But hey, if you wanna watch me sleep, go right ahead. Good night, angel."
"Good night, sweetie."

Matt closes his eyes, a tiny smile still etched on his face. He sighs, cracking one eye open.

"I thought you'd be better with pet names, pretty boy. 'Sweetie?' It's so cliche. Stick with the bird-related ones. I like those, not as much as I like *you,* but still."

"Are you being serious?" *Please say you're serious.*

"Yup," Mattie grins, "I don't know if it's the fever or the cough suppressant or both. I've wanted to tell you how great you are for a while, but I was too scared. I lost my filter when I got this cough, I guess. Anyway, you're precious and cuddly. You're, like, way too good for me. I love you, Sam."

At that, my brain buffers like a 2005 Dell PC that didn't take kindly to Windows 10. Finally, I stutter out,

"I love you too, Mattie. And nobody is 'way too good' for you, you're amazing."

The only answer I get are the soft snores from Mattie's hospital bed.

Matthew

I wake up shivering uncontrollably. I had the strangest fever dream, something about telling Sam I love him. My fever is breaking, which is good, but *god.* There's a dull ache in my lungs and a splitting pain in my head. I groan and stretch my arms up over my head, before dropping them against the cot. Well, one arm hits the cot, the other hits somebody's solid shoulder.

"Good morning," Sam mumbles, "Feeling better?"

"Yeah, a little. My fever is breaking."

"You were so sick yesterday, Birdie. You were kinda clingy, said I was your boyfriend to bypass the 'family only' rule. And you said-you said that you loved me. Was it just the fever talking, or-?"

"I love you, Sammy. I want to be with you, wanna have you, call you mine. I want to take things slow. I trust you enough to be with you."

"Mattie, I'm terrible with words," Sam stutters, "I love you, too. I just don't know how to say it with the same level of eloquence. Taking things slow is fine, great actually. I want you to be happy."

I smile broadly at Sam. He ruffles my hair and pulls me into a hug. I nuzzle his neck, my arms looped around Sam's shoulders. He squeezes me just a little tighter, and kisses my forehead. A nurse walks in, gives me discharge papers to sign, and sends me on my way. It's a tad embarrassing to have him walk in while I'm still entangled with Sam, but I'm too happy to care. Sam and I walk to the car, and he opens the door like he's trying to bring glamor back.

"Are you going to pull my chair out in fancy restaurants, too?" I smirk.

"Maybe," Sam beams, "Do you like the whole chivalry thing, or is it patronizing?"

"It's cute. You look so shy and timid, like I'm way out of your league or something."

"You are! You are totally out of my league. I'm dating my *idol;* the guy I liked as the singer in a garage band and as an actual human being. I am the luckiest man alive, Birdie." Sam murmurs the last bit, ducking his head.

"You're the best, angel. Let's go home."

I sit back on the couch, settling into the cushions. Sam plops down and wraps his arms around me. He reaches to hold my hand, glancing sheepishly at me. The universal *"is this okay?"* look. I nod and rest my head on his shoulder. Sam rubs his thumb across the back of my hand. It's so soothing and so achingly gentle, like he's nervous. This is what I've wanted for so long; somebody to cuddle up with and hold. I could stay here forever. Yeah, it's cliche as all hell, but it's true.

Sam's got his eyes closed, head resting against the sofa. He's absolutely divine. He checks all my boxes: caring, respectful, handsome, and he can cook. Sam's such a sweetheart, he does everything he can for the people he cares about. I hope he takes care of himself, too.

"You're so good to me, Sammy." I whisper.
"I do my best."

Sam squeezes my hand and snuggles me closer. He's so lovely. I turn around in his arms, pulling Sam to his feet. He tips his head to the side, looking at me curiously. I grin at him, walking backwards toward a speaker. Music drifts through the apartment, the song's barely begun when Sam says:

"Eric Clapton, huh?"
"Yeah," I laugh awkwardly, "May I have this dance, Sam?"
"Of course, Birdie." Sam smiles shyly.

I press myself into Sam's chest and sway to the soft guitar swing. Sam's taller than me, and still built like a swimmer. As much as I hate to admit it, I love the size difference. I love how strong Sam is, it makes me feel sheltered. And here I am -here we are- slow dancing in the living room. Sam's got his hands on my waist, tracing my sides, and eventually resting on my hips. I smush my cheek into Sam's chest and wrap my arms around him. He leans into me, pulling me just a little closer. It's so intimate, even though we're just in the living room.

The songs ends. Sam pushes me back so he can look at me, his gaze flickering between my eyes and the carpet. We stay there for a moment. Sam pulls away, interlocking our fingers and giving me a lopsided smile.

"You're precious, angel." I murmur.
"So are you, Mattie-Bird. How 'bout you go and lay down for a bit? I bet you're still tired from being so sick."
"I guess you're right, Sammy." I hadn't really noticed, but yeah. My eyelids are drooping, and I yawn.
"Get some rest, sweetheart. I love you."
"And I love you, Sammy."

I patter back to my bedroom and lay down on the bed. It's been a long-ass day, I just want to sleep. I wrap myself up in blankets, and I'm *so close* to sleeping when I hear Sam knock on my door. I grumble and get up to let him in.

"Sorry, Mattie-Bird. Were you sleeping?"
"Almost. Do you need something?"
"It's dumb," He sighs, "But I just started thinking about my mom and how I never called back, and now I can't stop thinking about it-"
"Hey, it's alright. Stay here tonight, and I can read to you again, if you'd like."

Sam nods and snuggles in next to me. He has a book in his hands, *Make Way For Ducklings.* Sam tosses a shy smile at me, barely making eye contact. I smile back and tuck myself into his chest. As I read, it occurs to me that Sam's probably never been read to before. His mom was busy and his dad, well, I don't know when he took a wrong turn, but I still feel special. Sam's breathing evens and slows, his shoulders slouching back into the pillows. I put the book down and press up against Sam. *I love him, love him so much.* I yawn, and finally fall asleep.

Chapter Three

Sam

It's not her fault.
It's not her fault.
It's not her fault.
It's not her-

I hate this. It had been years since Mom tried to get in touch, and then... She just shows up. Maybe she saw me on the news and thought, *he's finally made something of himself.* Or maybe she's accepted who I am and she wants her son back. The first is more likely. *And it's still not her fault.* She wasn't home, she never knew, *she was never there.* Maybe that's what hurts. She didn't know because she didn't see it. She only had to work like that because of Dad's drinking problem, and she never saw it because she worked. She wasn't home when I was a kid, wasn't at my 8th grade graduation, and I'd been kicked out of the house by the high school ceremony. Jackson's family took me out for ice cream, at least.

And it was worse for Krista. She wasn't there for Krista's fourth grade play (she had been so excited), wasn't there when Krista "became a woman." Krista didn't even know what was happening to her. She wasn't there when Krista almost got kidnapped. (Krista came to my apartment, scared and in tears, and stayed for a couple weeks.)

She wasn't there. And maybe that part hurts more than everything Dad's ever done.

I wake up next to Matthew, or perhaps more accurately; I wake up with Matthew laying on me. He's still asleep, one arm wrapped around my shoulders and his legs tangled with mine. I card a hand through his hair, feeling his breath on my neck. I usually hate it when anyone breathes on me, but it's okay right now. Mattie presses his face into my collar bone, soft cheeks adorably smushed. He's got so many freckles that I hadn't really noticed before. His hair's a mess, all curly with more cowlicks than I would've thought possible. Matt yawns and sits up enough to look at me, my hands still tangled in his hair.

"Morning, Sammy." He simpers, giving me a not-so-subtle once over.
"Good morning, Mattie."

He rolls over, so warm and so close to me. His whole body relaxes and stills; it takes a minute for me to realize he's sleeping again. I slip out from under the blankets and tiptoe into the kitchen. For as much as he complains about my "compulsive cooking," Mattie doesn't turn down the food. Then again, he told me a story about how his dad was a kitchen disaster and almost burned the house down. He might just appreciate pancakes that aren't charred and smoking.

I get dressed and go for a run. When I get back, Matthew's still asleep, curled up like a cat. I toss a blanket over him, put the to-go container on the counter, (I got junk food after a long run. It balances out, right?), and take a shower. After that, I step out of the bathroom to find Mattie sitting on the counter, eating a donut. The latter was to be expected, but the former?

"You do realize we have chairs, right?"
"I know," He smirks and hops down, "But where's the fun in that?"
"Alright, Matt. Enjoy your food, sit on the counters, live your life."
"You sound like a greeting card," Mattie giggles, "Sit on counters, live your life, and have a happy new year: this year's hit holiday collection."

I roll my eyes at him, even though he's right. Matthew's expression sobers unexpectedly, frown forming fast enough to give him whiplash.

"Did you ever call your mother?"
"Not yet. I was thinking about doing it today."
"You don't have to call her back, you know. She didn't call you for years, and not to be an asshole, but you're successful now, Sam. She might want to take advantage of you."
"I've thought about that. I still wanna call her."
"As long as you've thought it through, Sammy," Then he whispers so softly I almost don't hear, "I just want you to be happy."
"It'll be alright, Mattie. When I call her, though, can you stay with me?" I mumble and duck my head.
"Of course. If she says anything that hurts you, just give me the phone. Parents shouldn't treat their kids like that, and I'm not just talking about your dad. Your mom wasn't around when you were a kid, I don't want her to hurt you now, too."

I sit down on the couch, grab my phone, and dial. Matthew presses up next to me, his hand resting on my knee. The phone rings once, twice.

"Hello? Sam, are you there?"
"Yes, Mom, I'm here."
"Thank you for calling me back, son. How've you been?"
"I've been good," I grimace and inwardly kick myself for lying so quickly. Old habits die hard, "What about you?"
"I'm alright, thanks. That band you're in? Is it doing okay?"
"The band's doing great, Ma."
"That's good. You really don't have a girlfriend? Doesn't Jackson set you up with dates anymore?"
"No, I really don't have *a girlfriend.* The last girl Jackson set me up with didn't end well, so I'm not seeing any girls right now." *It's not a lie, but not exactly the whole truth, either.*
"Oh, so you're taking some time off the dating scene? I get it, a rough breakup and a new job, you just want a little 'me time,' right?" I can *hear* her faux-sweet grin.
"No, actually, I'm not 'taking time off.' I have a-" *Boyfriend. Boyfriend. Boyfriend.*

Matthew grabs the phone and curls impossibly closer to me.

"He has a boyfriend, and you're talking to him right now. I understand that this might be hard for you to swallow, and you think you're always right about anything and everything relating to your kids, but I wouldn't call you a mom at this point. Did you raise those kids? No. Did you help with homework? No. Did you love them unconditionally? *Clearly not.* All you did was become a mother, then run from every responsibility that came with those two kids. I've seen it once before this, and I'm sure I'll see it again, but that doesn't make it right. I'll give you the same speech I gave Ricky's parents: you can't fix your kid that isn't broken. Okay? Say it with me: you can't fix your kid that isn't broken. I'm hanging up, don't even think about calling back. Asshole."

He really does hang up, tossing the phone aside.

"Parents can't treat their kids like that." He whispers.
"I'm starting to understand that. I really thought I deserved everything, and I didn't," I pause, "You said something about Ricky."
"I know. His parents were homophobic as shit, so he ran away from home. He said they'd beat him, try to 'fix him.' He lived with me and my mom and dad for a few months, but went back because he felt like a burden. He wasn't. Then, Ricky's parents kicked him out-"
"Permanently?" I ask, horrified.
"Yes. They were batshit crazy, believe me. My dad decided to adopt him, even though we barely had enough money to feed ourselves. Mom's medical bills stacked up, then the funeral... but Ricky wasn't going into the foster system. Period."
"Is he doing okay now?"
"Yeah, he's fine. Still has nightmares, but even those are getting better."
I nod. *I had no idea.*
"Oh, and Sam? I know what it's like to think you deserve the abuse, trust me, but gotta get over that part. You did nothing wrong. You were just a *little kid.* Kids are supposed to be able to trust their parents. This isn't your fault; you're not weak, you're not disgusting, you're not any of the awful things they said about you. You're my angel, my Sammy, and you didn't deserve any of it."

"Thanks, Birdie," I pull him in close, resting my chin on Mattie's head, "What did you mean when you said you 'know what it's like?' Did you think deserved what he-?"

"I did, in a weird way. I knew what Nick was doing was wrong, that he shouldn't do it, but I felt like I had done something to make him do it. I felt bad, as if I was the person in the wrong. I felt like I had taunted him, egged him on or something. Like I had done everything to myself. The weirdest part is that I *knew* it was fucked up, but I thought *deserved* it to be like that. I knew it was abusive, but he had already gotten in my head enough for me to think I deserved it. That I deserved to be hurt, because that's what was happening, *and I knew,*" Mattie holds in a sob, "The only thing I hold against myself now is not leaving sooner."

"Look at me," I turn Mattie's shoulders so he's facing me, "From what you've told me, he was toxic enough to make it hard to leave. Awful to stay, but worse to go. You were scared of him, but you didn't know how to get out. Don't beat yourself up, Birdie. I'm just glad you're okay, that you got out. You're getting better; you're healing."

I yawn, feeling more than a little drained. Mattie wraps his arms tightly around my chest.

"Is it wrong to take a nap right now? I just woke up, like, an hour ago." He mutters.

"I was thinking the same thing," I trace Mattie's shoulder, "I'm exhausted."

"Go back to bed, Sammy."

Matthew stretches and rolls off me. He grabs my hand and pulls me to my feet. He starts walking towards his bedroom, encouraging me to follow. He flops down on the mattress, but I stay in the doorway.

"Come and lay down, Sammy. Neither of us should be alone right now."

He's right. I sit on the edge of the bed, then lean back against the pillows. Matt smiles at me, a silent *thank you.* I don't like being taken care of, it had never really happened before this. I'm not used to it.

"I know you hate it when I dote on you," Mattie says, "But please humor me. That phone call was dreadful, Sam. I wanna hold you and make everything okay, but I can't fix *everything.* Can I hold you, though?"
"Yes, Mattie. You can almost *always* hold me."

He grins and snuggles up against my back. Mattie slings an arm across my chest, sighing contentedly. Matthew's a certified space heater, and soon enough I'm lulled to sleep by his constant warmth.

Krista's yelling at Dad. She's pissed like I've never seen her; a boiling, seething rage in her eyes. Dad swings, missing by a mile, stumbles and falls.
"-hate you! You were too drunk to see Sammy's swim meet, you sick son of a bitch!"
"It doesn't matter, Krista. He'll grow out of it someday."
"But he hasn't yet. You just don't care."
"You're right, I don't."

Krista lunges at him. She's only thirteen-years-old, but she's already a ball of fury. She gets hit, again and again and again and-

---

"Sam!" Matthew is leaning over me, brow knit with worry, "You were crying, angel. Do you know where you are?"

"I'm in your room, in our apartment, in Chicago." *So much better than where I just was.*

"Good, that's great, Sammy." Some of the stress falls from his shoulders.

"I'm sorry, Mattie. I didn't mean to wake you up."

"Don't you ever apologize for that," Birdie stares at me with a furious intensity, "I want you to feel safe, and if that means waking up in the middle of the night, so be it. I love you, Sam. Please don't hesitate to ask for help."

I don't know how to respond to that, so I don't. I pull Matthew into my side and hope he gets the message.

Thank you for caring the way you do.

Matthew

It doesn't take long for Sam to fall back to sleep. His breathing evens, and I take some solace in that. He wants to run, I know that look, I've seen it on my face. He's warm and holding me tight, but I can feel the tension in his frame. *You wanted them to have changed, and they didn't. When you needed her, she was gone. Now that you're okay, she's back.* Sam's not used to being cared for, being able to ask for help. He works so hard to make everybody else happy. I sigh and run my hand through his dark blond hair. Sam's hair is "windblown" on the best of days, but usually it just sticks out at all angles. *Cute.* It's the one imperfect physical feature on my otherwise perfect boyfriend. I want him to feel safe in his skin. Sam's always been so patient and kind to me, I wish he'd be more forgiving of himself.

I awaken a short time later. Sam is still sleeping, tangled in the covers. He must've been truly exhausted; I never wake up first. Cautiously, I slip away and into the bathroom. I peer at my reflection and sigh. I would look good, if I could ignore the bags under my eyes and the slump to my back. I look stressed. Maybe I just need some fresh air. I throw on a coat and head for the door, then stop. *What if Sam wakes up while I'm gone?* I write a quick note and tape it to his face, figuring he couldn't miss it if he tried.

It's bitterly cold outside, the wind is biting, and it looks like it might snow. I wish I'd grabbed a heavier jacket. All the storefronts are lit up with holiday lights and cheer, and I smile, ducking into the nearest store. Pretty little trinkets blanket the shelves in a twinkling gleam. It's warm in here, Christmas carols crackle through an old-timey radio, and a grey old man tends the counter. It's like I've stepped back in time. Enchanted, I drift through the little shop until I see *the one.* On the lowest branch of the display tree, there's a tiny, blown-glass hippopotamus wearing a teeny santa hat. It's almost exactly like the one at Gram's house. Well, the one that *used to be* at Gram's house. Papa dropped it, which was fine, but then Grams stepped on it, which was not. For being so old, Grams sure uses a lot of curse words, especially when there are shards of hippo in her foot.

I bought the festive little pachyderm, of course.

The walk home is mostly uneventful. There's a kid dancing on the street corner, a bucket label "for college" nearby. The backing track ends, and she glances to the empty bucket. Something about her posture changes as she starts in on the next song. She's dancing with twice the fury she had before. I put $10 in the bucket, along with a list of the sites I used for financial aid. (I hope she can read it; I scrawled that list on the back of a takeout menu.)

Once back in the apartment, I write down the name of the restaurant that the takeout menu was from. It looked really good! I don't want to forget the name of the place. There's some scuffling in the kitchen, and a couple pots and pans clank together before Sam pokes his head out.

"Hey, Birdie," He beams, "Welcome home."
"Hi, Sammy. Sorry about leaving before you woke up. I really needed some air, you know?"
"I get it. I wasn't worried, Mattie. You left me a note, remember?"
"Yeah, I remember. I just didn't want to leave you right after all of that. I wanted to take care of you, wanted to snuggle you and make things better."
"Have I mentioned how much I love you?" Sam says fondly, "I feel like I don't say it enough."
"You do," I murmur, "You don't always put it into words, but everything you do says that you love me, Sam. All the little things, like making waffles every Saturday, watching *The Bachelorette* with me, just… everything. I know how much of a mess that ancient waffle iron makes, but you still use it, just because it makes me happy. I love you, angel. So much."

Sam just stands there for awhile. Right when I'm going to check for a pulse, he crosses the floor between us and pulls me in close. I wrap my arms tentatively around his shoulders, trying to gauge a reaction. Sam nearly goes limp, his head drooping until it rests on my shoulder. I hold him a little tighter.

"Are you feeling okay, Sammy?"
"Yeah, I've just been spread a little thin lately. Between my mom and all the recording sessions, I guess I'm exhausted."
"That's normal, pretty boy. I'm tired from just the recordings, I can't even imagine how you're feeling. Why don't you sit down on the couch? I'll bring you something to eat, you just rest and relax, alright?"

Sam nods and walks over to the couch. I enter the kitchen, grab a couple snacks, then patter back to Sam. He sighs and flashes a feeble smile, then scooches over so that I can sit. I snuggle into the space next to him, letting Sam cuddle up against my side.

"You need a self care day." I whisper.
"Do we have time? I mean, the record company is really pressing for a tour and-"
"And there won't be a tour if you keep working yourself to death. If there's one thing I know, it's that taking a little time for yourself does a lot of good. I love you to bits, I don't wanna see you hurting."
"If you're sure that I have time for this, then I'll do it. I know it'd be good for me, but I'm not at all used to taking time off. I've never been able to before."
"You can do it now, though. Seriously, angel, you have all the time in the world."

Sam nods thoughtfully, then flops gracelessly onto my lap. I make a very undignified little "oof" noise at the sudden move.

"Sorry, are you okay, Mattie?"
"Yeah, I'm fine. You just surprised me, is all."

Sam sighs and puts his head back down. I run my hands through his hair, hoping it'll relax him. Sure enough, Sam's shoulders finally release their constant tension and he sags into me. I stop playing with his hair for a moment; just long enough to pull him closer, his head on my chest. He mumbles some thanks, but I shush him. This isn't something he needs to thank me for. Sam huffs a disgruntled sigh, but allows himself to melt a little more.

We stay like that for almost an hour. Sam seems content with just companionable silence and an embrace. I know that I wouldn't change a thing.

"We should go to the Shedd Aquarium. I never went as a kid." Sam says, seemingly out of the blue.
"Sure," I pull him closer, "When do you want to go?"
"Could-" He stops, "Nevermind, I shouldn't ask you on such short notice."
"If you want to go today, we can go today," I snap, then more gently, "It's your choice, Sammy. You can ask for stuff and take days off, though, okay? And if you need to do something, you don't have to ask me. I know that you're used to people controlling you, but I don't want you to have to deal with that anymore. You don't have to work everyday from seven in the morning until ass o'clock at night just to survive anymore. So, if you want to go today, we could go today."
"I would like that, yeah." Sam smiles.

Sam

Something about taking time for myself doesn't sit well with me. I've never been able to do it before, and honestly, I just don't know how. Mattie's driving us to the Shedd, humming along to the radio and drumming on the steering wheel. He gives me a reassuring smile as he pulls the car into a parking spot. As we walk up the stairway and into the main building, Matthew seems to gain a little more bounce in his step. He's practically vibrating by the time we reach the front of the ticket line.

"Two main entry tickets," Matthew pauses to scan the exhibits, "And two for the beluga encounter!"
The man behind the counter arches an eyebrow, but rings up our total nevertheless.
"That's way too much, Mattie. Just the main entry would be fine."
"I wanna teach you that it's okay to treat yourself," He swipes the credit card, "Especially when you're recently famous and permanently stressed. Now let's look at fish and shit! Literal shit, 'cuz fish don't use toilets."

I snicker and follow Matt into the center room of the aquarium. There's a massive tank in this first room. I can see in from all angles and it's mesmerizing. I want to live here. Matthew already has his face pressed up against the side of the tank, his glasses smashed into his cheeks. I peer into the tank as well, silvery scales rushing past my eyes. Mattie giggles from a little ways away, and I glance over at him. (I hate to admit it, but I'm reluctant to stop staring at the fish.) Flapping at the glass in front of him is a stingray. Mattie laughs again, putting his hand up to the tank.

"Sam, you've got to see this!" He smiles, "It's got no teeth! It's just like the nature shows said, this little guy's got a mouth but no teeth. Look at the gills. What a beautiful animal, I think I love him."

"Are you leaving me for a fish, Mattie?" I chuckle.

"No, but I could've been a marine biologist. Finally put that degree to use."

"What did you major in, again?"

"Biology. I would love to work here, oh my god. If we didn't get famous, I totally would've applied."

"That would've been fun, I'm sure."

"Yeah, but not as fun as what I've already got."

I smile, delighted by that comment. Mattie comes over and wraps his arm around my waist. He points at some brightly colored thing, laughing about fake it looks. I allow myself to enjoy the face of wide-eyed wonder Mattie's making. I still do not like to treat myself, but maybe this'll be okay.

Mattie leads me into another wing off of the main room. Tanks line the walls, all filled with dull colored fish. When I look into the first tank, ten pairs of glassy eyes look back at me. I shiver and look at the sign identifying these unblinking beasts. All of them are native to the Chicagoland area. Matthew dragged me into the Great Lakes wing, apparently. I walk briskly to the next tank, and luckily these fish don't stare at me. I walk from tank to tank, and somewhere along the way I lose sight of him. I look around for him, and it doesn't take me too long to find Matthew leaning over a waist-high tank of sturgeon fish. He looks thrilled to be there; he's got his hand in the water, fingers grazing the bony back of a fish. He catches my gaze and waves me over.

"They're so cool, Sam," He says, "They're living fossils! And I'm touching them!"

I grin and nod. *He's so happy.* Matt pulls his arm out of the water and shakes it off. He then proceeds to give me an enthusiastic hug, still chattering about how awesome the fish were. I don't particularly think that they're too "awesome." I am now covered in fish water, but I'm not about to burst Mattie's bubble. His secret, weird, nerdy bubble. He's still absolutely adorable when he's geeking out like this, fish water or not.

Perhaps, it's alright to treat myself every once in a while. Mattie's smiling sweetly and holding my hand in his. We walk leisurely back to the car, conversation wandering aimlessly. *It's incredible.* I sink back into the passenger's seat, thanking Mattie out of habit. Again, he shushes me and says I don't need to thank him, that he wanted to do this. I smile and lean across the gear shift for a hug. I can feel my pocket buzz with my phone, but I ignore it.

It's about time for dinner when we get back to the apartment. I start a pot to boil, humming and bopping around the kitchen. *Pasta, roma tomatoes, canned tomatoes, cheese, other cheese, pepper, more cheese...* This the only recipe that I stole from Krista, not the other way around. It's only fair; I've always been better at dessert.

"Sammy, your phone's ringing!" Matt yells from... somewhere. "Where are you?"
"Bedroom, but your phone's on the coffee table."
"Thanks."

I pick up the phone and answer it.

"Krista?"

"Can I come over? I'm sorry, I'm so sorry, I just-"

"Take a breath, Kris," I sigh, "What's the matter?"

"The break-in was three years ago today and I don't want to be alone. I should be over it by now, I know, but-"

"You can come over, Krissy. I was just making the pasta you like, so come on over and stay awhile. You can sleep in the guest room if you need to."

"What about Mattie? It's his house, too."

"I'll ask him. It'll probably be fine, though."

I walk into Mattie's -our?- bedroom. *We would so often be tangled together at night, even before we were together. It was just for some silent company, some comfort in the dark.* I sit on the edge of the bed, and Matt looks up from his book with a lopsided grin.

"Hey, Birdie, would it be alright if-" I start to speak, but choke right after.

"What's wrong, angel?" Mattie tips his head. It's unseemly for someone so *good* to look so worried. Wordlessly, I had him the phone. He nods, listening to whatever Krista has to say. Finally, he exhales deeply.

"Of course you can stay here," He says, "The break-in... must've been rough. I'm no stranger to asking for a place to stay, Krista. And I wasn't even asking somebody *I knew.* You can sleep in the guest room and I'll just share a bed with Sam. No big deal. Okay, bye."

He hangs up the phone, then opens his arms for a hug. I give in to my craving for comfort and nestle up against his chest. Mattie tells me that my sister is in the parking lot to our apartment building. I look up at him, suddenly frantic. *I have to get the pasta served and-*

There's a harsh buzzing noise. *The doorbell.* Matt trots over to open the door. Krista brushes past him, scrubbing at her face.

"Kris." Matthew whispers.
"I'm sorry, I know I'm invading your home, I just need-"
"It's okay, you're okay. You're not a burden to bear, Krissy. C'mere, Sam's in the kitchen."

They walk in together and almost immediately, Krista flings herself into my chest. She huffs and moves quickly away, head bowed. I hate how guilty she looks. Mattie silently passes out the food.

"Eat," He says, "You can't recuperate on an empty stomach."

We all eat in a gloomy silence; it's like a storm cloud is devouring any conversation to be had. Krista's fork clinks against her empty plate, but her gaze is still cast down. She looks terrible, and I don't say that often. Her posture screams "exhaustion," but she says she can't sleep. I hate being helpless to comfort those closest to me.

"Krista." Matthew's tone is firm.
"Yes? I'm sorry, what is it?"
"No, quit apologizing. I want you to take a shower, put on some pajamas, and get some rest."
"But the dreams-"
"I know, Kris, trust me, but you need to sleep. Stand up and fight this. Take care of yourself, or else you're letting them win."

Krista's face hardens how it always did before a fight. Sure enough, she stands up and walks toward the bathroom. Matt throws her a towel, and she thanks him. He just nods and patters back to the couch.

"How did you do that?" I ask, amazed.

"I just played to her ego. You told me she never backs down from a fight, not until she wins at least, so I framed this as her fighting her weaknesses. She loves to prove herself to everyone, so I thought 'huh, maybe she should show herself what she's got.'" Mattie shrugs.

"Thank you. Krista's a lot tougher than she realizes."

"I know. If she knew how much power she has, she'd be ruling the world right now."

I laugh and sling an arm around Mattie's shoulders, "You really are the greatest, Birdie."

"Thanks, angel."

Matthew

As it turns out, both Sam and Krista try way too hard to keep everybody happy. While I'm not exactly surprised, (their childhood was far less than ideal...), I'm still absolutely *livid*. I'm not mad at Sam or Krista, of course not, but I'm furious with whatever or whoever told them that it wasn't okay to ask for help. I think it's high time for a role reversal. I'll take care of all the work, let Sam relax a bit. As for Krista? I'm considering inviting her to stick around for a little while longer. Sam's already off to bed, Krista's still in the shower, so I'm alone with my plans. Right as I'm considering doing a wellness check on Krista, I hear the shower turn off. She walks into the living room, her hair up in a towel and her pajamas all wrinkled. *I guess not ironing your clothes runs in the family as well.* She looks at me forlornly, then falls onto the couch.

"I feel fucking pathetic," She snarls, "Can't even sleep in my own bed. What kind of sad, loser scum have I become? God, and my roommate's at home; she's probably worried sick. She's my business partner, you know. Her name's Amy Buchanan, and she's the pastry chef at the restaurant too. I'm a disappointment. Shit, man, I'm crashing on my brother's couch again. I do this every year. Every year! And now he lives with somebody and I'm intruding on two lives, not just one. I'm fucking sorry, Matt."

Wow. That was a lot to take in. She talks so fast, too!

"You are not pathetic, Krista. Recovery takes time. You're not intruding, either, okay? Sam said it was fine to have you stay the night, and I agree. You set your standards so impossibly high that you're bound to fail. Just relax, Krissy. No one is judging you as harshly as you're judging yourself."
She nods stiffly.
"Go to bed, Krista. It's late, and you haven't slept in days, right?"
"Yeah, I should take better care of myself."
"Yes, yes you should. Rest well, Kris."

She plods into the guest room, where I can only hope she gets some sleep.

When I finally get to bed, Sam's already fast asleep, snuggled up under the covers. I cautiously climb in next him, being so, so careful not to wake him. I'm able to press myself up against him without disturbing him. I sigh contently and nuzzle my cheek against Sam's chest. I can hear his heartbeat, albeit faintly. I cuddle even closer and toss an arm around him. Sam's breathing is slow and even, except for the occasional snore. It doesn't take long for me to fall asleep.

I don't often have good dreams. When I do, they're usually about the band or one of life's milestones. It's typically something like getting married (but I never see the guy's face) or touring around the country (but I never hear the applause.) My dreams are seldom something to write home about, but *tonight...* Tonight, there's nothing missing. It might not be a special setting, just a corner bakery, but I have everything. I can see all the wrinkles in his T-shirt. I can feel the calluses on his hands, and how they hold mine. I can hear his laugh, smell the coffee on the table, taste the cupcake I ordered. *Everything is here.*

Unlike so many of my other vivid dreams, I don't wake with a jolt. Instead, I slide into a new little wonderland, although this one is so much more boring. I long for the bakery and my coffee *and my Sammy* to take me back.

A soft tapping on the door pulls me from sleep altogether. With an aggravated grunt, I tell "whoever's rapping on my chamber door" to come in. The door swings open and sure enough, it's Krista. I blink a couple times and, hang on just a second here, there's somebody with her. And that somebody looks kinda pissed.

"I did not get a single text or call from you, Krista. I tracked your phone like a fucking stalker, just to be sure you weren't killed by a stalker! I was so worried, Kris. I remember the break-in, you know."
"Amy-"
"Please just text me, Kris. I almost called the cops!"

"Okay, I'll text you next time. But, uh, this is Matthew. Matthew, Amy. Amy, Matthew."

"It's a pleasure to meet you. Maybe we could talk sometime, when it's not in the middle of the damn night." I grumble. I've never taken kindly to being woken up.

"Heh, need your beauty rest?" Amy smirks, "That's alright. Sorry about barging in and giving you an earful of a secondhand lecture. Thanks for keeping Krissy safe, I don't know what I'd do without her."

"Okay, you giant sap. Let's go home." Krista's already putting her coat on.

"You don't have to leave."

"Nah, it's alright. I think I'm ready to go."

I nod and say some goodbyes, then *finally* get to crawl back into bed. I sigh and curl up against Sam's chest. He snuffles and stirs, eyes cracking open. He looks at me groggily, trying to get his eyes to focus.

"Birdie?" He hums, "What're you doing awake? It's the middle of the night."

"Ah, well, Krista's overprotective and overly concerned roommate showed up. It seemed like Kris was getting a bit of a lecture from her, but whatever happened..."

"What? What happened?"

"I think it comforted Krista enough for her to go home. They just left."

Sam grunts and flops melodramatically onto his back, "But I was gonna make pancakes and be a good 'lil bro.' Krissy had to take care of me all the time; I just wanted to return the favor."

Sam, you stupid, selfless, little "knight-in-shining-armor," you.

"You don't owe her anything, Sam. She felt horrible about coming over-"

"What? *Why?* Was it something I did?"

"No, not even close. She said that she was 'intruding,' or something like that. You don't have to feel bad about all the small things you couldn't fix. It wasn't your job to take care of anybody back then-"

"But-"

"-It wasn't her job either, I know. I also know that Kris took care of you because *she wanted to.* She didn't have to, but she did. Don't beat yourself up about everything that's ever happened to you. It wasn't your fault, it wasn't your responsibility, *it's time to let it go.* You're in a different place now, Sammy. You're safe now, alright? Safe and sound."

Sam chokes on the lump in his throat, a couple tears threatening to spill.

"C'mere."

And that's all it took. All of the those walls come crumbling down, and Sam finally lets himself fall into my chest. I keep a gentle hand on his shoulder, running the other up and down his waist. He trembles miserably, clutching me and whimpering apologies. I shush him as gently as I can, holding him close. Sam snivels and sobs and it damn near breaks my heart.

"You don't cry much, do you?" I whisper, more to myself than anything, "That's alright, Sammy. I gotcha, I love ya, you know that. It'll pass, angel. Just let it out."

A part of me wonders how many years of pent-up emotions are all crashing out right now, but I put that aside. Sam's stopped crying, but now he looks almost scared. *He isn't scared of me, right? No, that's not it. Then what's the matter?*

"Sammy? Sam, angel, what's wrong? You don't look like yourself, sweetheart."
"I hate crying," He's barely even audible, "I hate showing weakness, Mattie. I know- I know it's not- that crying doesn't mean I'm weak but I was always told the worst things as a kid-"
"Sam. Look at me. You don't have to believe what people say about you. You're the only one who can really change yourself, right? It doesn't matter what they told you; you're not weak. You're not even close to weak, Sammy. Now, just hold me and get some rest, alright?"

He nods, his whole body sagging with relief. Sam pillows his head on my stomach, (I'm not exactly *thrilled* about it, but if Sam doesn't mind the extra cushion, then that's fine by me...) and he's asleep in two minutes flat. I wait a minute for *yet another random occurence* to keep me from my sleep, but nothing happens.

Success.

Sam

How and why did I have a meltdown? Poor Matt had to deal with it, but at least Krista didn't see anything. God, I'm so embarrassed! I completely and totally freak out, beg for comfort in my own sad way, then let Matt pick up the pieces. I'm more than a little shocked he didn't make me leave or sleep on the couch or something. But instead of waking up somewhere cold and lonely, I'm still all snuggled up next to Matthew. The guy's way too good to me, way out of my league, everything and more. For now, though, he's with me. Me! I'm just another white collar nobody, a good-for-nothing fool, but at least I have my rockstar. Speak of the devil, Mattie rolls over in bed, making his whole body weight press down on me.

I can't exactly breathe, and not because my ribcage is being crushed. (My ribcage *is,* in fact, being crushed, but that has nothing to do with why I can't breathe.) My face is sandwiched between Mattie and the pillow. *You take my breath away, Birdie.* Everything is so warm and so soft; I never want this to end. I fall back into a peaceful sleep, Matthew still laying across my chest.

As with all good things, this too ends. Matthew wakes with a start and springs away from me.

"Oh God, Sam!" He sputters, "Did I crush you? I'm sorry, angel, so sorry."
"It's alright, Birdie. You weren't crushing me. You worry too much, you know."
"Like you can talk." He cracks a small smile.
"Touche. Did you sleep alright?"
"I slept great, Sammy." Mattie tilts his head down, messy hair hiding his eyes but not his blush.
"Awesome. C'mon, songbird, let's eat some breakfast. We still have a practice session at the record company today."

He slips out of bed and stretches, body arching like he's posing to be drawn. I don't notice that I'm staring, I certainly didn't mean to do it, but Matt turns around, smirking.

"How long are you gonna stand there gawking, angel?"

I immediately look away, mildly ashamed. I shouldn't be ogling my boyfriend, even if it's in the privacy of our apartment. Matthew deserves better than me giving him a once over like that.

"I'm not mad at you, Sam. You weren't looking at me like- well, I guess the kids are calling it 'eye-fucking.' You weren't doing that. You were looking at me like I hang the moon and the sun shines out of my ass. I love you, Sammy. You can look at me with that smitten face anytime, day or night, because you're different from everybody else. You know me as a person, not as just another pretty face. *You* giving me that lovestruck look is different because you've seen my flaws, my imperfections, and *I want you to look at me*. It's mutual, angel; I want to be with you. I should stop talking now, but I-"

I pull Matt into a tight embrace, feeling him go limp in my arms. His head falls against my shoulder, his arms wrapping around my waist. I cradle him, bending over so he doesn't have to stand on his toes. We stay there for a minute, Matthew rocking back and forth on his heels. I'm eventually forced to lean away when the desire for food outweighs the desire for human contact.

Mattie stays plastered to my side as I cook. He sits up on the counter at one point, pouting and glancing at the omelets. I look at him with what can only be called a lovesick smile.

"I'm almost done, Mattie-Bird. If you're hungry, though, go right ahead and eat."

He grins, grabbing a plate and planting himself back up on the counter. I'm not sure what it is, but something about Matthew just makes me want to take care of him. Not in a creepy, possessive way, absolutely not. I just want to see him happy. I mean, how could you look at that face and *not* want to spoil him rotten? He's so precious; he's both cute and more than worth his weight in gold. I want to have nice, relaxing breakfasts like this all the time. Matt loves food more than most other things and/or people. If I want to see him happy, it makes sense to cook for him. Besides, Mattie's more than a bit of a kitchen nightmare. Sandwiches? Sure. Instant noodles? Absolutely. Anything else? It starts to get questionable.

I sit down across from Matt, see him smile at me when he sees me. I give a shy smile in return and start in on the omelet. It's so nice to have a guy like Matt in my life.

"I am so lucky." I don't realize that I'd spoken aloud until Mattie starts giggling.
"Yeah, well, so am I." He casually throws me a megawatt smile. I don't think he knows how handsome he is. I just sit there like a man wooed and turned to stone by medusa. Although, if my memory serves me, medusa turned men to stone because she had snakes for hair and was terrifying. So, I suppose I sit there like a smitten fool and nothing more. I can live with that.

We show up at the record studio right on time. Matthew is immediately whisked away by a sharply dressed woman. I think she's our boss, Mary May Jones, although I'm not sure. I stand at attention, waiting for someone to tell me what to do. No one does, so I'm left standing there like a very nervous scarecrow. Matthew and the pretty-and-scary lady come back a short time later. I must look scared and out of place, because Pretty-And-Scary tells me to "loosen up and follow." I trail her like a lost puppy.

"I'm Mary May Jones," She says, still walking, "And I'm your manager. You are recording today, correct?"

She glances over her shoulder, one eyebrow arched.

"Uh, yes, ma'am. I- er, we are recording. I think. Are we recording, Mattie?" *Ultimate fail.*
"Yeah! I mean, yes. Ma'am. Should I call you ma'am? You don't look old enough to-"
"Enough, the both of you," Mary May Jones turns on her heel, "Have you ever spoken to another human being before? Ever in your life?"
"Hey!" Mattie glares at her, clearly offended.
"Well, have you?"
"Yes, I have. It's been awhile, but I have in fact 'spoken to another human being.'"

The line is delivered with patented Matthew sass. Now he looks at her over his glasses, hip cocked out to the side. *You're a brave soul, Matt. Please don't get us fired.*

"There he is." She says simply.
"Excuse me?" The pose gains a slight lip curl. It's kinda hot, if I'm honest.
"You were so... *extravagant* on all the interviews. I missed that personality. You don't have to call me 'ma'am,' just call me Mary, or Mary May."
"Alright, Mary. If you wanted personality, you could've just said."
"Well, where's the fun in that?" She smiles devilishly and beckons for us to keep walking.

Eventually, we reach an enormous recording studio. It's beautiful. *All of my dreams are coming true right in front of my eyes.*

"I'd like for you to try your hand at a cover, if you don't mind. You like Queen, right?"
"Of course I do, who do you think I am? But to cover a Queen song is to set one's self up for failure."
"All you have to do is record, Matthew. It doesn't have to be released or sold."
"I guess that's true. Alright, I'll do it, but I'm picking the song."

Mary May nods and ushers us into the studio.

"Have fun and try not to break anything!" She smirks and walks briskly away.

I just stand there for a while, still in shock. Everything in here is so fancy! I cannot believe my luck. It takes me a couple minutes to even notice that Chris and James are already here. Chris has been Matt's friend for years and James joined the band in college. Chris is on drums, James on rhythm guitar. They smile and wave, Chris and Matt do some kind of complicated handshake. They probably made it as kids. It's nice to see everybody again, especially offstage. I think it's going to be fantastic getting to know Chris and James a little better. They seem pretty great.

We start recording "Don't Stop Me Now." I've always loved that song -sung it in the shower, in the car, and so on- but never in front of people. Now, I'm being recorded. Granted, I'm not singing, but it's still nerve-wracking. No one can do Queen how Queen did

Queen. Mattie's marvellous, (as usual), and all the music is blending together perfectly.

We might have just covered Queen fairly decently, but no one will ever do Queen how Queen did Queen.

The session takes several hours, and I am exhausted. It's almost five o'clock at night, and we got here early this morning. I didn't eat lunch! No wonder I'm so hungry. Chris is shrugging on his coat when he asks if we'd all like to get some dinner.

"Sure," Matt says, "I'm starved. With the recordings and then all that talk about a tour? I'm absolutely famished."
"You're dramatic as hell, that's what you are," James laughs, "But yeah, let's get something to eat."
"You coming, Sam?" Chris makes a puppy face at me, as if I needed convincing.
"Of course, where do you guys want to eat?"

We end up at a diner. They serve the best biscuits in town, apparently. Chris is loud and fairly funny, while James is quiet, almost shy. I find out the Chris is engaged to his longtime girlfriend, Claire.

"Claire Greensburg?"
"Yeah! Do you know her?"
"We were best friends as kids! Small world, man."

We all laugh and eat until the diner closes. James let some personality show about halfway through dinner and is still chuckling about something. Chris is flailing his hands around to emphasize "how fucking stupid you were in high school, I swear to God, Matt." Matthew's laughing along, probably tipsy. Come to think of it, so is Chris.

"Hey, Chris," I tap on his shoulder, "Are you gonna get home alright?"
"Oh, heh," He giggles, trips over his feet, then says, "Yeah, I'll be fine. Jamie drove me here 'cuz my car's in the shop."
"I'll make sure he doesn't do anything too stupid." James grumbles, but he's still smiling.

Satisfied, I start leading Matthew towards the car. He stumbles a couple of times and grabs my waist eventually.

"Thanks, Sammy," He slurs, "You're the best- the best- the best everything."
"You're welcome, Mattie. The car's not too far, now. Just don't fall."
"M'kay, angel. I love ya."

I freeze up. *It's not the first time Matt's said it but still. He's drunk, he might not know what he's saying, but he might know* exactly *what he's saying. Oh man, oh no, think, Sam, think.*

"I know, sweets. I love you too."

I hope I did that right. Dear lord, it's like I'm a nervous middle schooler again.

Matthew starts dozing off in the car, but doesn't fall asleep. That makes it a little bit easier to get upstairs and into bed.

"Sammy. I'm fine, just a little drunk. You can relax; I can hear you worrying from here!"

While I appreciate the effort, this does almost nothing to soothe my nerves. I've never done well with drunk sitting, but I haven't told Mattie that yet. I can't exactly tell him now; he's already snoring away under the covers. Besides, I don't *want* to tell him and I really don't want to tell him why. Logically, I know that having a beer or two while out with friends is something that lots of people do.

I still can't stop my mind from flashing to my father and how one beer had turned to one pack, and that had turned him into a monster. I guess that's why I don't drink at parties. I don't want to be around the "do it and you're cool" attitude. I'll have something when I'm with close friends, or just during a night-in with Matt. But I will never drink with people I don't know. I've always known that if I talked about it, I might feel better about everything.

That's something to worry about in the morning, though.

Matthew

Something was off last night and I still can't place it. Sam was even more nervous than usual. It was weird, concerning even. I don't know what's going on with him. Even now, he seems jittery. Maybe it was being around the band. Sam's a kind soul, but he's so shy. I'm not convinced that was the issue, though. He was fine up until we were getting into the car. It was kinda like he was scared of me. That would be weird, right? I mean, I'm about as intimidating as a teddy bear. Still thinking and overthinking, I walk into the kitchen.

"Did you sleep okay? Need advil? Coffee? I can-"

"Sam, what's the matter with you?" *I probably could've phrased that better.* Sam looks at me with wide, hurt eyes.
"I didn't mean it like that. You just seemed so nervous last night, and now you're throwing hangover cures at me. I'm fine, angel. I promise. So, let me try this again. What's wrong, Sam? Talk to me."

He just looks at me again and heaves a sigh.

"I always tense up around alcohol," He mumbles, "It's nothing about you or Chris or James. I just freak out, especially if I don't know the group very well. I'm scared of being pressured into a drink, and I'm *terrified* of turning into my dad. It wasn't about you. In all honesty, I was just barely holding it together before we got in the car. I projected my worry, which isn't fair to you, I know. I'm sorry, Birdie."

I pull Sam in for a (hopefully) reassuring hug.

"No need to apologize. I had no idea, Sammy. *I'm sorry* that you were so stressed all night. I love you, and I would never have put you through all that if I had known. Now come on, let's get breakfast out today. We can try the new bakery you saw."

He nods and cracks a twisted smile, "Thanks, sweets. I've been holding that in since I was a kid. I think I made it a bigger deal than it is, worked myself up and made myself think that no one would respect that fear. God, I'm sorry. It's way too early in the morning to talk about this kind of thing. Let's get something to eat."

I hold him a little closer. *Has he ever let his walls down before?* I have to stand on my toes to give him a chaste kiss on the cheek. Sam gives me a watery but sincere smile. We get ready to leave in silence; we drive to the bakery in silence. There's no conversation walking in, and it's infuriating. Sam is sitting across from me, coffee in one hand, bagel in the other. He looks up at me, then shamefully drops his gaze. *Why is he so scared to talk about this? It's not like I'm perfect, or anything.*

"Samuel. You know that I love you to death. Quit looking so ashamed of yourself. You didn't do anything wrong."
"Except that I did. I'm supposed to *talk about my feelings* and be open with you. I don't want to be closed off."
"Then don't be! It's not like I have the grounds to judge anyone, especially not you."
"It's not that easy," Sam's voice lowers, "I'm terrified. I have always been terrified of telling anyone about the shit I've been through. I'm not like you; I can't just bear my soul like it's nothing."
"What's that supposed to mean?" I frown.
"It means that I envy you!" Sam stands up and pushes away from the table, "I can't talk to people, I'm scared of everything, and I can't even go out with my boyfriend and our friends. I wish I could do all of that but I *can't.*"

Sam looks like he's about to cry. He looks so vulnerable and hopeless, but fierce at the same time. It's like he'd be willing to knock somebody out cold for me or for his sister, but would cower and take the blows if they were aimed at him. Then it hits me. *Sam has never been properly taken care of in his life. He has no idea how to take care of himself.* And it's not like he can't put food on the table or keep a roof over his head. It's that he doesn't do that for himself. Sam puts himself aside in favor of everyone else.

"Sammy, remember when we went to the aquarium?"
"Yeah, I do." He tries to steady his voice to no avail.
"You looked happy. You let yourself have fun. You can do that more often now, Sam. We don't have to worry about money

anymore. Besides, I think you're going to get an ulcer if you keep stressing like this. You're safe now, pretty boy. Nothing can- nothing from back then can hurt you anymore. You're going to be okay, angel. I don't want to fight with you, so even if you're not ready to talk to me about everything, please tell me if something's upsetting you in the moment. I don't want you to hurt."

"I don't want to fight with you either," He mumbles, head hung and eyes wet, "I'll- I'll try to tell you the stuff that brings up bad memories. I'm tired of hurting."

"Thank you," I whisper, relieved, "Now drink your coffee before it gets cold."

Sam finally meets my eyes, then. The best comparison for his facial expression would be to one of those scared, cornered dogs on the ASPCA commercials; the ones that have never known love. I get up and walk to his side of the table. I wrap my arms around his shoulders, my cheek resting against his neck. He lets himself be held and shakily puts his hands on my waist. I can tell that he's crying (my shirt is wet where Sam pressed his face into it) and he's clinging to me like a life preserver.

"It's alright, Sammy. I got you, you have me right here. I need to sit down, though, angel, my back is killing me."

Sam nods against my shoulder and lets go of me. I sit back down in my chair, feeling guilty despite myself. Sam wraps himself up in his coat, shrinking down to a nearly impossible size. I sigh and stand up again, taking Sam by the hand. I tell him we could take breakfast to-go, and he agrees. He has that same shameful look on his face, but I think it's for a different reason. He's apologizing to me again and again. *What has gotten into you, Sammy? I'm worried.*

Once we get back to our apartment, Sam falls gracelessly onto the couch. I snuggle up to him, resting my head on his shoulder. Sam sighs heavily and melts into my side.

"I think I know what's going on with me." He murmurs.
"Yeah? Do you wanna talk about it?"
"Yeah, I do," He takes a breath, "The holidays are coming up and I have a lot of bad memories surrounding them. My mom wasn't home and my dad was worse than usual. Krista would try to work, sometimes her boss would let me help out in the kitchen, but most years I was stuck at home. There were no big meals, no presents, none of that holiday spirit that the other kids would talk about. I still get so stressed this time of year; it's like all of my other fears are amplified."
"That-" I falter, "That sucks. Seriously, Sam, none of that was fair to you. Parents are supposed to care for their kids. Jeez, you had to hide out in a kitchen?"
"Yeah, Krista pleaded with her boss to let me come in. I was too young to get a workers permit, but then again so was Krista. I was nine, I think, the first time Krista's boss let me stay. She was twelve."
"That is never going to happen to you again. You will have somewhere to celebrate, angel, I promise."
"Thanks, Mattie-Bird."

Sam leans back against the couch, pulling me a little closer to him. I nestle into his chest, letting Sam tuck me under his chin. Of course, my phone starts ringing. It's my dad so I can't just ignore it.

"Hello?"
"Hey, son! Have you been busy lately? You haven't called in forever."
"Yeah, I've been booked. I'm actually a little busy now."

"Oh, is that right?" I can hear his smirk, "I'll make this quick, then. I've been wondering if you're coming to Thanksgiving this year. I mean, you don't have to, but-"

"I would love to go! Dad, you know me. Of course I'm going to the eat-until-you-can't-breathe event."

"Alright, fair enough. Bring a friend, if you want. Or if you have a date-"

"Yeah, I know. The more the merrier. It's been this way every year."

"Okay, see you in two days. Love you, kid."

"Love you, too, Dad."

I smile and put my phone on the coffee table. Sam looks up at me curiously.

"What was that about?"

"My dad invited me to Thanksgiving, told me to bring a plus one."

"Okay, I usually work at Krista's restaurant on Thanksgiving so I'm not lonely but she doesn't need the help this year-"

"Samuel! You are the plus one. You can come with me to my dad's place."

"Oh my God! Mattie, I'd love that!"

Sam grins and nearly tackles me in a tight hug.

"I can't believe it. I'm actually going to have a Thanksgiving dinner. And what perfect timing, too. With the phone call?"

"Yeah, Dad does that. I'm starting to think that he plants spy cams everywhere I go."

Sam chuckles and tugs me back onto the couch. He puts an arm around my shoulders, keeping me close. I've never associated being held with being safe and sheltered, (hell, I've never really put those words in the same sentence), but now I feel a little like a spoiled house cat. I'm being pampered and cuddled and loved, even though I showed up as an abused stray.

That cat metaphor might work well in a song... I'll keep it in mind.

Sam

I am so lucky. When I told him some of the fears I still have from childhood, Matt didn't scoff at them or turn his back or do any of the things I'm used to. He actually wants me to talk to him. He's my only chance at heaven and I don't want to let that go. Mattie's still curled up next to me on the couch. He looks at ease; his eyes are closed, a small smile on his lips. I run a hand through his hair, watching each curl spring back into place. Mattie's hair is lush and soft, much like the rest of him. *He's perfect.* God, I love him. Matt cuddles closer to me, resting his head on my chest.

"Are there any good movies on Netflix?" He murmurs, "Because I don't wanna get up. I just want to stay here with you, watch some TV, maybe have you pet my hair some more."

I smile, holding Matthew tightly as I reach for the remote.

Some time passes, enough to watch three movies. The low hum of the TV is relaxing, especially when Matt's got his arms around me. He looks so happy. He also looks a little sleepy; his eyes keep fluttering shut, but he's still trying to watch the movie. (Fast and Furious 4. Matt has all the movies on DVD. I had to get up and get them.) I doubt he'll be able to stay awake for the rest of the franchise. Shortly, Mattie slumps over and into my lap. I shake my head, smiling fondly. Glancing back at the screen in front of me, I decide to stay put. No harm in finishing up the movies; Matt only suggested them because I hadn't seen any.

About an hour later, Mattie starts whimpering in his sleep. I've heard it before, but only through the walls between the guest bedroom and the rest of the apartment. He hasn't done this in such a long time; I was hoping it had stopped altogether. Clearly, it didn't stop or it's back or something, but that doesn't matter anymore. Mattie's shaking, tears streaming down his cheeks. I know that he's having a night terror, but I don't know how to help. It's terrifying to see somebody you love be so hurt, *so scared* that they tuck themselves into a ball like a goddamn armadillo.

"Mattie," I whisper, pleading with God to keep myself from crying, "It's time to wake up. It's not real, alright? Whatever's happening in your head right now isn't going to follow you out. Just wake up, sweets. Please, Birdie, open your eyes for me."

He starts to stir, his whole body shaking with tremors bad enough that they could probably be mistaken for a seizure.

"That's it, sweets. You got this, Birdie. Wake up now, please," I sound a lot like I'm begging, "I need you back here with me. I'll be right here when you wake up, baby bird, I got you."

Finally, Mattie wakes up with a gasp and a shudder. He turns away, head hung low. He's still trembling. When he looks at me, his eyes are wet, gaze unfocused. He lets out a tiny, miserable sob, clearly trying to hold back tears.

"May I hug you?" I say.

Mattie nods, leaning cautiously into my arms. He presses his face against my neck, letting his guard down and coming back into himself.

"I'm so sorry, Sammy," He kisses my cheek, "Bad dream. I haven't had one in so long, but this one was so awful. It was-"

He chokes on his words. I softly rub his back, hoping to calm him down.

"It was brutal. I could *feel* everything and I- I'm still so *scared* of him. Nick did so much to me and I want to forget everything. I- He made me fucking starve myself. He fucking brainwashed into thinking it was totally normal and okay for him to do what he did. He raped me, more times than I can remember. I hate him, Sam, I hate him so fucking much."

I knew Nick was bad, but he still manages to get crueler with every new detail. It makes me wonder what else I don't know.

"My baby bird," My voice is already breaking, "I am so sorry that happened to you. God, sweets, I'm so sorry. I know I can't fix anything, not exactly, but is there anything I can do?"
"Stay with me for a little while. I don't wanna be alone."
"Of course. Whatever you need."

Matt sniffs and snuggles into me. I wrap both arms around him, nuzzling my nose into his hair. I want to ask him something, but I don't want to do it now. I want to know if he could press charges against Nick, more than the ones from the Gummy Worms Incident. That monster needs to be kept off the streets. But I won't ask now. Not when Mattie's clinging to me like this. I'd rather keep him safe and warm than keep Nick behind bars.

"I love you, Birdie." I whisper.

"I know, Sammy. I love you, too. Thank you for everything. I owe you my life."

"You don't owe me anything. I only do what I think is right. I want to make you happy."

He smiles feebly and holds me closer.

As much as I don't want to unpack everything Matt just told me, I can't help myself. I start thinking about every word he said. Nick convinced Mattie to starve himself. That would explain why his ribs showed through his skin when we first met. At least he's doing better now; he's got a soft tummy and faded scars instead of being so hollow-cheeked with fresh bruises. I hug him tighter. *I won't let anything hurt you, not again.* The faded scars on Matt's left wrist have always bothered me. I don't find them unattractive, nor do I think they "deface him." I just worry. Some look older than others, like they were done years ago, but some were probably only a couple days old when we met. I don't have too many opinions on self-harm, but I do truly loathe that Mattie got hurt so bad, he started hurting himself. I reach out and lace Matt's fingers with my own, lifting his arm up enough so that I can press a kiss to one of the scars.

"Please, don't do that. Don't look at those." Matt squirms. I drop his hand, apology at the ready.

"Don't apologize either, Sam. You stopped when I told you to."

"I'm sorry for making you uncomfortable, though. I just- I hate that you got hurt bad enough to hurt yourself. I don't want you to hurt anymore."

"Thank you, angel. I love you, Sammy, so much. Can we watch one of those nature shows with David Attenborough? In bed? I still need to sleep."
"Of course, Birdie."

Matthew

I fall asleep the moment my head hits the pillow. Sam has his cheek on my chest, listening to my heartbeat reverently. He's curled up around me, so close and so soothing that I can feel his presence even in my sleep. I rest easy all the way to morning.

Sam's gone when I awaken. I have a moment of fierce panic before my more rational side kicks in. I can hear Sam humming to himself from the kitchen. *Of course he's in the kitchen.* The smell of pancakes and syrup is enough to get me out of bed. I plod into the kitchen, hugging Sam from behind. He puts a hand over mine, the one that's not whisking eggs.

"Morning sweets," He smiles, "How'd you sleep?"
"I slept great," I let my head fall against his shoulder, "Did you open a bed and breakfast without me?"
"No," He chuckles, "I guess I did go a little overboard again, though."
"A little, Sammy?" I squeeze him tighter for a second then let go.
"Alright, a lot. If I'm worried, I cook. You know that."
"I do, indeed. What're you worried about, though?"
"Thanksgiving. I don't know how to behave within a normal family."
"You'll be fine, Sammy. I didn't tell anyone that you're coming, but that's a good thing. My family loves a surprise guest. They don't

know that we're together, either, so we could just go as friends. I know that you don't have the... *fondest* memories of bringing a guy home."

"I want to tell them the truth. Your family's pretty accepting, right?"

"Yeah, absolutely. They're pretty protective of everybody, but as long as the relationship is healthy, they're fine with it."

My face clouds a bit.

"Or if you can hide how bad things are, they'll be just fine until everything comes into the light. Then they'll feel guilty, and so will you even though you know it wasn't your fault."

"Nick met your family." Sam's face is unreadable.

"Yeah," I sigh, "He put up a front of being sweet and caring when he was everything but. They bought it and I don't blame 'em. He was a great actor and I hid every warning sign I could. There was nothing to see, nothing to make anyone think something was wrong. But *everything* was wrong, and now they're all blaming themselves for not seeing it. Especially Ricky. We've known each other all our lives and he keeps thinking that there must've been something he could've done. Except there was nothing to tip him off, nothing to tell him that everything had gone bad. I can't change his mind, though. He'll just keep on blaming and blaming until the day he dies. That much is my fault. I should've told him-"

"I'm going to stop you right there," Sam looks me in the eyes, "It's not your fault. You were *scared,* Birdie. What you do now is bring me over for Thanksgiving and let your family poke and prod me to their heart's content. Let them not trust me; let them worry that I'm like him. I hate Nick more than anyone; let me prove that to them. I will prove that you are so deserving of love, that you're allowed to be happy. Even if it's not with me. I just want you to heal. Let me take the brunt of this, baby bird."

"Thank you, angel. Uh, 'even if it's not with you?' What did you mean by that?"

"I meant that if you ever fall out of love with me, I wouldn't force you to stick around. I'd rather see you happy with somebody else than see you miserable with me."

"That-" I pause, "That is one of the most beautiful things I've ever heard. I'm glad you value *me* more than a relationship status."

And you said you wouldn't force me to stay. That makes me feel even safer than before.

Sam nods and breaks eye contact. He had managed some impressive eye-to-eye staring. I'm not sure that he blinked once through that whole rant. He also didn't burn any of the food during that time so, again. Impressive.

We sit down at the kitchen table to eat. Sam's back to his typical *I-can't-believe-my-luck* smile, chin resting on his palm. It's funny to me that Sam can still make that lovestruck face while I'm eating pancakes like it's going out of style. That stupid little twitch at the corner of his mouth, the half-smile that nearly makes me faint... And I'm lucky enough to have that look directed at me. Not just when I'm dressed up or in something too tight, but *all the time.* My sweet angel doesn't seem to discriminate between sweatpants and a suit coat. He just looks at me with those unfairly pretty eyes and that gentle smile. So, I smile right back and eat my pancakes.

Although, there is one thing that I don't understand about Sam's attraction to me. When I showed up in Sam's life, I was in desperate need of a place to stay. That much was obvious. I was also hungry, cold, and sickly. I hadn't eaten a real meal in weeks, maybe months. Probably months. I'd been eating for sustenance, just enough to survive. I ended up nearly bedridden once with Sam. He brought me soup and tea and homemade chocolate pudding. I went from emaciated to gaunt to average during that time. Unfortunately, one thing I've always hated about my body is that it holds weight like a sloth holds a tree. (And not like the sloths that mistake their arms for branches and plummet to their deaths. I can't drop weight for shit.) After starving myself nearly to death, I ended up eating all the time, just because I could. It was oddly freeing to have control over what I put into my body. Of course, that caught up to me. I got fat. Well, not quite, but chubby enough that it's impossible to hide. The thing is, Sam never stopped giving me that *look.* He still treats me like I'm priceless, constantly wrapping an arm around me or kissing my cheek. I'd been in a few relationships before Nick, and even then I went from a precious diamond to a half-eaten ring-pop the moment I put on any weight. I'm certainly not complaining about the change, but I'm so confused. Sam's carved out of God's own marble; I'm pretty sure his abs have abs. I'm the exact opposite, physically. I'm basically a teddy bear: soft, warm, and perfect to cuddle. I've got too much of a stomach, stretch marks all over, but at least the weight makes my ass look great. Plus, I'm short for a guy in my family, only a smidge over 5'7" when almost all of my relatives are over six-foot.

Alright, I should probably stop whining. I wouldn't want to jinx the great thing I have going on. I look back at Sam, and he looks so goddamn *smitten* with me. I can almost forget all the times I've been told nasty things, but not quite. It feels marvellous to truly be loved, but even that's not a cure-all for the past. I pick up my now-empty breakfast dish and put it in the sink. Brushing past Sam on my way to the sofa, I ruffle his already messy hair.

"You're amazing, Sammy," I say, "Thanks for making breakfast. And I doubt Thanksgiving will be as big of a deal as we're making it. My family already knows 'Sam O'Henry' as 'the guy that took Mattie in off the streets and then helped the band.' They'll probably worship the ground you walk on."

Sam smiles, looking a bit more relaxed. *He works himself up so much and worries himself to death. He's gonna have stroke when he's 35, at this rate.* I want to keep my angel around longer than that; I just have to teach him to loosen up a little. It can't be that hard to do, can it? Those are some famous last words, if I've ever heard any.

So much for not jinxing what I've got.

Sam

It's half an hour before we have to leave on Thanksgiving Day and I think I've already sweated through my shirt. Matt's forbidden me from driving us there, saying I'm shaking so badly that the car would be swerving. I fix my hair for the millionth time to try to keep from pacing. A pair of arms wrap around me from behind. I turn to face Matt, his arms still tight around my waist. He stands on his toes, eyes soft, and presses a kiss between my eyes. I try to relax, I really do, but I just can't.

"C'mon," Matt says, "Let's go to dinner. I love you too much to see you suffer like this. Let's just go and get the hard part over with, alright?"
"Yeah, that sounds good. Thanks, Mattie."
"Go get a coat, then."

I patter off to get a my leather jacket, tugging it on over my polo. I feel uncomfortably formal and stiff. Mattie comes back into the room then, and I actually take the time to look at him. He's sweet and plush in a navy cable-knit sweater and dark jeans. I feel my heart swell up at the sight, even as he's guiding me to the car. I smile stupidly at Mattie-Bird over the gear shift. He gives me a brilliant smile of his own as the car hums to life.

It doesn't take long to reach Matt's childhood home. It's a tiny one story house, no yard. It's hard to imagine Matthew, Ricky, and their parents all in that little house. Matt and Rick are loud on their own. I'm brought out of my reverie by Matt giggling and hopping out of the car. He runs over to my side of the car and opens the door, dragging me out and onto the driveway.

"Mattie, sweets, slow down there. I gotta get the pie!"

Mattie lets go of my arm and rocks back on his heels. I take the pie (french silk) out of the back seat and chase after Mattie, who's already halfway to the front door. It swings open, revealing an old lady with striking eyes and smile lines. She smiles broadly at Matt and hugs him so tightly, I doubt he can breathe. She tugs him into the house, then focuses her gaze on me. I squirm under her scrutiny.

"Hi there!" She says with some kind of a southern accent, "I'm Grams. You look so tense, kid. I'll take this pie, you go sit in the living room with Matt. No need to stress, we don't bite."

She steps aside to let me in. I wander into the packed living room, immediately spotting Matthew. He grins and waves me over, patting the seat next to him. I smile sheepishly and sit down.

"Hey Sammy," He snuggles into my shoulder, "I was just bragging about you."

"You don't have to do that." I cough and feel my cheeks heat up.

"I know, but I want to. You're too good not to be bragged about."

"Matt. You're embarrassing him." Everyone turns to look at the man in the doorway.

"Ricky! God, I missed you. How've you been?" Mattie's on his feet, launching himself at his brother.

"Jeez, dude. I missed you, too. I've been alright, nothing too crazy. How are you?"

"I'm okay. Better actually, much better. I've been sleeping and eating like a normal human being-"

"That's because you *are* a normal human being." I mutter.

"Are you the 'Sam O'Henry' I've heard so much about?"

"Yeah, I am. Hopefully you've heard good things? About me?" *Nice one, Sam.*

"I've heard good things. So far, I like you. But if you hurt him," Ricky points almost viciously at Mattie, "I will tear you limb from limb. *Alive.* Then, I'll blend you into a human smoothie and pour into the river. Clear?"

"Very." I shudder.

"*Ricky,*" Matthew snarls, "What did I say about this?"

"That it's obnoxious and creepy and I shouldn't do it."

"Yup. And don't try to act tough! You cried once because a dog was, and I quote, *too cute to actually exist.*"

"I was high!" That warrants several glares from around the room.

"Doesn't matter. Your tough guy thing? Total bullshit. You just watch a lot of true crime shows."

"Can we change the subject please?" I say, both disgusted and amused.

"He wouldn't actually do it. Ricky's bark is way worse than his bite, so to speak." Matt says flatly.

"Uh-huh. Still kinda gross when we're about to eat."
"True enough. Hey, what'd you do with that pie?"
"Gave it to Grams."

Matt hums and leans back against me. Soon after, Grams walks
into the living room and proudly announces that dinner's ready.
Mattie springs up and trots into the kitchen. He's promptly shoved
back out, laughing as his family claims he'll curse the food.

"Well, you are a kitchen nightmare," I smirk, "But if you didn't have
flaws, it'd be kinda disconcerting."
"Sap," Mattie rolls his eyes and bumps up against my hip, "C'mon,
food's gonna get cold."

Matt grabs my hand and squeezes it. We take our seats, Mattie still
holding my hand under the table. No one's reaching for the food
yet, just staring at it with big wistful eyes. Then, Grams sits at the
head of the table. Everyone starts grabbing food like madmen.
Grams clears her throat and everyone sits back down.

"Be civil, for heaven's sake," She sighs, "Pass the plates around the
table, there's more than enough for all of you, jeez."
"Sorry, ma'am." Comes the shameful response from the table.

And the dishes are passed.

"Every single year..." She mutters.

Mattie grins and starts in on a heaping plate of *everything.* His eyes
are sparkling and he looks so happy and in his element. He sighs
contentedly, eyes fluttering closed in enjoyment. I probably should
stop just staring at him, especially considering that his family

doesn't quite know we're together. So I eat my turkey and potatoes (both are amazing) and rest a hand on Mattie's knee.

Thanksgiving might not be so bad afterall.

Mattie's asleep on the couch, drooling a smidge after eating himself into a food coma. Dinner's over, but dessert hasn't been served yet. I'm surprised Matt's already knocked out; he's got a sweet tooth the size of the Sears Tower. The TV's on in the background, switching between football and the dog show. I cover a yawn with my fist, smiling at the peaceful expression on Matt's face. He leans into me in his sleep, tucking his face into my neck. I sigh and kiss the top of his head.

"So Matt found somebody new," A deep voice says flatly, "I'm glad."

I look up to see who's speaking. An older man stands in front of me. He was introduced to me earlier, but for the life of me I can't remember his name.

"Ha... yeah," I chuckle nervously, "I guess so. I'm Sam O'Henry, by the way. I don't think I ever told you my name."
"I know who you are. I'm Matthew's dad, Patrick. Matt told me about you on the phone, but it's nice to finally meet you face to face."
"Nice to meet you too, Mr. Lin."
"Look, kid, I'm just glad you found him," *Before something happened* hangs heavy and unspoken, "We're all lucky to have you."
"I think I'm pretty lucky, too."

Patrick smiles and sits down on the adjacent couch. I go back to watching TV. There's some crashing in the entryway and kitchen, but I don't pay attention to it. It wasn't enough to wake Mattie, so it's low on my list of priorities. Then the crashing and thumping gets closer to the living room. More and more people start looking around until a lady stumbles into the room. She has a bottle in one hand and a coat in the other. The tension in the air is palpable, not that this newcomer notices. She's still staggering around, pinching the cheeks of her relatives and ignoring the whispers of *did she drive here?* I grow stiff, a wave of panic and nausea overtaking me. I have to leave right now or I'm going to puke on Matthew's dad's couch. Mattie's finally starting to stir so I roll him off of me and bolt to the bathroom.

This is mortifying. I'd been trying so hard to make a good impression and now I've got my head in the toilet. I can feel tears prick at the corners of my eyes. I let out a sob that ends up being a wretch, throat already feeling torn up.

"Sam?" *Oh god no. Please don't look at me.* "Sweetheart, I'm here, I'm going to sit down by you. I'm so sorry she showed up, Sammy. The one year she shows... It'll be alright, though, Sammy. I got you, I'll take care of you."

I vomit again and again until I have nothing left to give.

"Shh... Let me wipe your face, angel. You just rest."

I'm too exhausted to try and fight it. I collapse into Matthew's chest as he rubs my back. I feel like I'm going to fall asleep here, until Mattie pulls me to my feet. He gently leads me back towards the living room. I do my best to stall.

"I don't want to go back in there. I made a fool of myself and-"
"-And everyone's worried about you. You're more like family than she is. Nobody's mad at you, Sammy."

I trudge awkwardly into the room, Mattie's arm around my waist. I'm immediately asked how I'm feeling, if I'm okay, and so on. *I don't know what to say. I've never been cared about by a family.* I start tearing up again, blinking furiously.

"Oh honey," Grams cooes, "Don't get yourself worked up all over again. Take a breath and come help me put dessert on the table."

I exhale deeply and trail her into the kitchen. We set up the desserts in silence. She gives me a brief hug before yelling that dessert's ready.

"You don't have to be so hard on yourself, Sam." She murmurs, then takes her seat.

I smile a little and tuck into the table. Matthew's already seated, passing plates and taking treats. That same contented look crosses his face again, the one from before he started eating dinner. He mumbles something into his food, it sounds a lot like *I missed this.*

"How's the pie, everybody?" I ask.

Nods and hums of enjoyment come from around the table. I smile again, casting a quick glance to Matthew. He's chowing down with fervor, making the occasional noise of pleasure. As nice as it is to see him treating himself, I don't think I've ever seen him look around so much. He keeps checking to make sure nobody's watching him, like he's self-conscious of eating. It's Thanksgiving. Why would he be concerned today, of all days?

"You okay, sugar?"

"Of course, Sam. Why wouldn't I be?"

"You're looking around a lot. It's lovely to see you eating your fill, though."

"Yeah. I didn't eat like this last year, not with Nick around. I missed it, god I missed this so much. Actually enjoying family events and not having to put up an act? I never thought it'd happen again. I'm kinda making up for lost time. Thanks for not staring at me while I stuff my face."

"You don't have to worry, Birdie. You look so goddamn happy right now, it's precious. I'm glad you get to be happy. Enjoy yourself, sweetheart, Thanksgiving only comes once a year."

He smiles shyly and goes back to eating. I shake my head fondly and start back in on my food. Mattie leans back against his chair, huffing a sigh. Then he hiccups, blushing brightly and hiding his face. The rest of the table laughs or cooes, or asks if he ate too fast. I put a hand on his back and start to rub gently. Matthew groans and lays a hand on top of his stomach. He slumps over into me, his breathing already starting to even out.

"Do I need to carry you to the car, songbird?" I purr.

"Probably. Or I could sleep here…" *He sounds nearly drunk off of food and a little wine.*

"Take him home," Mr. Lin laughs, "And Matthew? Don't make Sam carry you. You can walk."

"I'm not so sure." Mattie mumbles, easing himself out of the chair.

I smile and help him up, letting Matt put nearly his full weight on me. It's hard to walk to the door like this (Matt should really just lay down) so I lift him up and carry him. He sighs, relieved, and wraps his arms around my neck. It's not too tough to get him to that car after that.

The drive goes quickly. Pulling into the parking lot, I walk over to Mattie's side of the car and open the door. He blinks awake and reaches out for me to pick him up. I really can't resist that sleepy face, and so I end up carrying him all the way to the elevator, then again to our apartment. I lay Mattie down on the bed. He stretches languidly, curling up on his side. I kiss his forehead then go to get pajamas. I come back already changed, carrying a shirt and sleep pants for Mattie. He thanks me and starts fighting with his sweater as I turn to leave. When I come back again, Mattie's already sprawled out on his back, taking up nearly the whole bed. Smiling fondly, I cuddle up next to him and loop my arm around his hips. It's easy to fall asleep when I'm pressed up against Mattie's soft hips and space heater warmth. I try to get impossibly closer to him, and finally start snoring.

Matthew

The one year she shows up. Sam didn't deserve that. I never wanted to have to cradle him while he throws up.

I'm awake, though I don't want to be. It's the middle of the night and Sam is asleep next to me. He doesn't look like he's sleeping very well, but I try to ignore it. I rest a hand on Sam's shoulder, then kiss his jaw. He's still tossing and turning, muttering in his sleep. I debate whether it would be better to wake him up or let him tough through it. Sam sits up suddenly, eyes wide and terrified. I flick on the light. Sam startles and looks at me, tears streaming down his face.

"Sammy, honey, what's the matter?"

He doesn't answer, just launches himself into my chest. His arms lock around me, hands fisting in my shirt. I run a hand along his back, his shoulders heaving. Sam leans away from me, still looking shaken.

"Sweetheart, look at me. What can I do for you?"
"I need a hug. I had another nightmare. It was the one with the fence."

The one with the fence? Sam tucks himself into a ball and curls up against my stomach. He nuzzles his nose into my shirt, his hands loosely grabbing my waist. He looks so small like this; I might think he's fragile if I didn't know better. *A vulnerable moment where you let yourself be "weak" doesn't make you a weak person. It makes you strong. Showing one's flaws is the bravest thing one can do.* Sam presses closer to me, looking up and opening his mouth as if to speak. He rests his head on my chest with a sigh.

"It was right after he ripped my college fund," Sam says, his voice quivering, "I came home after dive team practice. Dad was waiting for me, already hammered, lecture at the ready. I didn't want to see him, 'cause if I got hurt I wouldn't be able to dive. I was trying to get a scholarship. So when I saw him, I just ran. He chased me, and he didn't fall or even stumble. He was drunk, but he could still move around. He wasn't knocked out yet. I climbed a fence, thinking he couldn't catch me up there but he grabbed my leg and-"
Sam's ranting cuts off with a sob, then, "He grabbed my leg and I fell off the fence, but my sleeve was caught in one of the links. It was a big, metal fence and when he pulled me, I broke before the fence did. I dislocated my shoulder, and then I had to lie to the

team about how it happened. I told them I'm just accident prone. They bought it, of course, probably because I was always covered in random bruises."

I listen in horror as Sam tells me about the lies he told the dive team.

"They worried about me, always kinda thought something wasn't right, but they never said a thing. The only one I ever told the truth was Jackson. His family took me in after my run-in with the fence. I never went to the doctor about my shoulder, either. Never had the money. Still hurts sometimes."

Now that he mentions it, Sam does rub his left shoulder a lot. He says it gets stiff when holds his guitar for too long.

"Well, you have the money now. Insurance and everything. You could see a doctor or a physical therapist or somebody. Maybe they could help you," I murmur, "You don't deserve to suffer."
"I really should see a doctor. It's getting worse, not better. I'll set up an appointment in the morning. For now, let's just sleep."

I nod and snuggle up in the blankets, Sam still latched onto my hips. I smile sleepily and run a hand through his hair. He squirms and nestles in close to me.

"Thanks for being here, baby bird," He whispers, "I love you."
"It's an honor, angel. Get some sleep, my love."

Sam tightens his hold around me, turning to look at me and grin. He yawns as his head falls onto my chest. His breathing starts to even out, that peaceful smile still on his face. I lean back into the pillows and close my eyes. Sleep is quick to envelope me. I don't try to fight it. I let myself fall instead.

Chapter Four

Sam

When I wake the next morning, Mattie's already out of bed. I can hear him talking to somebody, or maybe he's on the phone. I check the time. It's only 8:30 in the morning. Who could he possibly be talking to? Maybe Ricky, he calls at ungodly hours all the time. I stretch and get out of bed. I'm hungry and I doubt Matt's cooked anything; he could probably set cereal on fire. I plod into the kitchen and pull out the omelette pan. Sighing contentedly, I get to work on breakfast. Matt walks in and gives me a brief side hug. He's got his phone against his ear, nodding even though whoever's on the other end can't see him. Cute. Anyway, as I'm cracking eggs and such, Matt keeps meandering in and out of the kitchen. I can only catch bits and pieces of his conversation. (I'm only listening because I'm fairly certain it's about the band.)

But I still have no idea who he's talking to.

"Sammy!" Matt shouts, sounding almost giddy, "Listen to this. Mary May, I'm going to put you on speaker."
"You all have gained popularity nearly overnight. We think it might be in your best interest to go on tour. Are you both interested?"
"Absolutely! I've always wanted to go on tour. Sammy?" Matthew is vibrating with excitement.
"I would love that," I'm surprised to find that my voice is barely above a whisper, "I'm going to cry, oh my god. I- I'm a success."

"Of course you are," Matthew quips, "And I'm thrilled to have you on tour with me."

"Alright now, settle yourselves. I still have to call Chris and James. I doubt they'd say no, but-"

"We're going to be huge, just like I always wanted. I can't believe we did it, Sammy. I'm so proud."

"*We?* Mattie, this was almost all you!"

"If you hadn't come in, there wouldn't be a lead singer. Or at least, they wouldn't be me."

"But you're here now and we're going to be rockstars."

"Sammy, we're already rockstars. I'm getting ready for sold out shows."

"Yes, that's great," Mary May says primly, "I'm emailing you the tour dates now. Chris and James have both sent me confirmation of their participation."

I snatch my laptop and look over the dates.

"The first Chicago concert is in six months and the actual first concert is in less than two!"

"Yes, that's right. You'd better get practicing. Gertrude, our costume designer and tailor, will meet with you in a week to get you fitted for outfits for promotional photos and the concert. Come in to the studio today. We have a lot of work to do."

Mary May hangs up without so much as a "goodbye."

"Well, I'd better get dressed. I can't wear my pajamas to work." Mattie shrugs and heads off.

I turn the stove back on and finish up breakfast.

Mattie comes back, dressed in jeans and that black turtleneck I like. I'm not sure if Matt knows how good he looks in it. I should tell him sometime. He looks good in everything, but this shirt fits him *perfectly.* I snap out of my little trance and hand Matt his breakfast. He thanks me, kissing my cheek and telling me I should get changed too.

I find it harder than it should be to get dressed. My hands are trembling with a nervous thrill I haven't felt in years. I don't think I've been this ruffled since junior prom. Still bouncing off the walls (and regretting that coffee), I trot into the living room. Mattie's already got the car keys in his hand, grinning ecstatically. We nearly sprint to the elevator, just to get stopped by Rosa. Yes, *that Rosa,* our elderly neighbor who thinks we're married. Maybe (hopefully) she'll be right someday, but it's awkward right now.

"Where are you two off to, in such a hurry?" She asks, sticking her head out of her apartment.
"The recording studio! Our band's going on tour soon and we have to practice. We'll see you later, Rosa, but we gotta go. Bye!"

Matt waves and drags me down the hallway. We get into the elevator and it cannot move fast enough. Still trotting, we get into the car.

"Send Rosa some of your compulsive baking," Mattie laughs, revving the engine, "I think she'd like it."
"Or maybe we could go over there and have some kind of late Thanksgiving with her. Her family never bothers to visit." I suggest.
"Yeah alright," Matt hums, "But we have to tell her that we're not married. I will not fake a relationship of any kind, especially not

when acting as family to someone. I've faked enough in front of my family."

"Of course, sugar. I didn't even think of that, and I'm sorry."

"It's not your fault, Sammy. There's no comparison between what Nick made me do and had me say, and faking being married to you because you went along with Rosa's assumption. Nick was awful to me and made me *lie to my family* so that he wouldn't have to stop. You love me in a way that compels people to write poems and songs and movies. You didn't ask me to lie to her, Sam. I told you that I wasn't going to and you said that was okay. It's not your job to think of every little thing that might bring something up for me. What you just did was perfect, so don't apologize for it."

I search for a response but come up empty. Mattie sighs and drums his fingers on the steering wheel. The car is uncomfortably silent for a few minutes, but I can't think of anything to say.

"You know what I just thought of?" Matt says, smile evident in his voice, "While we're on tour, the hotels will probably be nice and have room service and stuff. I could have an entire cake brought to me."

"That sounds lovely, Mattie. I'm just glad I get to come on tour with you instead of staying home. The plan's for four months on the run, and I don't want to be lonely for that long." *As grateful as I am to not be left behind, I sound so clingy. It's embarrassing.*

"Yeah, I wouldn't want to be away from you for that long, either. I'd probably try to bring you along, smuggle you backstage. We don't have to even think about that, though, 'cause you're going be onstage with me. God, I'm so excited, Sammy." He chortles with laughter, looking fierce and unstoppable.

"Yeah, Birdie. Me too."

Walking into the studio is easier now. Mary May greets us at the door, her sharp attitude replaced with an air of pride. She looks us over and a smile settles onto her painted lips. It's a simple "welcome back" smile, with a hint of contentedness that I cannot place. She ushers us into a small room. Well, the room itself is enormous, but the stacks of half-sewn garments make it seem almost cramped. Mary May whistles as if calling a dog, then turns and tells us there's no other way to get Gertrude's attention. You can call her name for hours, apparently. There's some scuffling in the back, a clang and some muttered curses, and then a short, silver-haired woman steps out from behind a rack of dresses. She wears huge black-framed glasses, her hair pinned back in a messy bun, and a set of overalls that should be hideous, but somehow look *right.*

"Ah, so these are my rockstar clients? Ricky's brother, yes?" She has an accent, possibly Eastern European.
"I'm Ricky's brother," Matt says, hand extended to shake, "My name's Matthew Lin, but never refer to me by my last name."
"Alright, Matthew. I like the turtleneck," *I trust her fashion sense entirely,* "Although I think something in dark red would look even better. It would bring out the lighter parts of your hair, and make your eyes look bluer. Less grey."
"Okay. I'll try anything within reason." He gives a smile and little half-shrug.
"Good, good. Now, you," Gertrude spins and turns to me, "What's your name? You look bland, grey t-shirt, loose jeans. You're tall and strong, dark skinny jeans on stage would make you look too long and stringy unless..." She darts off to get something. Matthew is trying not to laugh.

124

"Alright, I gotta apologize to Ricky. I told him Gertrude couldn't be *that hard to handle* and I was very, very wrong," He chuckles, "Tell her your name when she gets back. That's assuming she can find her way out of that labyrinth of fabric."

"I am back!" Gertrude announces, "And I have boots and jeans for you. They might not fit right quite yet, but I can fix that, just try them on..." She looks at me expectantly.

"Sam O'Henry. That's my name."

"Yes! Go, Sam, there are plenty of places to hide around here." Matthew snorts.

"And you!" She says, twirling, "This is a jacket for you. It would be exceptional over that shirt and with those jeans."

I can still hear Gertrude's sing-song voice praising both her own work and Mattie's existence. Shaking my head fondly, I pull up the new jeans, hopping around a bit to get them on. I put on the boots, even though they look clunky and obnoxious, and walk back out towards Gertrude and Matt.

I'm greeted with a sight I doubt I'll forget. Gertrude is jumping up and down, gushing over how "it's almost like you were made to wear this, Matthew!" and I'd have to agree with her on that. She runs into her fabric fortress and comes back with a full length mirror. Mattie turns to see his reflection and his jaw nearly hits the floor. I finally walk over to Gertrude and tap her shoulder. Her face lights up and she says,

"You look fantastic. I might make them a bit looser so that you can walk, but this could be a stage look. I think Matthew's jaw is stuck like that. Fix it for him."

She walks away, whistling to herself. I walk towards the mirror. (And not because Mattie's still standing there and I want to see whatever red jacket he has on. No sir.) When I'm standing a few feet away, I cough. Not loudly, just enough to announce my presence.

"Sam!" Mattie squeaks and whirls around, "I didn't see you there." "I haven't been here very long." I say dumbly. Any intelligent response I had was stolen when Mattie turned around. I gape at him, my mouth opening and closing like a fish. He is *incredible,* but he tilts his head down and tugs on his turtleneck as though he can't see it.
"Hey, earth to Sammy," A smile of false confidence crosses his face, but even that wavers, "You okay? You're just staring at me and making a weird face."
"Yeah, I'm fine. Do you have any idea how amazing you look right now?" I blurt, then cover my mouth. *Stupid.* I try desperately to recover, "I mean, you always look amazing, but-"
"Thanks, angel," He says, but his smile doesn't reach his eyes, "Hey, can you even sit in those pants? You look great, but it also kinda looks like you're losing blood flow to your feet."
"I can barely walk in them. I have to waddle."

Mattie laughs, that brilliant, blazing smile back in its rightful place. I waddle and wobble my way back to corner I changed in, grabbing my regular, baggy, *wonderful* jeans. Mattie's in just the turtleneck again by the time I get back. Gertrude is on a stepstool, inspecting his hair.

"I love your curls, Matthew. Do you know that you are handsome? You keep looking at the floor. I think Sam would agree that you're very attractive," *Is she playing matchmaker?* "Right, Sam?"

I stand frozen, shocked by Gertrude's immediate scheming, but quickly snap out it. "Of course. Ah, Gertrude, can I talk to you for a second?"

She nods and skips over to me. "What do you need?"

"I think Mattie's a little uncomfortable with being scrutinized."

"But I'm telling him that he's wonderful-"

"I know, but he's not used to that. People can be cruel. Maybe go easy on the poking and prodding?"

"Yes, of course! I wouldn't want to hurt him," She nods, "But what flaw could anyone possibly find in him?"

"He's a work of art, I know, but modern beauty standards tend to demand a cut-and-paste muscle man. It's ridiculous."

"Such a shame. Where's the individuality? Where's the love for the rest of us? I won't poke at him any more. I'd hate for him to be miserable here. I want to make everyone comfortable in their own skin."

I smile appreciatively at her.

We walk out of Gee's studio a couple hours later, exhausted. Mary May tells me to go home, but asks Mattie to stay behind. He shrugs and follows her. I'm not exactly suspicious, but I don't like being left in the dark. I head home, taking an uber so Mattie can still get back, an icky feeling settling in my gut.

Please be okay, songbird.

Matthew

I walk with Mary May into her office. She sits me down across from her, a large wooden desk between us. It's ominous, but not uncomfortable. She smiles and asks how I'd feel about an interview with a magazine company. I'd be the only one getting questioned, so it's my decision.

"Is that why you made Sam leave?"
"Yeah, I figured he might influence you whether he meant to or not."
"Well, I'll think about it. But I don't know."
"You've got time to decide. Now go home, Matthew. I know that Gee can be tiring."

I take my leave, walking out into the parking lot. I slide into the front seat of the car and rev the engine, silently wondering how Sam got home. *Sam!* I should text him and tell him what Mary May wanted. He looked so worried about leaving me, the poor guy. I sigh and put the car back into park. One probably reassuring text later, I finally start the drive home. The drive isn't a long one, and soon enough I make my way into the apartment building. I open the door to Sam's apartment. Well, *our* apartment. I live there too, even if I got there by unconventional means.

I have to step over Sam's discarded coat to get in the door. He's currently pacing the floor. And what is that *smell?* It's like a donut shop in here. *Oh no.*

"Sammy, I'm home," He whips around, eyes wide with relief, "I take it you didn't get my text?"
"No, I didn't even look," He shakes his head, "I'm sorry about the mess. I got all in my head about what Mary May wanted from you and I stressed myself into a frenzy. I'm so sorry, Mattie."
"Don't worry about it, Sam. I'm home, I'm fine, and I'm not mad at you for worrying about me. That'd be ridiculous. Mary only sent you away because she wanted to ask me about a solo interview.

And if I'm the only one being interviewed, she didn't want you to influence my decision. Even if you didn't mean to do so-"

"-There would still be a chance," Sam murmurs, "God, I'm such an idiot. I shouldn't have gotten so worked up about this. But I did, and now we have a massive amount of cupcakes scattered throughout the house."

"It's okay, angel. There are worse things than too many treats."

Sam heaves a sigh and sinks heavily into the couch. I trot into the kitchen and grab a tray of "death by chocolate." (Dark chocolate cupcakes filled with chocolate ganache, coated in chocolate frosting, and drizzled in caramel. My personal favorite for obvious reasons.) I sit down next to him and extend a sugary olive branch.

"Eat. I know you haven't eaten lunch, or dinner for that matter." I say, glancing at my watch.

"I guess I sort of forgot. I'll make something quick-"

"No, you won't. You'll sit and relax and I'll order a pizza," I try to be firm, but soon fail, "Please, Sammy? Try to take it easy."

"Alright. I guess I can do that. Can you order-"

"The Chicago Classic from Lou Malnati's, a medium so that we supposedly have a couple meals worth even though it'll be gone by tomorrow night. I got you, angel."

"Thanks, Birdie." Sam grins.

The pizza takes twenty minutes to arrive. I tip the delivery boy more than is needed, thinking back to when me and my friends would pick up jobs like this. We were always thrilled to get a big tip from somebody. May as well pay it forward. The guy thanks me profusely and shuffles off, just like I used to. I bring the pizza into the living room and set it on the end table.

"Food for you," I smile, nudging Sam's shoulder, "How about a movie night? But with Mystery Science Theater 3000."
"What exactly is that?"
"You'll see."

I plant myself on the couch, settling in against Sam's side. It's good to see him a little more relaxed. He's eating, finally, and laughing at some snappy commentary that I must've missed. As nice as it is to see him like this, it always makes me wonder if he took care of himself *at all* when he was living alone. Give Sam half a reason to worry and he won't sleep or eat for days. He won't take care of any of his own basic needs until whatever's bothering him has been fixed. And here's the kicker; it takes virtually no effort for somebody else to calm him down or reassure him. So when I got home today, whatever could've happened was cut off at the pass. It pains me to think of long he could've gone on like this. And who was it that pulled him out of these cycles before? Krista? Jackson? Claire? Or no one at all? I shiver at the last prospect and press up closer to Sam. I suppose it doesn't matter at this point. All that I really care about is the here and now, and now I can help.

I turn my focus back to the movie. A low budget sea creature is terrorizing the beach on screen. I love crappy sci fi. I guess Sam does too. He's fully relaxed, his arm slung around my middle. It's comforting to have him so close and so constant beside me. I sigh contentedly and reach for another slice of pizza. As I lean across Sam's lap to grab my food, he tightens his arms around me and kisses the top of my head.

"Thank you," He whispers, "You know that I get trapped in my head. Thanks for pulling me out of there."

"Not a problem," I huff and sit up, "Besides, you're getting so much better at calming yourself down. I'm thrilled to see you already at ease."

"You really are too good to me." He sighs and kisses my cheek.

"Not true."

I wrap myself around him, cheek pressed against his shoulder. Sam runs his hands idly through my hair, before letting them rest on my hips. He gently, almost reverently, traces the scarring and stretch marks that reside there. It's just on the right side of intimate, not too much. I shift on Sam's lap, seeking more of that precious contact. Sam pulls me in closer, holding me like he doesn't quite believe that I'm his. I smile against his neck, placing a tiny kiss there. My arms are wrapped around his shoulders, hands in his hair. He moves to get up from the couch, keeping me tucked into his chest. I make a weak noise of protest because *excuse you I was comfortable,* but Sam just chuckles and says,

"I was about to fall asleep, darling. Let me carry you to bed, we can still cuddle there."

I nod groggily. I had already been planning to sleep on the couch, but as long as I'm warm and preferably being held close, I'll be fine. I let Sam lift me up and carry me. I'm placed on the bed by careful hands. Sam curls his arm around my hips and rests his head on my chest. It occurs to me that I'd never been carried to bed like this before. I had been grabbed and thrown like a doll, probably because that's what I was to *him.*

"Thank you for treating me like I'm a good thing." I mumble, nearly asleep.

"Of course, Birdie. You *are* a good thing."

Sam nuzzles his face into my collar. I loop an arm over his shoulders, feeling the telltale relaxation of his tense muscles. I can tell I'll be asleep soon, a soothing aura coaxing me closer. Even still, a part of me wants to stay awake, stay here with my Sammy. I drift off, though, not wanting to fight the warmth and safety I can finally find in my dreams.

Sam is holding tightly to my shirt when I wake. He mutters and hums in his sleep, lips twitching into a smile. I watch him fondly, waiting for him to stir. He blinks suddenly and his whole body goes rigid, then limp. Sam looks up at me, trying in vain to cover a yawn. He ducks his head back towards my neck. I play with the longer bits of his hair, not wanting to get up.

"Morning sunshine." Sam says, his face smushed against me.
"Morning. Did you sleep okay?"
"Yeah, I did. I don't think I've slept like that in years."
"I'm glad to hear that. Not the part about you not sleeping well for so long, but you know."
"I know, lovebird."

With that, he starts kissing my cheeks, winding down my neck and cradling me. He cups my face in his hands, calluses on his fingertips tracing me. They're from his guitar, which is another thing he's this gentle with. To him, I'm something worth worshipping. It's a little odd to me, for someone so marvellous to look at all the parts of my body I hate and tell me how lovely I am. Currently, Sam has his hands on my hips, which I've always thought are too soft, too wide. But there's nothing other than pure adoration on Sam's face. He's careful, possibly overly so, to keep his touches light and chaste. It's sweet of him. Just as I'm about to fall back asleep, my stomach growls. It's obnoxiously loud in the near-silent room.

"Hungry?" Sam chuckles.
"Clearly," I mutter, embarrassed, "Maybe I'll have some of those cupcakes you made."
"For breakfast?"
"Sure, why not."
"Cupcakes are not really a breakfast food, but hey. If they sound good to you, go for it."

I sigh and roll away from Sam. Propping myself up on my elbows, I let myself gaze at Sam's stupidly impressive swimmer body. He walks into the kitchen, and I stretch lazily. I am not nearly as much of a morning person as Sam. Eventually, I do manage to get out of bed. I find Sam sitting at the kitchen table, eating a bowl of cereal. He pushes a plate towards me. It's got a cupcake and a couple strawberries on it. He smiles and glances at me. I tuck into my food as Sam talks about plans for the day.

"So we have nothing to do today," He starts nervously, "There's this restaurant I've been wanting to try, but it's mostly for couples so I haven't been yet. I was wondering if you wanted to go. It's a steakhouse, by the way."
"For dinner? Tonight? That sounds amazing, but wouldn't we need reservations?"
"No, actually. Krista's friend runs the place and we're kinda celebrities so I think it'll be okay."
"Alright. Is it fancy?"
"Yeah, but it's not hoity-toity or anything like that."
"Perfect. I'd love to go with you, Sam."

He grins brightly at me from across the table. I nod sheepishly and duck my head. I never used to be this quick to fluster. I'm not upset about the change, but it would be nice to have some sense of smoothness back. Oh well.

Sam

I'm thrilled to be going out with Mattie tonight. It's a real date to a nice place and I really could not ask for more. It's already almost time for us to leave. I'm trying on a dress shirt, with and without a tie. I settle on without, as the shirt itself is one of the nicest things I've ever owned. I stride into the living room, buzzing with excitement. I'm not particularly nervous about tonight, nor do I feel bad about treating myself to something. It's strange and stunning to be so free and light. Mattie's already waiting for me, chin resting on his fist. He's truly something to behold, with all of his charm and that sweet smile dimpling his cheeks. I can't help but pause and revel in my bewilderment. I would never in a million lifetimes have guessed that this gorgeous man would even look twice at me, let alone stare. I give him a love-dumb smile, one that reeks of infatuation and pure idiocy, I'm sure. But he looks at me, eyes framed by thick glasses and smoky eyeliner, and he doesn't look away. I offer my hand to him with a very thin guise of lifting him from the chair. In reality, I just want to hold that hand and treasure who it belongs to. Matthew rolls his eyes at me and for a moment I worry that I've overstepped.

"I don't need help to stand up, love," He smirks, "But I would like to hold your hand, and I'm pretty sure that's why you offered it."

He looks me over fondly and takes my hand in his. I've known for a while that I'm completely smitten, but even still, an emotional surge bowls me over at every little gesture. Right now I'm caught up in a tidal wave adoration, one that crashes into my chest and leaves me breathless. I don't want to surface, I'd much rather drown in this feeling. Mattie's looking at me curiously, head tilted and eyes bright. I force the storms in me to settle before squeezing his hand lightly. I know I have to drive us to the restaurant, but I'm afraid I won't be able to keep my eyes on the road if Matt keeps being so fantastic. He slides into the passenger's seat and lets his eyes slide closed.

"Wake me when we get there," He says, "You know how I sleep in cars."
"I know, sugar. Rest well."

It's about an hour drive, and Matt's just starting to stir from his nap when we pull into the parking lot. The restaurant is cozy but high-end. Matt seems right at home here, looking around for the waiter to arrive with our food. He's sitting across from me in a 50s-style booth, hands clasped on the table. The food comes out and his eyes go wide.

"Oh, Sammy, this is amazing!" He raves, his smile threatening to split his face, "Thanks for taking me here."
"Any time, Birdie. I've always wanted to try this place, you know."

By the time we've finished dinner, Matt looks sated and sleepy, a soft look of contentment spread across his face. I can't help but smile at him even though none of this is out of the ordinary.

"I want to file charges against Nick." This takes me by surprise, though. Maybe he was coaxed into saying it by the easy atmosphere of the restaurant. Or maybe it was the food.

"Really? That's great, Mattie, but-" I stop short. There's a lot that goes into filing charges. *A lot of recalling things and explaining things and-* "You'd have to talk to the police about what he did to you. And you'd have to be specific. It's your decision, of course, but I want to make sure you know what you're getting into."

"I know a little bit already. I've been looking online for what I need to do and where I need to go and stuff. I still don't know any details, but those weren't exactly on the CPD website," He takes a deep breath, "I need to do this. I can't stop thinking about all the what if's. Like, what if Nick's trying to find another stupid, naive, and lonely heart to break? What if he's already found one? I can't let what happened to me happen to somebody else. I want him locked up, or registered on some government list at the very least. And yeah, I would be happy to see him pay for what did, to see him get what he deserves, but mostly I just don't want him out on the streets."

I gawk at Matthew for a shocked moment, gauging the tension in his jaw. I try desperately to snap myself out of it, but to little avail. He tilts his head as he looks at me, worry evident on his face. I finally crawl back out of my own head and into the real world.

"That's a solid plan, Mattie. Glad you researched it, too. It's always nice to know a little something going in."

"Thanks, Sam," A fraction of stress slides off of him, "I might want you to come with me, if they let me bring you in. I don't know if they would, you know, the investigators or whoever. But I'd still want you there for some moral support."

"Absolutely. I'll be right next to you if I'm allowed and I'll be waiting outside if I'm not. Even if I'm not allowed in the room with you for whatever reason, I'll be right outside that door when you leave."

"Thank you, Sammy."

Matthew

I just want to get this over and done with. I'm looking at the number to call and report a crime for the hundredth time. I want to call, I want to be *done* with him. I still can't bring myself to. I'm scared, even after talking with Sam last night. I don't want to explain to some stranger everything that he did to me but I know that I'll have to if I call that number. If I call that number, I would suffer, but for what end? Would Nick get any punishment? What if all the cops and lawyers can't sentence him? Then what? But if he gets even the smallest consequence...

I dial before I can change my mind again.

"Hello! You have reached the Chicago Police Department. If you have a tip, press 1. If you'd like to report a crime, press 2. To speak to a representative, press 3. If you're currently in an emergency situation, hang up then call 9-1-1."

Shaking, I press 2. I start pacing back and forth across the apartment floor before collapsing in a nervous heap on the couch. Sam's somewhere nearby and I can hear his hurried footsteps getting closer. He sits next to me and tucks me into his side with a whisper of "moral support." Great, now I'm going to be tearing up before my call has even connected.

"Hi, thanks for calling the Chicago Police Department. My name's Sheryl, how can I help you today?"

"Hi, Sheryl. My, uh, my name is Matthew Lin and I'd like to report a domestic violence case," I'm already gasping for breath, "Do I do that over the phone or do I need to come in to the station?"

"Either way works for us, whatever makes you comfortable. How do you know this person?"

"He raped me multiple times. We were in a relationship and it turned abusive."

"Alright. I'll need your name again and the name of the offender."

"My name is Matthew James Lin. His name is Nick Garcia. I don't know if he has a middle name."

"That's fine. I'll also need..."

It takes hours. I give everything I know about him, everything he's done, and I give it away to someone who can use it. Sheryl is understanding of the need to take a breather every once in a while, when I have to come back down from a flashback. It's exhausting, more so than I expected. So when Sheryl asks me to come in, I almost say no.

"I understand that you're tired and under undue stress, but there's an ongoing investigation into a case very similar to this one, right down to the names of the victim and perpetrator. It was reported by someone claiming to be your brother."

Ricky fucking Black. When did he plan on telling me this?

"I'll be right over."

Apparently, my testimony is enough evidence to put Ricky's investigation through to court. That doesn't mean I'm not furious at him. Despite Sam's pleas to just go home and relax, I drive to my brother's house.

"I can explain." *Of course those are the first words out of your mouth when you open the door.*
"You'd better. Start talking, asshole."
"I wanted him to pay. I know I should've asked you but I didn't-"
He stops abruptly, "I didn't want you to say no. I know how bad that sounds but I needed him to pay, Matt. I couldn't watch you suffer, and I know you did, and let him get away with it. I can't just beat him up like I would've when we were kids. So I went to the police like a real, law-abiding citizen."
"But not like a good brother."
"I know that. I did something horrible, Matt, I know. I lied to you, I hid from you, and I didn't ask for your permission because I thought you wouldn't give it. I wanted Nick to pay for what he did and in the end, I did the exact same things as him," He looks about ready to cry, "I'm sorry, Matt. I knew it was wrong and I did it anyway."
I scour his expression for any fault in his story. Finding none, I say, "I forgive you, sort of. I understand why you did it, I believe that you're sorry, and you helped get a whole load of charges added to Nick's sentence. But you still lied to me and broke my trust and divulged the most traumatic and personal parts of my life to someone I've never even met. I'm not mad at you, per say, but it'll take some time to rebuild that blind trust I had in you. I'm still not mad, Rick."
"Thank you. I really don't deserve this." He whispers, head hung.

"Yeah, you do. You're my brother, you've always been there for me. Sometimes you screw up but you always have the right intentions. I'm going to head home now, though. It's been a long day," I pause, "Hey, where'd Sam go?"

I saw him slip in through the door behind me, but I wonder where he wandered off to. He could get lost in Ricky's house; the place is enormous. Ricky shrugs, clearly having as much of a clue as I do: none. The only lead I have is that if he found the kitchen, he's probably in there. Upon reaching the kitchen, I find Sam nursing a pot of something and holding polite conversation with Timmy.

"Did you two work things out?" Timmy says, eyebrow arched in a typical *what did you do now* expression.
"I think so," Ricky mutters, "Have you both been here the whole time?"
"Yeah," Sam pipes up, "Your kitchen is amazing! I never thought I'd get to work with such nice equipment."
"He's making dinner for twelve," Timmy laughs, "And I'm not sure why. You just came in here, grabbed stuff, and food started appearing."
"Nervous habit."

The room stills, any tension dissipating. Sam takes this as our queue to leave, escorting me out to the car. The drive away feels starkly quiet against the rest of the day. I start to fall asleep in the passenger's seat as I so often do, but rabid dreams keep my eyes open.

It's going to be a long night.

Sam

The walk in from the parking lot of our apartment building is too quiet for my liking. Mattie's always cracking jokes or singing to himself but right now he's listless. It's almost more than I can bear to see him like this. I scoop him up in a hug the second the door closes behind us. He relaxes minutely, I barely even notice, but I'll take what I can get. He falls, exhausted, onto the couch and I bring him a blanket to curl up in. I find myself wandering into the bathroom and splashing water on my face, desperate to get out of this trance. I come back to the living room to find Mattie wrapped in the blanket like a burrito, only a bit of curly brown hair sticking out of his makeshift nest. I sit next to him and the entire cocoon he's made scooches toward me. It should be comical, but it isn't. I tuck him in close to me, holding him with gentle arms. Mattie pokes his head out from inside the blanket to look at me. I can see tear tracks on his cheeks, new ones bubbling in the corners of his eyes. I pull him in tighter and he wraps his arms around me. He's shaking and whether it's from relief or the sobs racking his body, I don't know. I keep the blanket around his shoulders, even as he squirms out of his cocoon. The warmth and security of a well-worn blanket can work wonders for someone in pain. Mattie calms down surprisingly quickly, his sobs fading into sniffles. I untangle myself from him and retrieve some leftovers from the fridge, heating them in the microwave.

"Are you hungry, Birdie? We didn't eat lunch today."

He nods from the couch and burrows back into the blanket. I bring back two plates of warm pasta, setting them on the coffee table. I keep one for myself, and I'm heartened to see Matt emerge from the blanket to eat. He wouldn't have done that a couple months ago. It's comforting to know Mattie's not starving himself anymore.

I used to worry too much about that. It was so hard for him to break out of the mindset the Nick put him in; I almost didn't go to work several times to try and help him. But I knew that he wouldn't think highly of that kind of thing. It was always "go on Sam, you don't have to worry about me." I didn't exactly believe him but I went along with it, mostly because he's stubborn as all hell. I'm so glad everything worked out. No more abuse, no more self-torture, and I haven't been this happy with anybody *ever*.

"I love you, Mattie. Thanks for existing."
"You're welcome? I'm glad I exist, too," He sighs, "I love you, Sammy. Thank you for being there for me today. I mean, you're always there, but especially today."
"No problem, lovebird. Eat your pasta."

And he does, looking just a touch more at ease. I toss an arm around his shoulders and pull him into my chest. He's okay, he's *okay*, and I love him so much. I want to give him kindness and sweet things and everything I have. I have never felt my chest ache just seeing someone have enough to eat and warm clothes and a home that doesn't hurt. I want to give him soft blankets and hot soups as a reminder that nothing has to hurt anymore. I want tender mornings where we have nowhere to be, nothing to do, just a sense of security. I will always worry, but at least I can hold Mattie and for now I will let those worries go.

It was already late when we got home and after such a long day, it's no wonder I just want to crawl into bed. I'm almost asleep now, finally. Mattie's already sound asleep. I need to roll over before my leg goes numb but I don't want to wake him, not with how long it took him to fall asleep. He was so tired but all the memories stirred up today kept him awake. At least he's asleep now; it scared me, how miserable he looked. He's at peace for now, his face relaxed in sleep. He sighs and settles deeper into the pillows. I take that as an omen to move my leg. Mattie whimpers as I move away and I can't get back to him fast enough. It's not for his sake, but for mine. He tucks himself into my chest and I curl protectively around him. I never want to see him hurting, especially not like this. I would do anything to keep him safe, I'd go hungry, I'd go homeless. Matt would tell me not to think like that, call me self sacrificial. This isn't news to me. I know how quick I am to self sacrifice. I've always been this way and even though I know it's not healthy, but I can't bring myself to care much. I really need to sleep but I can't quite get there. So instead, I roll over and the TV on. I keep Mattie close, not wanting a repeat of that heartbreaking whimper. I turn the volume down low and sigh. I would love to be read to or get a massage. *Wait, what?* I haven't thought like that since I was a kid. I haven't let myself want things in so long. I have to admit, I'm a little proud of myself. I'm about to turn off the TV when Matthew stretches and wakes up.

"What are you doing still up?"
"Can't sleep," I yawn, "I was just thinkin' being read to might help."
"I'll bring something for you. Get comfy."

He stands up and pulls a book off the shelf. It's one of mine, an old one. He plops back into bed, pressing himself under my arm. He starts reading, and I start falling asleep. I melt against the mattress, finally feeling secure and calm. I barely notice Mattie peck my cheek and curl up to sleep. It's nice to be taken care of sometimes.

Matthew

I wake up in Sam's arms. It's odd, but not at all unheard of or unpleasant. He doesn't usually sleep in; I guess yesterday really drained him. I glance over at the time and blanch. It's almost noon. I hate to wake Sammy by getting out of bed. He's gotta be exhausted to have slept this late. I slide out of bed, nevertheless. Sam rolls over and settles back in, thankfully. I tiptoe into the kitchen, watching for the spots where the floor creaks. There's nothing already made, nothing to microwave, no "just add water!" meals. I really can't cook without setting something on fire, despite many efforts to learn. Maybe I should ask Sam to teach me. Not right now, obviously, not when he needs to sleep, but some time. I still want food now, though. I guess I'll order something with one of those delivery apps.

My breakfast arrives half an hour later, and Sam still hasn't woken up. I decide that I should probably check on him. I find him curled in the fetal position, trembling and tugging at the sheets. Yeah, definitely time to wake him up.

"Sam," I say, "Wake up, angel. You're having a bad dream."

I shake his shoulders until he opens his eyes. I sit on the edge of the bed while Sam gets his bearings. He gently wraps an arm around my waist. I know that in a moment, he'll be clinging to me. This is the calm before the storm. I open my arms and wait for him to crawl in. I find that I mustn't wait long. Sam tucks his cheek into my chest and I hold him there. Sam stops shaking quite so badly. I push him away from me to get a good look at his face. He looks scared instead of sad, which is odd. It's not at all how he usually looks after a nightmare. I kiss his forehead and pull him back into me. He sighs and goes nearly limp in my arms.

"What happened, Sammy?" I whisper, "I want to make you feel better."

"I had another dream about my dad," He says hoarsely, "About the time he finally kicked me out. My ex-girlfriend told him that I was dating a guy even though I wasn't. She wanted something bad to happen to me. Before she told him what she did, I told her that I'm pansexual and she didn't take it well. She dumped me on the spot and told my dad a couple weeks later."

"Did she know what he's like?" I murmur.

"Yeah, she did. She shared a lot of his opinions, but I didn't know that."

I don't know what to say, so I stay silent and just hold Sammy close. I try to process what he told me. He was kicked out of the house for something that wasn't even true. Someone told his dad a fucking lie just to hurt him, knowing full well what kind of hurt they could be inflicting. I give Sam a tight hug and I don't let go. I nuzzle my face into his shoulder, revelling in the way his breathing has evened and smoothed. I finally pull away, giving Sam a quick peck on the cheek and pulling him towards the kitchen.

"I ordered waffles," I say, "I wasn't sure what you'd want. It's noon but we haven't eaten breakfast yet. Feel free to have a couple waffles."

Sam just nods. He's never very talkative after a nightmare like that. He stays right at my side throughout the day. I don't mind him being clingy. I actually enjoy it, in a way. He's letting me take care of him, and I'm so proud of him for that. It's four o'clock by the time Sam's talking again. I think that's the longest he's been silent in all my time knowing him. He's resting, his body slumped over in the arm of the couch when he says softly,

"Thanks for all this, Birdie."

"Of course, Sam." I smile, even though I barely heard him from the opposite end of the couch. It's still progress, still such a relief.

"Is it too early in the season for me to make Christmas cookies?"

"I don't think so. At least, not if I can eat some."

"That's the best part."

Sam hauls himself up off the couch and into the kitchen. I follow him and watch, smitten and delighted, as he lays out sugar and flour. I take my usual perch on the counter and eat half the marshmallows that were supposed to go into the fudge. Sam gives me his *I should have known* look and quietly takes the bag away. Everything about it is so domestic and sweet that almost have to pinch myself to make it real. *But it's already real!* It is heartwarming and aching and real and it's mine.

"Sam? Would you teach me to cook? I've always been a kitchen nightmare," I say, then sheepishly tack on, "And I want to be able to make stuff for you sometimes."

"Absolutely! I think you'd be good at it, but no one's taught you properly. Think of cooking the same way you think of science; you need to be precise with your reactants, or ingredients in this case."

"Okay, so then what? If I measure everything right, how do I make it taste good?"

"Trial and error. Remember that you can always add more of something, but you can never take it out once it's in."

I hop off of the counter and try to get a feel for what Sam's doing. He looks over at me, then takes my hands and presses them into the cookie dough. He tells me to knead it, fold it, care for it. I do my best. Sam takes a step back to observe, and he nods. He tells me how good it looks and that I'm doing better than most do when they start out.

"Not as good as you." I say, and he laughs.
"Yes, but I've been doing this for years. It takes practice."

He curls his arms around my chest, which is very distracting. Somehow, though, it makes the process easier. When the dough is sufficiently "cared for," I cut it into little trees. Sam's at my side, stirring a bowl of green icing. The cookies go into the oven, but my work isn't done. (Apparently.) I'm handed a bowl of white icing and some food coloring. Sam tells me to go nuts. The result is a pepto bismol pink sludge. Sam tells me it'll make nice ornaments on the cookie trees.

He wasn't wrong about that. While cookies for dinner is not recommended, I certainly enjoyed it. Sam is off picking up our take out order from the hole in the wall Chinese restaurant. They have fabulous shrimp; it's one of the best things I've eaten in my lifetime. (Sam's stress baking not included, just because it far surpasses all other food.) The door swings open and Sam drifts in, balancing two fragrant bags. I swoop in to help, getting my food in the process. I plop back onto the sofa, Sam tucked into my side. I kiss his head and turn the TV to another Mystery Science Theater 3000. Sam has decided he loves this show and I like it well enough, so why not?

Later that evening, as I'm burrowing into bed, Sam says something that nearly tears me to pieces.

"I love you," He says, "Every single piece of you. I can't begin to tell you how much you've helped me. I want to hold you and hug you and kiss you and make you happy. I will give you the world someday, lovebird. I can't even believe that you're real."

Does this angel really think that he's *the lucky one?* I want to ask him, but I don't. Instead, I say, "I'm right here, Sammy. I'm real and I'm yours and I love you, angel."

And I press myself into his arms, falling asleep within minutes.

Sam

I wake up with Matt sprawled across me. He moves so much in his sleep; it's a wonder he gets any rest at all. I yawn wrap myself around him. I know that I won't be moving for a while, not when I'm so cozy with Matt. He's curled tightly around my chest and hips, his cheek against my neck. I smile at my sweet lovebird, unable to help myself. I am so lucky to have him. I didn't think someone like him, so handsome and funny and *confident,* would ever be interested in me. I've never been special enough to get a second glance. I'm attractive, but not outstanding, I don't have an exciting life; nothing sets me apart. I must have *something*, though. We did get together, afterall. Matt says I'm warm and caring, maybe that's what it is. Or maybe it's just that I met him at the right time, or that he sees something in me that I don't. I don't understand it. In my mind, I'm still the kid having a panic attack in the bathroom between classes.

I wish I knew what he sees in me. Maybe then I could see it in myself.

Matthew insists that we go holiday shopping that afternoon. He says it'll be fun and get us into the holiday spirit. That sounds all well and good, the only problem is that I've never had any holiday spirit. I know that he knows this, I've told him so, which leaves me thinking that he must be plotting something. I don't think I mind.

The mall is packed. I've never liked crowds, but at least now I can press closer to Matthew everytime it feels like my throat is closing. I'm tugged into a store filled wall to wall with ornaments, wreaths, and holly. Matthew stops walking to take a look around. I stop beside him to catch my breath.

"Are you alright, Sammy?" He asks, head tilted with concern. "I want this to be fun for you, you know."
"I'm fine," I say, even though I know I'm lying, "I just don't like crowds."
"Oh, okay. Well, let's just stay in here a while. It's not so crowded."

I trail Mattie like a lost puppy through the store. He shows me little trinkets, clearly trying to cheer me up. I appreciate it and start to relax a bit. It's hard not to when he's pressed against my side - a constant, comforting presence. I find myself in an aisle full of miniature figures ice skating, sledding, and various other winter time activities. I'm hit with a wave of nostalgia, wild and unexpected. Krista and I used to do that kind of stuff. We'd sneak out to the hills by our house and sled until our toes were numb. I take the miniature sleds to the counter where Matt is waiting for me. He lights up when he sees what I'm holding.

"I wanted to buy that," He says, "Couldn't quite pull the trigger, though."

"I guess you didn't have to," I smile and edge up to the counter, "I'm going to get it. It reminds me of sledding with my sister."

"Well then, by all means."

Mattie rests his head on my shoulder and the store clerk looks curiously between us. I'm not nearly as comfortable with initiating PDA as Matt. *Receiving* affection is another thing entirely. I tuck Matt under my arm and grab the bag with the other. The clerk wishes us a polite happy holidays, and I'm able to remind myself that the world is not against me.

Back in the more crowded central area of the mall, I'm still nervous but less so than before. I find a gift for Krista (a silver frying pan necklace) and something for Matt as well. I don't buy it yet, worrying that I'd ruin the surprise. (It's a blanket with little music notes all over. It's also one of the softest things I've ever touched.) Matthew comes running up behind me while I'm looking at it, leaning on me and politely demanding a break for soft pretzels. I chuckle and abandon the blanket in search of more important things; namely, a cinnamon pretzel. Once found and purchased, Mattie sits down at one of the mall's rickety tables, eating a pretzel and humming along to "silver bells." I sit beside him and he offers me a piece of the aforementioned pretzel, which I decline.

"I'll eat when we get home. I don't like eating when I'm nervous."

"That's a little odd, Sammy, for as much as you *cook* when you're nervous." He teases.

I laugh and nudge his shoulder before settling against his side.

"I've had a really good time today, Mattie-Bird."

"'M glad," He mumbles, mouth full, "Want you to be happy."

Despite my good mood, my heart still sinks when I turn to look at the line of kids waiting to get their pictures taken with Santa. Sure, there's the screaming, the crying, but I expected that. My mom is there. *Why is she here today?* And if I've seen her, maybe she's seen me. I slide down in my chair, pulse pounding in my ears.

"Are you sure you're alright, angel?"

"I just saw my mom. I can't let her see me, Mattie, I can't. Can- can we leave, please? I'm sorry, I wanted to have fun today, and I did, I really did. I can't let her see me, please, Matthew, please God I need to go home."

"Darling, breathe. Just breathe for a minute. Of course we can go home, love. Alright, now where did you see her? Because I'm gonna take you out the other doors." He cups my cheeks before pulling me into his chest.

"I saw her by the creepy santa photo station. I just can't let her see me."

"Alright, Sammy, I'm taking you out the back."

I nod. I cling to Mattie's shirt and walk on shaky legs to the backdoor. I see her again, just a flash of blond hair *(too much like mine)* and pointed cheekbones *(I hate mirrors, hate looking like her, like him)* walking past. Matthew drags me towards the door still and I am grateful.

"Sam?" I hear her calling through the ringing in my ears, "Samuel O'Henry, stop running from me."

She cuts in front of Matt and halts. She's saying things, lecturing me I'm sure, but I can't hear her. My knees buckle and I fall heavily into Mattie's arms. Matt struggles to hold me up.

"I'll tell him," He snarls, "But unless he calls you, stay away from him. I'm sorry for what you went through, but that doesn't justify what you did."

"I know and I'm sorry. I am so sorry for everything."

Matthew hustles me out into the frigid December air. I fall into the front seat of the car and watch Matthew start the engine. He wipes the tears from my cheeks and wraps his arms around my shoulders. He sighs heavily and starts to drive home. I doze off on the way, sleeping until Matthew opens my car door.

"C'mon, love, let's get inside."

I stand and hug him right there in the parking lot. Matt pulls me in tight, letting himself melt against me. He's soft, so achingly soft and tender. I stand straighter and let myself be led inside. Once in our apartment, Mattie leaves me on the couch and treks into the kitchen. I pull a blanket around myself and wait for him to come back. Matt returns with a plate of brownies and a salad. An odd combo but still good. I take both and tuck myself under his chin. Matt wraps his arms around me. I eat the salad and let Matt kiss my hair. He might be a little overprotective, but that's fine by me. Overprotective isn't the word for it, either. Coddling, maybe. Excessively caretaking and sweet on days like today or just 'cause. I appreciate it, how much he cares.

"Thanks, Birdie." I mumble.

"Of course, my love. I didn't want to see her make you cry, give her that power. She doesn't deserve it," He sighs, "Just want you to live your own life. She wanted me to tell you something, though. She's getting divorced. She knew about your... father and what he did. She worked all the time because in her words, 'she knew what he was like with his vices and feared what he'd be like without them.'

She's leaving now because she realized that you and Krista aren't in danger when she isn't home. She said she's sorry for lying to you about him and sorry that you suffered. I told her not to call, to let you get in touch with her if you so desire. There's no pressure on you that way. Think it over and I'm here if you need anything. Truly, Sammy, anything you need, you can have."

He looks at me then and kisses my nose. I curl up in his lap and rest for awhile.

I wake up in bed the next morning. Matt is wrapped around my chest. *He must have carried me here!* I fell asleep on the sofa and now I'm in bed. Matt starts to stir and brushes his lips against my cheek. I hold him tightly and he smiles when he looks at me.

"Sorry about waking you. I just thought you'd be more comfortable in bed. That, and I don't think I can carry you. Sorry about that too. It's nice to be carried." *So he didn't carry me, I was just too out of it to remember climbing into bed.*
"It's fine, Bridie. I'm just glad you've been taking such good care of me."
"It's the least I can do. You take care of me when I'm down, and I do the same for you. That's how a relationship is supposed to work, Sammy. I know that neither of us have ever really had that before but still. That's the way it's drawn up on paper."
"I'm lucky to have that, though. Anybody would be lucky to have you."

He smiles and rests against me.

Matthew

I stay pressed against Sam for most of the morning. We don't talk (I think Sam fell back to sleep for awhile) but it's comfortable. I try to burrow under the covers and keep my angel close. I have no reason to get up and so I linger. Sam rolls out of bed a long time later and I follow. I patter into the kitchen and find Sam on the phone and stirring something aggressively.

"Don't overwork the batter, angel."

He startles then grunts in acknowledgement. I decide to stay close. Just in case.

"Hey Ma." He murmurs. *He might be forgiving to the point of self-endangerment.*
"He told me, yeah. No, this is not- no. I don't want you back in my life right now. I finally found a good job, a partner that respects me, and I have real friends that are more like a family than you ever were. I need some time to recover from everything you and Dad put me through."
He pauses. His mother must be speaking. *And I might have spoken too soon.*
"No, I guess seven years isn't enough time to recover from child abuse and years of living paycheck to paycheck. And think about Krista! She had to- no, do *not* call her. She had to work from the time she was ten. No worker's permit, just a half a prayer that nothing would happen to her 'cause lord knows she couldn't do a damn thing about it. She took care of me, cashed your checks, and paid the bills. She's successful and so am I. We don't need you and we never have. Goodbye, Ma. I'll call you, not the other way around."

And he hangs up. I'm proud of him for standing up to her. He didn't do it without some stress baking: there are pancakes on two plates already. I smile and slink into the kitchen. He kisses my temple absently, probably still drowning in other thoughts.

"Eat," I say simply, "These don't reheat well."

So he sits and starts in on a pancake. He pours on a truly unholy amount of syrup, much to my amusement. Some of it drips down his chin as he wolfs down his food. I'm struck by how fast he's eating.

"Nobody's taking your food away, darling. You can take your time."
"Was I eating too fast?" He says, still hovering over his plate.
"Yeah, you were. It's alright, angel, I just worry sometimes."
"I used to eat like this when I still lived with her. Sorry."
It's the apology that does it. "Don't you dare be sorry, Samuel. This isn't your fault," I steady myself to say, "Have you ever considered seeing a therapist for this? I've been thinking about seeing someone, you know, to process everything that happened with Nick. I think it might be good for me and for you, too."
"I should talk to somebody but I'm scared. I need to though, probably, before my anxiety really spirals out of control. I don't want to be so afraid. But... why are you so willing to help me?"
"Because I care about you, I love you, I want you to be happy? Sammy, you don't need to face everything on your own. I'm going to keep telling you that until you believe me. Forchristsake, angel, come here."

He does, holding tight to me on the sofa. I want to tell him how worthy he is of nice things but I don't think he wants to hear it. I recline against his chest and try to think of ways to bring Sam's self-esteem up a little. I'm still pondering when he starts to talk.

"No one's ever been able to help me," He mumbles, "Krista was too young, Jackson didn't know enough, and I was too busy trying to stay alive. It's not completely foreign to me, the concept of being cared for, but it's not *allowed*. I can't let myself rely on someone like I used to. It's not fair to you. You shouldn't have to be the proctor for my mental state."

"And I won't be. You're in charge of that. I'm asking you to find some way to take care of yourself in ways beyond the physical. I know you haven't had much of a chance to do that before but that doesn't mean it's not okay for you to do it now."

He nods tightly, "I'll try if you do."

"Deal."

We book an appointment with a therapist for the next day. It's nerve-wracking to walk in. The receptionist gets us checked in and I go in first. The room's alright, and talking comes easier by the end of the session. Sam goes in for the second half and I sit in the lobby. It's only a half hour that he's gone, but it feels like forever. I read bits of the magazines in the waiting area. It does little to ease my mind. Sam comes back, though, and tells me he's glad we did this. That is enough to placate me.

The next few days fly past. I wake up to breakfast in bed on the twelfth of December. Sam is smiling at me.

"Happy birthday, Birdie!"

"Oh, it is my birthday, isn't it?"

"You forgot?" He says softly, brow furrowed.

"It kinda slipped my mind. I wasn't excited or anything. It's not all that important. I'm twenty-five. Nothing special. I haven't celebrated for a few years and I guess I forgot that I could."

Sam stares miserably at me before wrapping his arms around my shoulders. I sigh and hug back. He says something about celebrating a little extra today. I pull away from him and smile.

"That sounds nice, angel."

I eat my breakfast. Sam insists on taking my plates to the kitchen. I sit up and snuggle under the blankets again while he's gone. He comes back with a neatly wrapped package, extending it to me. I thank him profusely and tear the paper off. Inside is a blanket, soft and grey and speckled with music notes. I hold it to my face and let my eyes flutter closed. I murmur more thanks to Sam and curl into my new blanket. He grins and sits beside me, tucking in under the covers and resting his head on my chest. His hand hovers dangerously close to a love handle and I suck in my stomach too late. Sam seems to notice but doesn't pull away. He turns on a movie and presses closer to me. He doesn't move his hand, instead letting it rest where I'm soft. I slowly relax, deciding that he's earnest in his affection; he wouldn't turn around and tell me... Well. I cradle the small of his back and feel him settle more fully against me. He's still curled around my stomach (there's plenty of it for him to curl around) and I'm starting to really consider the possibility that he *likes* me like this. Maybe he doesn't care about the extra cushioning or maybe he likes it. Sam slides down and rests his head on my tummy. He hums, eyes closed, and tangles himself with me. I'm caught in an onslaught of love and warmth. I put my hands on Sam's shoulders and haul him up to eye level. He looks confused and concerned but I shake my head at him, smiling. I kiss him firmly on the lips. It's about time, I think. Sam tenses at first, but falls into my chest the next moment. It's chaste and gentle and so much more exhilarating than anything I've felt before. I lean back and gaze wonderingly at Sam.

"Can we do that again?" He whispers, smile flickering over his face.
"Yeah, but only that. No tongue, nothing under the clothes, nothing below the belt. I am not up for that yet. I want- I need to take physical intimacy slowly."
"Of course. Whatever you want, Mattie. Nothing more, nothing less."

I smile breezily. He leans nervously into me and I cup his cheek. He's nearly trembling as his hands come to fall on my hips. I kiss him softly, tracing his waist. I pull away, then go right back to Sam. It's sweet how he touches me. He skims over my belly, though he doesn't avoid it. Quite the opposite, actually. He's tender and nearly worshipping as he kisses me. He's so sweet. I let go of him eventually, regretfully. I stay close to him as we go into the kitchen. There's a cake, not yet frosted, sitting on the counter. Sam asks if chocolate frosting would be alright. I say it'd be wonderful. I cuddle up with Sam on the couch, kissing some more. He's a good kisser, careful and loving and everything I want that I couldn't have before. He keeps touching my face, sides, and stomach with reverence. Eventually, I just lay against his chest and hold his hand. I love him with my whole heart. I nuzzle against the nape of his neck. He's massaging my stomach casually, pressing lightly and squeezing. He's getting a little more handsy than I would prefer. If I were smaller, it wouldn't be so uncomfortable but-

"There shouldn't be enough for you to squeeze," I mutter, "You don't have to touch me there, if you don't want to."
"I want to, though."
"I'd understand- wait, what?"

"You're so handsome, Matt. I like your tummy. I know that some people haven't been the best to you, but I'm not lying. I would never do that. I love every inch of you. I loved you skinny, I love you now, and I would love you fat. And anywhere in between! If you want to lose weight, that's fine, but *please* don't worry about changing for me. You are so, so gorgeous. I don't know what to do to prove that to you, but someday I will. I wish you could see you how I see you. My sweet, soft Birdie..." He kisses me and pulls me into his lap.

"Are you sure I-" I trail off, "That I'm not too heavy?"

"I'm sure. You're perfect, lovebird."

I kiss him this time, searching for grounding in his form. He holds me closer and trails his fingers along my sides. He's gripping me as if we could fuse if he could only get close enough. I tangle one hand through his hair, the other falling to his hip. I press a kiss to his forehead then lean back. I rub his shoulders and let him -really let him- touch my chest and stomach and hips. Soon, I'm covered in a litany of praises I want so desperately to believe.

"I don't know the words to tell you how stunning you are, Matt. You are so lovely, gentle, and warm. I can't even begin to explain it. I'm so in love with you, Mattie. I wanna hold you and love you with utmost care. I want to be with you. You are so much more than I ever expected or hoped for and I need you to know that."

"Thank you, Sammy. You're an angel, I swear. I'm lucky to have you."

"I think I'm luckier, lovebird. Oh! What do you want to do for your birthday?"

"I want lasagna."

"That's not an activity, sweets."

"Try me. But seriously, lasagna, wine, and that cake? Perfect. I wanna watch reruns of the X-Files with you and cuddle under my new blanket. I haven't celebrated in years, angel. I think taking it easy would be amazing."

"Alright. So, I gotta make lasagna?"

"No! We could order or-"

"I'm kidding, Mattie," He laughs, "Sorry. It's your birthday. I'll always make you food, especially on your birthday."

"Thank you, my angel."

Sam

I never realized that Mattie is at least a little self-conscious. I mean, we have mirrors in the house. He's seen himself. I don't know what he's seeing that he isn't liking. He seems to dislike the weight he's gained, though I can't fathom why. He was absolutely emaciated when I met him. He's finally got some color to his cheeks and some real substance to him. I don't care what size he is, but he seems to enjoy food. If some chub is any measure of his happiness, then I think I'll end up liking it in more than just the physical sense. Maybe I just think it's a measure because he put on weight after getting away from Nick. And I do love all of him, like I told him. He's so wonderful, I wish I could convince him of his own charm.

I try to get a handle on my thoughts as I frost the cake. Matt is sitting next to me, singing along to an Elton John album. I'm starting to think "Tiny Dancer" is on repeat, but that's fine with me. It's a great song, and my little songbird seems to think so too. He's singing every word and has started to dance around the kitchen. I smile stupidly and hand him the almost empty bowl of frosting.

"C'mere, birthday bird. The frosting bowl ain't going to clean itself."

"You're making me do dishes?"

"No, silly. I'm giving you a spoon and the rest of the frosting. What happens next is up to you."

He laughs and scampers off, bowl in hand. I finish the cake and walk into the living room. Mattie's under the new blanket, eating frosting with a spoon. The TV's on and an episode of *The X-Files* is already queued up. I'm warmed by the sight. I cuddle up next to him and kiss his temple. I have to get the lasagna out of the oven, but I'll sit for as long as I can. I snuggle against Matt and he starts the episode. He knows it line for line and I'm disappointed when I have to get up and grab the food. Matt's face lights up when I come back. I kiss the top of his head and hand him the plate. It's comfy cozy with good food and drink, Matt happily leaning against me. I loop my arm around his shoulders and wish him happy birthday again. He mumbles something sleepily and I laugh. The constant drone of the TV is a comforting background noise as I hold Mattie close. The cake is on the table and Matt is eating some. He's sighing contentedly and snuggling into my side.

"I didn't sing happy birthday to you yet!" I exclaim.

"Meh. I wanted cake. You can still sing if you want to."

I decide that yes, I want to sing, and so I do.

"Thank you, angel. Second best birthday."

"Only second?" I smirk.

"First was my tenth birthday. I went dirt biking with Ricky, Chris, Jamie, Luci, and Johnny. It was awesome. I fell and ate grass and got this scar on my ankle. Didn't stop riding, though. We paid for a three-hour rental, we were getting a three-hour rental."

"I'll take second, if that's first."
"I thought you'd say that."

I pull him tighter against my chest and end up falling asleep. I had the foresight to turn off the TV, at least. It's warm and safe here, with Matt in my arms. Before I truly drift off to sleep, I kiss his forehead and ask if this is what he wanted for the day.

"It was perfect, Sammy. Thank you."

I fall asleep smiling.

I'm stiff when I wake. Not surprising, considering how I slept. Mattie is still curled tightly to my chest, though now we're both lying across the sofa. I have an arm around his back, hand resting on his soft side. I've never held someone like this before. I make a mental note to do it more often. Matt lifts his cheek off my chest and smiles sleepily. I kiss the top of his head. He rolls off me and grabs the leftover cake from last night. I assume he's going to eat it for breakfast.

"I'm not eating this now, if that's what you're thinking. I'm putting it in the fridge."
"Right. That would make sense."
He laughs.

Matt's got a dance lesson today. I don't need to go because I'll just be holding my guitar for the whole concert. Kinda hard to dance. Matt is looking forward to it, I think. He said he likes dancing and he's a good dancer, according to his family. I don't doubt it. Right now, he's smiling to himself and eating boxed cereal. I walk into the kitchen and drape over his shoulders.

"Good morning, love."
"Morning, Mattie-Bird," I whisper, "How are you feeling?"
"I'm excellent. I have that dance thing today, you know. I'm excited; I do love to dance."
"I'm glad. Hopefully you'll enjoy it."

Matt smiles at me. It's amazing how warm that smile makes me feel. I kiss his temple before making myself something to eat.

He heads out within the hour. I'll be on my own for most of the day, so I decide to pay Krista's restaurant a visit. She greets her customers fairly often and besides, I might want to stay for a quick bite. I don't talk to her often enough; we're both so busy. It's not far from the apartment, so I stop in for lunch. Sure enough, Krista's in the doorway. *It must not be very busy today, then.* I wave at her as I walk in, seeing her eyes light up.

"Look who it is. Mr. Famous," She laughs, "How's life?"
"I'm alright, Kris," I keep walking until I'm seated at a table, "And I thought I told you not to call me 'Mr. Famous.'"
"I'm sure you did, but I'm your sister and you're in a rock band that's on the radio. I'm going to keep calling you Mr. Famous. Anyway, where's your boy?"
"He's not *my boy*. Matt's at a dance lesson for the tour."
"Well, you knew exactly who I meant."

I can't argue with that. Krista says she'll make me something and bring it out in a minute. I don't bother protesting; she's too damn pushy. I really have to pick my battles with her. She comes back with risotto. It's one of her best dishes. I thank her and start to eat, scanning the dining room for nothing in particular. There are several couples on dates, laughing and giggling. I check my phone, feeling a little lonely. Matt texted me a video a couple minutes ago. I open it, smiling and watching his attempt at some dance routine. He laughs on the screen and trips over his feet. He's adorable and I text him so. It's funny to me, how bad he is at the simple steps and good he is at the tough ones. I must still be smiling when Krista returns, because a slow grin spreads across her face.

"Did somebody get a message?" She smirks, "You look awfully happy there, Sam-Bam."
"I think that's worse than Mr. Famous," I grumble, "But yes, if you must know, I did get a message from Mattie."
"Oh, I didn't ask if it was from Mattie. You told me that all on your own."
"You know, Krissy, sometimes I really hate you."
"No, you don't."

And I can't argue with that.

Matthew

The dance lesson is alright, I guess. The steps aren't that difficult, but my nerves keep getting to me. I'm going to have to do this on stage in front of a lot of people. What if I screw it up, like I'm doing now? Sam texted me back, and that helped, but I'm still so scared of-

"You'll be fine," The instructor says, "I know there's a ton of pressure for you to perform perfectly. I've been dancing on stage longer than you've been alive, probably. No one'll know if you mess up. It'll be ok, Matt."

I start to feel a little better and dance better, too. I guess my nerves really *were* interfering with my performance. It's nice to have someone so experienced tell me mistakes happen. Makes it more believable. I keep practicing the steps and missing less and less of them. I move with the music more, allow myself that freedom to screw up, and it feels amazing. The instructor is clapping for me and I smile at her. She's so talented and she's clapping for *me*.

"Bravo, Mr. Mayhem. Good luck at your show, not that you'll need it. Break a leg, Matt!" She calls as I leave. I know it's a performance thing, but I've never liked the saying "break a leg." I always worry that someday, as clumsy as I am, I actually *will* break a leg and it will be really embarrassing for me and whoever wished the break upon me.

I text Sam to see if he's willing to meet me at central park. I want to take a walk in the snow; it's so pretty. I think it'd be nice to have a little company. I've always wanted to go on a winter date, with the hot cocoa and beanie hats. It's not long before he texts me back. *See you there.* I grin at my phone and start the car. The dance studio isn't far from central park. Sam's sitting on a bench, probably getting snow on his ass. I smile when I see him, hands in my pockets. I should've brought gloves. He hugs me tightly, his scarf tickling my neck. I don't hug him back, instead, I lean in and tuck my face against his chest.

"Sorry about not hugging you right now," I say, "If I take my hands out of my pockets, they'll freeze off."
"It's okay, lovebird." He laughs.

I stay leaned against his shoulder as we wander around the park. Eventually, Sam gets too cold and has to duck into a coffee shop to warm up. I saunter up to the counter and buy a pastry and a hot cocoa. Sam gets a hot cocoa for himself and we sit in a booth. I peel off my coat. Sam is curled around me, his cheek against my shoulder. I kiss the snow in his hair. It's pleasantly warm in here, a change of pace from outside. Sam has stopped shivering. I was worried about that, the guy has no insulation. He's using me as a heating pad, not that I mind. I have more than enough *padding* for both of us. I'm starting to see that as a good thing, though. I feel more like myself, look more like myself. It's comforting to see my reflection in the mirror and recognize the face looking back at me.

I love Sam. I love how he looks at me, talks to me, the things he says. I've never been with somebody that loves my body as it is. I like getting used to it. I like being told that I'm handsome. I like being cooked for and pampered and treated well. I missed it even though I'd never had it before. I don't want it to end. Sam's looking at me now, his head barely lifted off my shoulder. He smiles and cups my cheek with his hand before settling back into me. I feel secure like this; protected and safe. Sam keeps himself wound around me in the coffee shop, which is a little odd for him, I think. He isn't usually so affectionate in public. It's good to see him coming out of his shell. He's such a sweetheart; I've always wanted to show him off a little. I'm not sure why I want to do that sort of thing. It feels disrespectful to show somebody off like gold and diamonds. They aren't an object. But, I don't want to show off Sam's looks, I want to tout our relationship. That's not much better, but hey. I love him and I want to show that love off. That *sounds* better, at least.

"C'mon, Birdie," Sam whispers, "Let's go home. It's almost time for dinner. Did you even eat lunch today?"

"No," I say shamefully, "I forgot."

"I figured. You ordered massive chocolate pastry even though it looked like it'd been sitting out all day."

"It's disgusting but I'm too hungry to care."

"Yup, we're going home and you're eating something worthwhile. Finish that if you want but I'm making you dinner."

I stand up and walk with Sam to the car.

"Wait, how did you get here? I had the car."

"I've been taking the bus all day."

"The bus? Oh Sammy, I'm so sorry."

"I still don't understand why you hate the bus so much."

"It's *gross.* People clip their toenails on the bus."

"Not on any bus I've ever been on."

"You just haven't been on enough buses. Lucky you."

I nudge his shoulder and slip into the passenger's seat. Sam likes driving more than I do and after a day on *the bus,* I dare say he's earned a drive. We aren't far from home, so even in this weather, the drive doesn't take long. Sam parks in his usual spot in the parking garage. We take the elevator upstairs, my arm around his waist. He smiles softly, a kind of gentleness reserved for private moments like this. (Even if we are only in the elevator.) Stepping into the apartment, I hang up my coat and find Sam already in the kitchen.

"At least take your coat off, angel."

"Maybe."

He shucks it onto a chair. I sigh and hang it up properly. If he's set on cooking for me before he even bothers with his coat, it's only fair that I help with that part. Still, he's so desperate to be helpful.

It sounds like a good thing, but to the point where he sacrifices his own comfort?

"I can wait, Sammy. You don't have to do this now. You could take your shoes off, maybe rest a minute?"
"I know you can wait, but I don't want you to have to."
"Still. Take your shoes off. You're home, you can relax while you're doing this."
He ponders this for a minute, then says, "Yeah, that makes sense. Thanks, Birdie. I forget that it's okay to rest, you know that."
"I know," I murmur, trying very hard to not look as sad as that statement makes me feel, "I'm going to go put on flannel pants. The dance pants are very nice for exercise, very breathable, but now I'm cold."
"Make yourself comfortable, love."
"Same to you."

He nods. I patter off to the bedroom and put on a well-worn pair of pajama pants. They've got little fish in santa hats printed on them. I can't remember the last time I wore these and they fit. They were too big for so long when I had gotten so small. I look at myself in the mirror and smile, reassured. I look like me again.

Back in the kitchen, Sam has kicked off his shoes and seems less tense. He kisses my cheek as I walk past. I sit on the counter as I so often do and watch him cook. He has chicken and rice in a pan, sizzling and steaming. It smells fantastic. Sam starts to dish up, but I tell him to go sit on the sofa and relax.

"You've done enough, love. I can take care of the rest."
"Thanks, Mattie." He says, though he looks reluctant to leave.

I bring him a dish, carrying a second for myself, and take a seat beside him. I feel him lean heavily into my side. I switch on the TV, resting my hand on Sam's knee. I change the channel to that trashy reality show that Sam loves. I'm not exactly a fan, but that's alright. He watches *The Bachelorette* with me. I can tell he's exhausted. He flops over onto me the moment he's done eating. I give him a little kiss on the top of the head. He's limp in my arms, completely relaxed. I'm relieved to have him here. He's tangled with me like the ivy and the wall at Wrigley Field.

"I love you," Sam whispers, "I love you so much. Can't even explain it, Birdie."
"Darling, I love you too. My sweet angel, you're the best thing that's ever happened to me."
"Perfect. My perfect Mattie."

I smile and tighten my grip on him, wanting to be closer than physics will allow. Sam rests his head on my shoulder, tugging a blanket around us. He's always cold, I swear. He's like a leech for body heat. Not that I'm complaining, mind you. I'll take any excuse for a cuddle session. Like now, with Sam pressed against me from knee to shoulder. He's watching the TV as if it holds some sort of merit. I don't see it, so I focus my attention on Sam's ever-tense shoulders. I put my hands on them and rub the knotted muscles. He goes lax against my fingertips. I dig my thumbs a little harder into his back. He makes a hurt little noise that goes straight to my heart.

"Too much?"
"Yeah," He mumbles, "It hurts too bad for you to press quite that hard."
"I'll be more careful."

He nods slightly. I try to press his shoulders more gently. He sighs softly and leans into my hands. It must hurt for him to be so tense all the time. It's reassuring for me to feel all those tight muscles come undone. He starts falling asleep in my arms. It's sweet, but I haul him up and take him towards the bedroom. I pull the blankets around him and kiss his forehead.

"Rest, my love. I'll be in sometime later. You just sleep."
"M'kay, Mattie. Goodnight."
"Goodnight, angel."

I stay up a couple more hours (it was *early* when Sam went to bed) but soon find myself yawning. I try to slide in silently next to Sam and keep from waking him. He rolls over and slings an arm around my waist. I kiss him softly and turn out the lights.

Sam

I wake up to Mattie laying beside me. He's tucked under my arm, holding the collar of my shirt as he so often does. I run a hand along his side, committing each curve and dip to memory. He stirs, looping his arms around my hips. He scoots up the bed and kisses me, satin soft and gentle. I kiss back and cradle the back of his head. He's warm in my lap, solid and comforting. I break the kiss and pull him into me. He wraps his arms loosely around my shoulders. I nuzzle the top of his head.

"You're the best." I murmur.
"Thanks, Sam."

We plod into the kitchen and eat reheated waffles. Yes, I saved waffles. I learned to be frugal when I was a kid and even now, old habits die hard. Matt doesn't mind it when I do stuff that I don't technically have to do anymore. He's the same way. Saving every scrap of *everything,* that kind of thing gets ingrained in a person. It's alright, though. We got by then, before we met, growing up with next to nothing. Even though we have the money to buy name-brand and on-trend, it just feels wrong. For me, at least, I can still only buy what I need. I bought the new car because my old one broke down. It's a cadillac, but I've wanted a nice car since I learned that they exist. We could afford another car, but we don't *need* one.

I think Matt bought his little bluebird pin because he knew he'd wear it on stage. It's useful for him. I don't know if he would've bought it if it wasn't. Right now, Matt is rapidly typing something on his phone. I smile at him, admiring how much of a mess his hair is. It's getting long, loose curls falling down his neck. He's so cute. The furious typing stops and Matt looks up at me.

"We have to be at the studio by ten. Mary May was very insistent."
"Sure thing. I'll grab my jacket."

We barely arrive before ten. Traffic's terrible, we get caught behind a snow plough, and then there's nowhere to park.

"Who are all these people?" Matt gripes as he finally pulls into a spot, "We're at a studio, not the mall."
"It's fine, Mattie. It's not like we can't walk a little further."
"But it's cold."
I step out of the car and laugh. This is a mistake. I start coughing, the cold air burning my lungs.
"And you laughed when I said it's cold." Matt smirks as we finally get inside.

"Hindsight is twenty-twenty."

"You're here!" A familiar voice calls from the hall, "I thought you'd skipped out on me."

"We would never." I say, eyes widening.

"It's fine," Mary May shrugs, "Just hurry along. Matt, that interview we talked about? They rescheduled for today. Terribly sorry for the inconvenience."

"Oh. I'll be fine." *Not convinced, Matt.*

"Well, head in there. Sam, stay here with me. I need to ask you a couple things."

"Right."

After that strange interaction, I feel uneasy both for myself and for Mattie. Mary May takes me to a side room and asks me how I'd like my hotel rooms for the tour.

"How I'd *like* them? I've never been in a hotel. The few times I've been on vacation, I slept in my car." *I miss my car.*

"So, whatever Matt, Chris, and Jamie want would be alright? Or do you have a hotel fantasy?"

"Whatever they pick is fine by me. How many rooms will there be? Are we expected to share, or-"

"You don't have to, but you may. I know you and Matt live together-" *That's all she knows? Really?* "-so if it'd put you more at ease, you could certainly share a room."

"I'll ask him, but yeah. That'd be nice if you could arrange it."

"Excellent."

Mary May and I continue to talk for another half hour. There's a commotion in the hallway, enough to send Mary May out of her office to check on it.

"Sam?" She says, frantically, "Come here right now."

"I'm on my way."
"Hurry."

I arrive in the hall to see Matthew looking around wildly, desperately. I approach him slowly, sending my most menacing glare towards the suit Mary May is mouthing off at.

"I swore I'd never work with your company again, but you paid my client enough that I reconsidered. Now, here we are. I ought to ask for a little compensation, huh? How about that girl you currently employ? You there! Whatever he's paying you, I'll double it."

Yikes. I open my arms towards Mattie and when he finally sees me, he launches into my chest, knocking the wind out of me. I gently hold him there and kiss his head. I bring him towards Gertrude's fabric fortress. She'll let us stay. Matt grabs the back of my shirt, burying his face in my shoulder. A patch there soon grows wet with tears and I start walking faster. Eventually, I think *screw it* and lift him up to get him out of here as fast as possible. Matt clings to me and I can't help but wonder, *what happened?*

Matthew

I take a seat in a strange, though not uncomfortable, armchair. There are two cameras, a producer in the corner, and an interviewer in front of me. Right now, I feel confident with the prospect of an interview. Then, I see the interviewer cringe at the list of questions in her hands. She stands to talk to the sharply-dressed man in the corner. They talk for a minute, she nods every now and then, before she sits back down. She introduces herself as Shelby.

"Your social media is full of links to help for victims of domestic violence. You have given personal anecdotes and seem very invested in the subject. Is there any particular reason for this?"

"Wow, jumping right to the deep stuff, huh?"

"I suppose."

"Alright then. I was a victim myself. My ex was abusive and I was lucky enough to get out. I want to help other people do the same."

"Why do you call your ex abusive?"

So it's this kind of interview. "He beat me and raped me. I would venture that most people agree that that's abuse."

"Er- Yes. It is."

"Any other questions or can I go?" *I'm getting rapidly tired of this shit.*

"Ah-" She glances at the producer or whatever he is, "I'm sorry about this, but I have to read my prompts."

"So read them!" He shouts at her.

She flinches, then starts asking me more questions. She apologizes intermittently, which is sort of comforting, but I'm starting to drown. I'm asked everything about my life. *How did you get fat? (I ate food, it's not complicated.) Are your parents aware of your sexuality? (Yes.) Are you and Sam O'Henry a couple? (If I decline to answer, you'll say we are, but I'm going to try this anyway. Please respect our privacy.) Do you think he'll leave if you put on more weight? (He wouldn't be the first.) Are you pressing charges against your ex? (I don't want to talk about him.) Why did you get in a stranger's car after running from your ex? (I wanted to die anyway. It didn't matter.) Why not go to your brother? (I was ashamed.) Why didn't you ignore him and just jump? (I don't know!)*

I don't remember what happens next. I'm vaguely aware that I'm having a panic attack on camera. Mary May is talking somewhere nearby. Sam is here. When did I get into the hall? Sam's carrying me somewhere. It's quieter now. I'm dizzy and sitting in a chair. Where's Sam?

"Sammy." I don't realize the name has left my lips.
"I'm right here, Birdie. We're in Gertrude's fabric forest. She's getting you a glass of water."

Sam has his arms around me. He's holding me. I start crying openly, finally. Sam strokes my hair, my shoulders, my back. I think I'm shaking. I don't know what's happening anymore. I'm scared.

"They made you live through all that all over again! The nerve that company has, I swear-" Mary May stops short.
"It's alright, Mattie. I got you. You're safe." Sam curls tighter around me. I shake harder.
"None of that footage will see the light of day," She sighs softly, "Stay here you two. Holler if you need anything."

I tremble for a while longer. I don't know how long. There's a glass of water next to me when I'm back in my mind. I take the glass and look at Sam. He nods at me. I sip at it, holding the glass a little too tightly. Sam kisses the back of my hand.

"I'm so sorry they hurt you, Mattie. If you want to talk about what happened, I'm here. I am always here. I love you."
"I don't even want to think about it. I love you, though, Sammy. Thank you."
"Of course, darling."

I can't bring myself to talk for a long time. Sam drives us home. I don't talk then either. At the apartment, Sam immediately wraps me in a blanket and brings me some pastries. I don't really taste it, but it's sweet of him to try. I feel numb, sick to my stomach. I'm filled with dread and restlessness but I want to sleep. Part of me never wants to wake up.

"Alright, this has gone on long enough. I'm going to make dinner. We're going to watch a movie. Something light-hearted. It's okay if you're not up to talking," *No, it's not,* "But I don't want you spiraling into some awful hole."

Sam makes lasagna, of course. It's my favorite. I cuddle up to him when he sits down. He wraps his arm around my shoulders and turns on *The Naked Gun.* Also my favorite. I relax a little into his chest. It's pleasant, warm, and cozy. I press a kiss to his cheek.

"Thank you." I whisper.
"Oh, sweetheart. You are so welcome."

I nod and rest against him again. I feel safer now. Sam has his arms around me and his cheek against the top of my head. I've settled into my skin again. Not restless, not scared, not numb. I place my hands over Sam's and let myself feel better. Sam laces his fingers with mine. I feel worthy of all this, of being cared for.

"You make me happy. I want to feel this safe all the time. I love you so much, Sammy. My guardian angel."
"You should always feel safe, lovebird. I love you, darling."
"You're too good to me."
"Never. Feeling safe isn't too good. It should be given. I know it isn't, but it should be."
"Thank you, Sam. I'm feeling much better now."

I lean my head on Sam's chest. I can hear his heartbeat as he cradles me. I watch the movie absently, laughing at jokes I've heard many times. Sam cards his hand through my hair. His other hand is resting on my hips, loosely holding my tummy. He strokes gentle circles there with his thumb. I finally feel the tense muscles around my shoulder blades relax. I stay tucked against Sam's side for a long while. I start nodding off, and he asks if I want to go to bed. I say yes. At once, Sam lifts me up and carries me to bed. I smile slightly against his chest. He kisses my forehead and pulls a blanket around me. I watch him leave, turn out the lights, and come back. He lays down next to me, wrapping me in a full-bodied embrace. I fall asleep with less trouble than I had expected.

Sam

I wake up to screams and flying elbows. Matthew is writhing next to me, not fully asleep or awake. I try to wake him up. He whimpers and cries out when I put a hand on his shoulder. *Does he think I'm...?* I get up and turn on the light, watching him intently. He's shaking, thrashing, sobbing hard enough to move the bed.

"Mattie. You're safe. I know today was awful, but you are safe. I love you, Birdie. I got you. I'm here. Wake up, darling."

He does, sitting up abruptly and gasping for breath. I sit on the edge of the bed, close enough he can touch me if he chooses, but that I'm not touching him. He looks at me with a terrified blank stare.

"Sam?" He whimpers.
"Yeah, it's me. I'm here with you. We're home."

"I had a bad dream."

I nod and extend an arm to him, not touching him yet. He leans away.

"I'm scared. The dream was about Nick. I thought he was here, thought he hurt you."
"Hurt me?"
"He was jealous." Matt says miserably.
"Alright," I murmur, "Nick's in prison. He can't hurt anyone anymore. He's got over thirty years in there already and more charges pending. He's not getting out anytime soon. He's gone. I know you're scared, Mattie. It's normal to be scared of someone who abused you. You don't need to be scared, but it's okay if you are."
"Sammy… Thank you. Could you hold me, now? I wasn't ready before," He lets out a shaky breath, "Thanks for not touching me when I woke up, just offering to. That was nice of you. I like it when you do things like that. I've never been asked if I want something to happen. I appreciate it."
"You're welcome. I'll keep asking about stuff like that, if it makes you more comfortable."
"It does. Thank you."
"No problem, Mattie-Bird."

And I snuggle up next to him, now that he's ready. I smile at him as he presses his frame against mine. Mattie's phone buzzes. Probably Mary May. I'm not waking him for it.

Chapter Five

Sam

I sleep through the rest of the night. I check my messages to see if Mary May called me as well. She didn't, but the detective working with Matt to keep Nick locked up did. If she called me in the dead of night... I listen to the voicemail.

Hey Sam, it's Sheryl. Nick pleaded not guilty to the additional charges. We're going to trial. You don't have to testify, and neither does Matt. I called Ricky and he already agreed to testify. Call me back. Stay strong.

I did not need this call. Why now? After yesterday and whatever happened in that interview? Knowing Mattie, he's going to want to testify. He'll march into that courtroom and stare Nick down as some kind of closure. I don't know if I can handle that. If Nick tries anything, I might just shatter. I glance over at Mattie. He's still sleeping, blissfully unaware. I call Sheryl back.

"Good morning, this is Sheryl, how can I help you?"
"It's Sam."
"Thanks for calling me back, Sam. Are you calling to find out about the trial?"
"Yeah."
"Alright, here's what we got. Nick plead guilty last time to everything involved in the kidnapping and-"
"The gummy worms incident. Just call it that."
"-And the gummy worms incident. He's fighting the domestic abuse charges, and the assault. He has multiple counts of almost everything he's charged with, because he did what he did repeatedly. The next step here is to go to trial. Witness and victim testimony can impact a jury in an emotional case like this. We have

physical evidence, too, so this doesn't depend on anyone's testimony."

"What physical evidence do you have?"

"Well," She sighs over the phone, "There are pictures, some digital, some printed. The victim never appears to be conscious in them."

"Oh, god." *The victim.*

"You don't have to be present at the trial."

"I know. When's the trial?"

"Thursday."

"That is *tomorrow!* What's with the short notice?"

"It was the state prison's decision, not mine. Nick is going to be there and give his own testimony. Please call me back with a decision on attendance of the trial."

"Wait! Does Mattie even have a lawyer?"

"The best we could find. He's got a soft spot for abuse victims and wins most of their cases. His name's Dan Veeto. You're going to meet him at the courthouse, if you meet him at all. It's an unorthodox trial, I know and I'm sorry."

"Alright, I guess. I'll call back later today."

"Thanks."

She hangs up. Left in a silent home, all I can think of are those pictures. I try to rid myself of the egregious mental image but to no avail. I pace the floors as my mind begins to decompose. I can still hear Sheryl's voice ringing in my ears, "the victim." I leap half a foot in the air as Matthew puts his hand on my shoulder. I whip around and look at him; he stares at me.

"What's the matter, Sammy? You were pacing and muttering to yourself."

"Sheryl called. There's going to be a trial tomorrow. Nick's going to *be there-*"

"I know. I got here voicemail, called her back. She said she just got off the phone with you. I'm going to the trial. I'm testifying."

"You're willing to see him again?"

"He'll be in handcuffs. He can't hurt me. You said it yourself last night."

"I just don't want to see you get hurt."

"I won't."

"But what if something happens? What if-"

"You seem more scared of him than me."

That stops me dead. I gape at him, wide-eyed. He's not wrong. I just didn't notice.

"I'm right, aren't I? You ended up terrified up of him, 'cause you're scared of me getting hurt."

"That's- yeah. You're right. I never realized it, but I would be devastated if he hurt you again. You've been through enough. More than enough."

"I know. I want to go out and tell my story so that maybe somebody could escape before things get bad. Maybe they could recognize warning signs I didn't."

"That's really mature of you. I don't think I'd be able to do that."

"Maybe not yet. You'll get there."

And he *hugs me,* so sweet and gentle. It's comforting to the point that my chest hurts with the bursting feeling inside. I can feel tears pricking at my eyes and for once in my life I don't hold them in. Through sobs, I tell Mattie that I should be the one comforting him. He shakes his head and escorts me to the couch. He tells me it's alright to be stressed about this, even if it didn't directly happen to me. *You care about me,* he whispers, *of course you're invested in the trial.* I calm down a little and rest my head on his tummy. He combs his hands through my hair, trying to make it lay flat. It doesn't work. I sit up and hold him for a minute, then go off to make breakfast. Silver dollar pancakes sound good, I think.

"Feeling better, angel?" Matt asks.
"Yeah, I am. Thanks for all that."
"Wow, chocolate chips? I guess you really are feeling better."
"Eh, just a little treat."

He smiles sweetly as I bring him a plate stacked with pancakes. I settle in next to him, bent on pampering him for the rest of the week. Matt seems to have picked up on my intentions.

"You spoil me, Sam."
"Good. Everyone deserves to spoiled from time to time."
"Is this going to last all day?"
"All week, if you'd like."
"I would."
I nod.

Mattie snuggles against me and turns on the TV. The morning news is on, blathering on about some grand fuck up. Nothing new. I'm about to change the channel when Mary May pops on screen.

"They've topped the charts week after week, sold out countless shows-"
"Twenty-seven shows, actually." Matt snipes.
"-and now, meet Mayhem's manager. Me! I'm Mary May Jones, and this is Shelby. She's my newest assistant-"
"That's the girl that interviewed me! The one that clearly hated the experience as much as I did."
"Yeah, Mary May stole her, chewed up her boss, and cut ties to his company. Apparently, this isn't the first time they've done something like that." I mutter.

"Huh. Well, good for her. Mary May doesn't steal employees out of spite."

"No, she doesn't. She knows that Shelby's talented."

"Saved her from an awful career." Matt says, mouth full of pancakes.

"Chew before you speak. This is why I've done the Heimlich maneuver on you twice already."

He laughs, and promptly starts choking.

"No! No, this time it's my fault."

"I'm alright, I'm good."

"Don't do that!"

"Don't make me laugh when I have food in my mouth!"

"I didn't even say something funny."

"You know I'll laugh at anything."

"Anything."

"You piece of meat." He snorts.

"*Piece of meat?* That one's new."

We never end up changing the channel. I laugh so hard I almost fall off the couch, grabbing the coffee table to catch myself. That makes Mattie laugh so hard he has the hiccups for the next ten minutes. Eventually, we're both exhausted. Matt's laying across my lap and holding my hand against his chest. It's great to be with him, all spread out on the couch. It's safe.

"I'm going with you to the trial," I say firmly, "Even if it's just for moral support. I want to be there with you."

"Thank you, Sammy. Let's call Sheryl."

We call her on speaker. I agree to testify where and when I first met Mattie. It was brutal just agreeing to the terms. I can't even imagine what the trial's going to be like, but I'm proud. I can do this. I can help give Nick what he deserves. I can help Mattie face the worst thing that's ever happened to him. For now, though, I kiss his cheek and find a kid's movie on Netflix.

"Really? Mulan? I didn't know you liked this movie."
"I love it. I watched it in the theater with Krista. It was a huge deal to see a movie in the theaters. She loved it too. I was maybe six, she was nine. Dad took us. He hadn't changed yet. I still watch it for nostalgia, I guess."
"Well, *let's get down to business.*" He sings the last bit.
"So you like it too!"
"Yeah, of course! I just didn't think it was your type of movie."
"C'mon, it's got a dragon and a badass girl that totally owns that entire war. How would that not be my kind of movie?"
"Touche."

Matthew

I feel special to cuddle up next to Sam and watch something that's so close to his heart. He knows all the words to all the songs and sings them quite loudly. I rest my head on his shoulder, and he wraps his arms around my waist. He runs his fingertips up and down my sides. I don't feel self conscious about how soft I've gotten. I feel good, even about seeing Nick tomorrow. It's refreshing to be free of the constraints I've put upon myself. I love myself how I am now, and it's a bonus that Sam loves me. I don't have to change myself for other people. I won't change myself for anyone but me.

Sam's steady breathing is a comfort at my side. The movie is still playing, and occasionally I can feel him laugh or gasp or hum along to the music. I lean into him a little more. I want to kiss Sam. This is not unusual. It's the depth of intimacy I'm willing to give him. I hadn't really thought I was going to be ready for anything beyond the gentle touches we're sharing now. I didn't think I'd ever get over the fears Nick left with me. I'm not fully recovered yet and I don't know if I'll ever be exactly how I was before, but being able to *want* someone? To *want* love and sweet touches? I never thought I'd want that again. Yet, I do. I lift my head from Sam's shoulder and nervously look him over. I want him, but does he want me?

"Sammy, I want to try-" I take a deep breath and try again, "I want to kiss you. Like more... vigorously? That sounds *so* not cute, sorry. This is much more difficult than I thought it'd be."
"It's alright, Birdie. Take your time." He's smiling, somewhere between amused and smitten.
"I want to try being more intimate with you. I'm still not sure how much I'll be comfortable with, but I want to try."
"That sounds great, Mattie. As long as you're doing this for you, and not because you think I want it. I don't want to do anything unless you're okay with it."
"This is definitely for me. I'll tell you if I'm not okay with anything."
"Good. Please do. I want you to enjoy yourself."
"And you're alright with this?"
"Yeah, I am."

Sam pauses the movie and I lean in, still jittery. Our lips touch, chaste as always, but slowly I press flush up against Sam. I don't even realize I'm doing it. I pull away in favor of resting my forehead against Sam's. He cradles my hip with his hand and cautiously connects our lips again. He's holding my hand between us and I shiver with the pleasant and greatly missed contact. I fall into his embrace the next time I surface from a kiss. I let my lips part against his, his hands toying idly with the hem of my shirt. He laughs breathlessly, head lolling onto my shoulder. I clamber into his lap, rendered graceless by his honey-eyed gaze. I feel like I've fallen into a long-forgotten fantasy of body heat and midnight smiles. My hands move on their own accord, touching Sam's chest through his shirt and feeling him tremble.

"You're shaking." I whisper, awestruck.
"Can't help it," He says, eyes closed, "I never thought that I'd find somebody like you, let alone have them live with me, love me. I'm overcome here, Mattie-Bird."
"Never thought anybody would be 'overcome' by me," I smile a little, "I love you."
"Love you, too."

Sam lays his hand gently over my heart and smiles softly. I pull him in close, trying and failing to kiss him. I mostly just lick the side of his face. We both burst out laughing. I tip over onto my side, dragging Sam with me. My back is against the seat of the couch, Sam laying on my chest, still laughing. I kiss him softly and successfully, his hands slipping under my shirt. I wasn't expecting it, but it's nice. He's ridiculously careful, and I think I love that.

"Is this okay? I got a little ahead of myself." He says sheepishly and nods to how my shirt has ridden up.
"It's fine, angel. I would've told you if it wasn't."
"I'm glad."

Then, he kisses my jaw and *that* is wonderful. He peppers my face in feather kisses and my body in the lightest touches. I didn't know anything could feel like this. I must've made some kind of a noise (probably an embarrassing one) because Sam stops and looks at me worriedly.

"Too much?"

"No, this is incredible. Why, what'd I do?"

"You, uh, whimpered and I thought maybe you were hurting."

Definitely embarrassing.

"I'm not hurting. Actually, quite the opposite. I always knew in my head that being touched is supposed to feel nice, but I'd never experienced it until just then. I had my mind blown and everything you were doing was so relaxing and *good.* That's all it was."

"That's a lot, lovebird. I'm so happy I made you feel like that, made you feel good. I love you, Mattie. I'm glad this was a worthwhile experience for you. I feel so lucky to have been the guy that made you happy like that I-"

"Sammy, angel, calm down. I know it's important. You don't need to get so worked up about it. Oh no, don't start crying, what happened-"

"I'm really happy, Matt. You know I cry at everything."

"Alright, sweetheart. Just let it out, then."

I hug him as he sniffles and whispers soft praise. He's never let himself be emotional before, I know, so it's natural for everything to be spilling over now. I kiss his forehead and nuzzle into his hair. Sam's pulling away from me, now, looking me in the eyes. I smile at him and take his hands in mine, squeezing just a little.

"Better?"

"Yeah. I got overwhelmed by how good that was. I needed it to feel like that for you, too. When you told me it did, I just..." He shrugs.

"As long as those were happy tears? I declare this a success."

"The happiest."

I grin and sit up against his side. He unpauses the movie and settles back into the couch. Soon, it's lunch time. Sam goes to pick up the shrimp I like from the Chinese place around the corner. We cuddle up together on the couch to eat. I'm warm with food and love and *Sam.* He's fondly rubbing my shoulders, running his hands through my hair. He tries to tie my hair back, but it's too short. I don't end up with a ponytail so much as a pony *poof.* Sam fails to hide his laughter, and I drag him down for a selfie. I ask if I can post it and he agrees. The caption reads "dear new hairdresser, please stick to guitar." He laughs when he sees it and says it's the hair's fault, not his.

I wish I could spend tomorrow like this. And maybe the days after, too.

It starts like any other day. Wake up, eat, shower, etc. I'm at the courthouse by seven. Sam is close behind me, send the most menacing glare I have ever seen at the reporters gathered outside. Someone leaked that I'm involved in the case, and that wouldn't be an issue, except that I'm famous now. I'm swarmed by microphones and cameras, making an already terrible experience *that much worse.* Sam hustles me through the door, his arm hovering behind me like a shield. I walk stiffly into the courtroom, *third door on the left,* just like the secretary said. It's clinical, immaculate, threateningly clean. I spot Nick, already seated in the defense booth. He's wearing a prison jumpsuit and cuffs. He's surrounded by guards. None of it makes me feel safe. I sit on my side of the aisle and look to the man seated beside me.

"I'm Dan Veeto. Sheryl informed me of your case. Tell the truth. That will be enough."
"Yes, sir."
"No need to be so formal. Call me Dan."
"Sorry, Dan."

I duck my head and look away. Sam and Ricky are with Sheryl in a booth for witnesses. I look away from them, too. I'm ashamed for reasons I can't understand. I know that I didn't do anything wrong, but I feel tainted. Like I *let* him do what he did. I don't want to believe it, but the feelings of worthlessness and like I'm a slut, not a victim, are getting harder to ignore.

The trial starts. Dan lays out his case. He paints Nick as manipulative and cold, and me as madly in love, not wanting to believe Nick was capable of what he did. Then, eventually, becoming too scared to leave. He isn't wrong. I stare at my hands clasped in my lap. Dan calls Ricky to the stand, asks him questions.

"Did you think your brother, Matthew, was in danger at anytime during his relationship with the defendant?"
"Yes. Matt was always covered in bruises and I asked about them a couple times, never got an answer from him. He dropped a lot of weight, to the point where I thought he'd just fade into nothingness if got any smaller. I was terrified."

I don't like knowing how awful I'd made Ricky feel. He takes his seat after a brief cross-examination.

The defense's case revolves around all acts being part of some fetish. They probably were, but that doesn't mean I consented to it. Dan shreds them for never saying that it was consensual. He claims it practically voids their argument. It does, I guess. If they're fighting rape, abuse, and assault charges, the difference between sex and something criminal is consent.

"Well, I clearly *implied* that this was a consensual act-"

"You're a lawyer! You should know better than to 'imply' something in front of another lawyer."

I smile a little bit at that and lift my head. Even that slight movement must've caught Nick's eye, because he yells at me from across the courtroom.

"Of course it was consensual. I *owned* Lin. He did what I said 'cause I made the money. I could do anything to him. He knew better than to say no. Even now, I could have him do anything for me. Right, Lin?"
"No, I won't live like that again! You can't- don't-" I have so much more to say. I don't get to say it, though, as my vision goes black and I no longer hear the chaos of the courtroom.

Sam

That fucking pyscho. It takes every ounce of restraint I have to not vault into the defendant's booth the second Nick opens his mouth.Then, Matt speaks, trembling with fear and adrenaline, absolute determination on his face. He hits his head as he falls, the *thwack* of it leaving the courtroom in sickening silence. The judge smacks her gavel and says the rest of the trial with be held with only the lawyers. The defence has no witnesses, she says. The remaining witnesses for the prosecution are dismissed. I'm relieved; Mattie can go home. He hasn't gotten up. Why hasn't he gotten up? He should have come-to by now. I nudge Sheryl.

"Mattie isn't moving. Somebody help him."

She stands abruptly, her steps too loud in the quiet. The judge nods at something she says, and Sheryl steps out. I stare at the door as it closes, then back to Mattie. He's still in the spot he fell over the table in front of him. I look back to the door. Sheryl is marching back in.

"Ambulance's on its way. He hit his head. I'm not willing to risk it."
"Thank you. If I'm dismissed, can I leave? Can I go with him?"
"Yes, Sam. That's what I asked the judge. She has no issue with you and Ricky both leaving with him."
"Rick?" I try to wave him down.
"Yeah? What's up?"
"Can you ride in the ambulance with Matthew? I need to drive there anyway so I have the car at the hospital to drive him home."
"Sounds good," He says, "Don't worry, Sam. He'll be fine."

I shift my weight between my feet and overall look uncomfortable. The paramedics show up shortly after. I see them off, before scrambling to start the car and follow them. I drive faster than I should, but I can't let Mattie out of my sight for any longer than I absolutely have to. I dash through the hospital entryway, throw my keys at the complimentary valet, and find the check in desk. I tell them I'm meeting the ambulance here and I'm promptly escorted to a room. Mattie's laying motionless in a bed, IV in one arm, blood pressure cuff on the other. I tiptoe in and sit at his side. He twitches and his eyes flutter, but don't open.

"You poor thing," I murmur, "Oh, Birdie. Wake up soon."
"He did," Ricky says, lingering the doorway, "Woke up in the ambulance and panicked. They had to sedate him with something."
"Really? What happened?"

"He was confused, didn't know where he was or how he got there. He tried to get out of the ambulance while it was moving. It was... intense."
"I hope he feels better when he wakes up this time."
"Me, too."

We lapse into nervous silence until the doctor arrives. She explains that Matt will wake up in a few minutes. He'll still be groggy and "easier to keep calm." I close my eyes and try to rub the exhaustion from them. Mattie starts moving a little, stretching. He opens his eyes and squints at me.

"Where am I?"
"You're in the hospital. You fainted and hit your head." I whisper.
"I didn't mean to make a scene."
"It's alright, Matt." Ricky says, finally sitting and not lingering ominously.

I fall forward with relief, resting my head on Mattie's chest, listening to his heartbeat. I was so worried. He rests a hand on my shoulder and rubs tiredly. It's relaxing after such a long and stressful day. I can see Ricky smirking at us, not maliciously, but instead proudly. He nods at me. *Yay, validation and familial approval.* I sit up and push Mattie's hair out of his face. He smiles at me and presses his head to my chest. I finally sit in my chair and hold his hand. It's been a terrible day but at least everything will be fine now. We'll be out of here soon. I curl into the chair. It's uncomfortable but better than nothing. The doctor comes into the room with discharge papers and we leave. I help get Mattie into the car, his arms around my neck. We drive home, tired and drained. I grab Mattie by the hand and take him to the apartment. I lift him up and carry him to bed. I pull blankets up around him and bring him pajamas. I let him change into them before laying beside him. I nuzzle against him and kiss his shoulder. He presses his back into my chest. I kiss his hairline and spoon up against him. He sighs heavily, chest heaving with his breath. I close my eyes and let myself be still. Mattie's already asleep, and I'm getting close. I rest my head against his shoulder and finally fall asleep.

I wake up in the middle of the night, no particular reason, I just wake up. Mattie's curled around me, legs wrapped around my waist. He looks peaceful and relaxed. I rub his hip and pull him against my chest. He wraps his arm around my back, hand fisting in my shirt. I smile and return to sleep. When I wake again, I find Matthew still clutching me. I don't bother untangling from him. It'll be nice to let him wake peacefully this morning, especially. I want to hold him a little closer today. He rolls over and yawns, peeking at me. I ruffle his hair and move to let him snuggle up to me. He gets up and patters into the living room, plopping down on the couch. I follow and sit at his side. I bring him a soft, knitted blanket and get to work on breakfast. I make waffles with chocolate chips, whipped cream, and strawberries cut to look like roses.

"This looks amazing! How did you make the little strawberry flowers? They're adorable." Matt gushes.
"Thanks, Birdie. I cut them to look pretty, wanted to make it a little fancy for you."
"Still pampering me, then?"
"If it's alright, yes."
"It'd be wonderful, Sammy."

I sit and cuddle up against him, eating leisurely. He seems to be doing okay after yesterday's events. He's leaning against my chest, eventually resting his head on my shoulder. I loop an arm around his shoulders and kiss his temple. I ask if there's anything he wants to do today.

"I want to have a quiet day in, if you don't mind."
"Sure thing. Is there anything you want to do around the house, then? Watch a movie or anything?"
"You're so sweet. Maybe we could watch a movie later. I don't have any plans."
"Okay. Whatever you want."

He smiles tiredly and falls into my side. He turns so he can bury his face in my chest. I run my hands along his sides as he grips my shoulders. He's shaking, tears soaking my shirt. It's all so sudden; he looked *fine.*

"Breathe with me, Birdie. In and out." I exaggerate my breathing and hope he follows my lead. He does, slowly but surely coming down from the panic that hit him. I rub his shoulders, back, and hips, letting him rest his head on my chest. Leaning away, I grab tissues to dry his eyes. I tip his chin up and wipe the tears from his cheeks. He thanks me before putting his head on my shoulder.

"What happened, love? It's alright, now, my dear. I got you. Tell me how I can help you."
"I don't know what I need. I'm just so glad you're here. I felt awful, you know, for not testifying. If he's found not guilty, I don't know how I'm going to live with myself. Yet you're still so good to me. You make me ridiculous food and spoil me rotten and it's all *so much.* After everything with Nick, I didn't think that my life could possibly turn around and it did and I'm just overwhelmed. All I need is good food and some cuddles. Just hold me for now."
"I can do that."

I trace his sides, holding on to the softness there. I nuzzle the top of his head, letting him tangle around me. He's sitting in my lap, tucked under my chin. He rests against me, my heart beating under his cheek. I almost fall back to sleep on the couch. I turn the TV on to reruns of *Golden Girls*, curling against the arm of the sofa. Matthew sprawls onto my chest, idly running his thumb along my knuckles. I reluctantly let go of his hand to better wrap my arms around him. His face is soft, eyes closed, and I revel in this. I doze off, *Golden Girls* still playing in the background. Mattie's more asleep than I am, starting to snore with his cheek smooshed against me. It's oddly relaxing to hear. Even when I'm getting ready to turn in for the night, those gentle snores are a constant comfort. I like the consistency, I suppose. I drift off into a deeper sleep, listening to his soft breaths.

Mattie wakes before I do. He's in the kitchen making lunch. Or at least, I think he is. I smell food. It doesn't smell burnt, for once. He's gotten substantially better at cooking. I walk in to greet him and I'm amazed with what he's made. There's a platter of grilled cheese sandwiches and a tray of sugar cookies on the counter. Mattie's standing in the middle of a fairly messy kitchen, looking anxious but proud.

"I can see why you do this so much. It's fun and I'm not even that good." He mumbles.
"I don't know about that," I say, "This looks good to me. I'm impressed."
"Well, we'll see how it tastes."

I take a bite from one of the sandwiches. It's fantastic. Mattie agrees and we take the platter back to the couch. I hold him loosely, one arm over his shoulders. His legs are tossed across my lap. I like sitting like this, with his warm tummy against my side.

He's always so much warmer than I am and with how much he likes to cuddle, it's like having the world's best heated blanket. Obviously, this is not all I think of Mattie, but it's a nice little benefit. I curl up against him, thinking about how much life has changed since we met. I would still be miserable with my job, my love life, and everything about myself. I don't really want to think about where Matt would be. I already know. Matt's phone rings, thankfully dragging me out of that train of thought.

"Hello?" Matt answers irritably, "Oh! Dan, how are you? Sorry, yesterday was a lot. Didn't want to be bothered today- what? No, you can keep talking. I meant a spam call or something. Yeah, I'm alright, no headache. All charges, huh? That's great. Thanks, really, you did great. Uh- yeah, yeah. Bye." And he hangs up.
"Was that the lawyer?"
"Yes. Nick was found guilty on all charges. He'll die in prison."
"That's awesome!" I nearly throw Matt off the couch in my excitement.
"Yeah. He's finally gone. It doesn't even seem real."
"It doesn't have to feel real yet, Matt," I murmur, calming down, "All that matters is that he's gone. He's never getting out."
"Thank God," He says and he falls on me, shaking like mad, but not crying, "I'm so tired of being afraid. I'm glad it's over."
"Me, too," I whisper, "But it is over now. You can rest."

He sighs and rests on my chest. I lean over and lay on the couch, Matt laying on top of me. I keep my arms locked around him. It feels good to know that things are getting better, but I don't *feel* better yet. I trace his spine and feel his muscles relax under my touch. I grab the remote from beside him and turn on some documentary. Mattie presses his face against my shoulder to see the TV. I play with his hair and twirl a few strands between my fingers. His hair is always so smooth, never tangled up in knots like mine. I let my hand rest where it is and close my eyes. I'm still tired from yesterday. At least now that I'm full from lunch and feeling safe, I might be able to sleep well. It's been a long time since I've felt consistently safe. I'm not used to it, but I want to be. I want to come home to hugs and movie nights on the couch, no fear or pain. I want to go on tour with Mattie and be on stage without worrying about Nick or my parents ruining everything. I want to kiss him in the hotel bed and order room service on a whim. I might actually get what I want this time. I relax into the couch and let sleep take me.

Matthew

I stay on Sam's chest for hours. He's asleep, so I watch TV with the volume low. I cuddle into his grip, feeling the muscles of his arms tense when I move. I hush him, tell him I'm not going anywhere. He settles, resting his hands on my back and hip. I sometimes wonder if he worries about losing me, even though I wouldn't leave him and he knows it. I know that some fears are irrational, but I wonder if he worries about Nick taking me away again. I worry about that sometimes, too, even though he's locked up. It's natural to be afraid of someone who's hurt you before. My therapist would say that, Sam says it all the time. I believe them.

Time marches on and soon it's time for the evening news. I figure that's around the time to wake Sam. He should eat dinner. I run my hands through his hair, down to his shoulders, trying to bring him gently into wakefulness. He rarely gets the chance for that, it seems. His face brightens as his stirs and stretches. I consider slipping away to let him wake the rest of the way up, but I stay. I kiss his hairline and he presses his face into the nape of my neck. I feel his lips curve as I sit up, pulling him with me.

"You must've been sleepy." I mumble against his temple.
"Didn't sleep well last night," He says, "Thanks for staying with me this afternoon. I needed this."
"You're welcome, angel."

I lean into his side, situating myself so that there's almost no space between us. I love the close contact. I think I've started to crave affection again. Sam's on the phone, ordering a pizza. He says he doesn't feel like cooking and *apologizes*. I tell him it's no big deal, that he has the right to be tired or just not want to do something. He smiles, if forlornly, and mumbles something about how he keeps forgetting that. It tears me open to hear him say things like that. I sit firmly in his lap and bracket his face with my hands.

"I know you keep forgetting. I'm going to keep reminding you. You are not a machine even though you've been treated like one far too many times. At your old job, in your old home, in old relationships. But Sammy, that's just it. Those are all old things. You don't need to please any of them ever again. You don't need to live up to some astronomical standard. It's more than enough to be yourself. You're human, darling, and sometimes you won't feel like doing something, or you'll be tired or sick. It doesn't make you less. You don't need to be sorry. I've wanted to tell you that for a while, so *I'm* sorry if it was a lot to take in."
"Thank you, Birdie. I appreciate the reassurance, love. It's good to hear that I'm enough. I don't always feel like I am."
"That's alright, angel. It takes time."
"I know. When we first met, I thought maybe I could do something useful, help somebody. Then, I needed help myself. I kept up all my walls to keep myself in, not to keep others out. I didn't want to be

vulnerable. I'd been hurt before. I wouldn't let it happen again. I made myself miserable. I couldn't keep it together around you. Mattie, I didn't stand a chance. Even that very first meeting, I physically couldn't keep driving. I came crashing through every wall I had built and it felt *good*. I don't want to go back there. You make me more human than I have ever been before and I'm ever grateful for that. I don't know if I ever would've been truly happy if it wasn't for you."

I stare at him, momentarily speechless.

"I know that was a lot to dump on you-" He starts, but I cut him off. "I had no idea! I'm so glad you told me, happy I could help. And, thanks for pulling over. You saved my life."

"What else was I supposed to do? I couldn't just leave you there."

I smile and launch at Sam's chest. He lets out a little puff of breath upon impact, but wraps his arms around me all the same.

"One of these days," He wheezes, "You're going to break my ribs." "Nah," I laugh, "But enough with all the serious talk. How about you just cuddle me until the pizza gets here?"

"That sounds good to me."

We end up entwined together, laying on the couch. It's not at all big enough for both of us like this, but that only serves as an excuse to be closer. I'm against the back of the sofa; Sam's towards the edge. I have a leg hooked around him to "keep him from falling off." His arm is laid across my middle, caressing a bit of pudge that is exaggerated in my current position. He whispers something that sounds a lot like "soft," but in a voice so reverent, I don't think I can be offended. Maybe *soft* is a good thing to him. The doorbell rings and Sam slides off the couch to answer it. He brings the pizza in and I nearly start drooling. It smells amazing. We eat straight from the box, not bothering with plates. It's been a long couple of days. I sit back and sigh contentedly with Sam right beside me. His hands are in my hair as they almost always are, his face gentle. I touch his cheek and lean in for one of the light kisses we so often share. It's sweet and chaste but still passionate as anything. I'm cupping his jaw and he's holding me by the hips. He's not holding me tightly, just enough so that I feel secure. I press forward again and slide one hand under Sam's shirt, placing it on his side. He shivers and pulls me closer, head tilting back. I kiss the dip between his collarbones. His fingers curl in my hair and then tighten, the slight tug not enough to hurt, not even close. Still, Sam freezes and asks if I'm alright. I tell him that I am and that if he does that again, it would be fine, nice even. He nods, relieved, and kisses the soft little pooch under my chin. I'm starting to discover how much I love it when he does that. He isn't trying to draw attention to my softness; he's enamored with it. He's worshipping me. He's tracing my sides, every once in a while glancing up at me with an enchanted expression. He's so tender, kissing my chest and stomach through my shirt. He seems taken by the experience as he drops his cheek to rest on my tummy. I don't dare breathe, eyes wide, completely open and vulnerable. It's suddenly too much, even though Sam's been so sweet, I don't want to be touched anymore. I don't want to go further.

"Stop," I rasp, "I need to stop for now."
"Of course."

He moves away to sit next to me, a small space between us. I thank him, leaning over into his chest. I tell him that everything was so great until it wasn't, that I don't know what happened. He nods and says that it's okay for me not to know. It's always a comfort when Sam says things like that. He can say he loves me all he wants; he doesn't have to mean it. When he says and does to make me feel safe, that's when I know he loves me.

As we head to bed for the night, I ask if he'd like to go to my dad's for the holidays. It'd be a lot like Thanksgiving, so I'm a little worried he won't want to come. Thanksgiving wasn't the greatest experience for him. Sam agrees to come with me, though, and I'm thrilled. I think I might be lonely without him.

The tour kicks off a week from today. It's a whirlwind getting ready and holiday shopping at the same time. The days fly by. We're working from seven to seven, seven days a week. Sam's baking is flying off the handle. We have more bread than we can push on our neighbors and so we've started calling loaves presents and giving them to coworkers. My big family celebration ends up being five minutes to say "Merry Christmas, Happy Hanukkah, and now we have to leave." But it's worth it. We're finally at the airport, heading out to L.A., where December weather is much nicer than in Chicago. I've been in an airport and on a plane before, as have Chris and Jamie. Apparently, Sam has not.

"I've never even been in a hotel! Why is it so crowded? Will it be this crowded on the plane?"
"It's airport rush hour, basically, so it's busy. It won't be this crowded on the plane. We'll be flying first class, so you and your lanky legs will have enough room."
"And so will Matt and his paunch." Chris jibes.
"Hey! It's just winter weight. I'm not usually *this* heavy."
"Sure…" He chuckles, "It's just good to you back to normal. You were skeletal, man."
"Thanks, I think."

Sam, who had been glaring daggers into Chris's back since his little jab, lets the tension fall from his shoulders. He walks a little closer to me, although whether it's because he's nervous or because he's feeling protective, I can't say.

"Does it bother you when Chris talks to you like that?" *I guess he's being protective.*
"No, it's fine. We didn't always talk to each other like that, but as we got closer, little taunts like that got more common. It's a brother thing, I think. I do the same thing with Ricky."
"Alright. I just really don't like the idea of you getting hurt, especially if it's somebody close to you."

I give Sam's hand a quick squeeze as we head to the gate. I can tell he's anxious about the flight. We sit and wait at the terminal, sadly that just gives Sam enough time to think of every way a plane can crash. Boarding is alright; I find a window seat, Sam's against the aisle. The first class section of this plane has two seats per side of the aisle. Chris and Jamie are across from us, already set up with that book series they've been reading and geeking out about. Sam has a death grip on the armrests. I consider pointing out that in a crash those will not save him, but decide that'd be entirely unhelpful. The plane taxis down the runway, and I hand Sam a piece of gum.

"Chew it when we take off so your ears pop with all the pressure changes. I've heard yawning works too, but it doesn't for me. Try both and see what works best."
"Thanks." His tone is clipped. *He's so stressed.*

I pry his hand off the armrest and lace our fingers. I trace the back of his hand, over the scar map of times he's forgotten to use an oven mitt or, more memorably, the time he tried to pet a raccoon when he was little. *I thought it was a cat!* He had said, while I was in stitches laughing. *And I'm the one that needs glasses...* I laughed, not at him, but at the thought of a young Sam, who's now very smart, thinking a raccoon and a cat are the same animal. I smile a bit at the memory. The plane is taking off, lifting off the ground. Sam is nearly breaking my hand with his grip, but once the plane is in the air, he relaxes.

"That wasn't as bad as I thought it'd be." He says.
"I'm glad," I say, and discreetly flex my hand, "Go ahead and rest, then. Being stressed for that long is exhausting. I'll wake you when we get there."

He nods and shifts in his seat, pushing up that poor armrest so he can lean on me. I give him a quick kiss goodnight, even though it's morning, and wrap an arm around his shoulders. Soon, his breathing slows and evens, his head heavy on my shoulder. One of the flight attendants comes by and asks if we need anything.

"Orange juice would be nice."
"Alright, I'll be right back with that. One glass or two?"
"Just one. I think he'll sleep through the flight."
"Okay," She smiles, "Say, aren't you those guys from that band?"
"Yes, we are *those guys from that band.*"
"You two are even cuter in real life than on your instagram! I'm sorry, I'm a huge Mayhem fan, I didn't want to come off as weird if you weren't actually who I thought you were-"
"It's alright. Do you want me to sign something?"
"Oh my god, yes! Here, sign this menu. It's got the airline on it. That way when I'm old, I'll remember where I got your autograph."
"Perfect."

I sign the menu and get my orange juice. Sam doesn't wake up for any of it, which is kind of a shame. He missed being called cute. I'm not sure if she was going for a *cute couple* kind of cute or a *you're both very attractive* kind of cute. Eh, a compliment is a compliment.

Sam

I'm woken up when we're preparing to land. I look up at Matt with big, sleepy eyes. He thinks I'm precious like this, he's said it before. My hair's all flat on one side and sticking up on the other. I fluff it a little and kiss his forehead. I'm still groggy when we get off the plane. We grab our luggage and find the ride Mary May arranged to take us to the hotel. It's an excessively large SUV, but that means it's big enough to fit all four of us. We ride in silence and anticipation. The hotel is extravagant. I didn't think it'd be this luxurious but I thought wrong. Jamie and I hang back to admire the outside of the building. Chris and Mattie get everyone checked in to our rooms. I discover that I'll be sharing a room with Matt. It'll be nice to come back after a concert and have him there. Probably less stressful for both of us. Jamie and I finally enter the lobby. We all take the elevator up, carrying luggage and buzzing with excitement when the doors finally open. Matt tosses his suitcase aside and look around the room. I'm doing the same, standing in a bedroom that's probably bigger than our entire apartment. Matt finds the room service menu and comes bounding into the bedroom.

"They'll bring a whole cake up here!" He pauses, "Should I order one?"
"Do it." I say and grin.

We set to unpacking after the order is placed. Matt breaks the news that *no, Sam, not all hotels are like this.* He ends up on the bed, curled up in fleece pants and an old t-shirt that he stole from me. I don't think I'll be getting it back. The cake arrives, just as elegant and decadent as everything else here. Mattie tears into it like he hasn't eaten all day, which makes sense. We got on the plane at ten this morning and it's a four hour flight. Then, we had to drive an hour to get to the hotel. We never had lunch and it's past three in the afternoon. Poor guy's probably so hungry. I manage to get a slice without losing a finger, but the vast majority of that cake is gone. He lays back on the bed and cuddles into soft sheets. I know he's well on his way to a food coma, but I decide to spoon up against him until he falls asleep. It doesn't last long, but it's comforting. He's warm and solid in my arms until I slip away. I'm not particularly tired, and besides; I need to find something to eat other than stollen cake. I order a panini and hope that the people doing room service don't hate us. I should've ordered it at the same time as the cake, instead of making them take two trips. The guy that shows up with my panini looks like he's twelve, but not like he's angry with me. I consider it a win for my social standing, and hope it's legal for him to be working.

Mattie's sleeping soundly as I eat my panini. He makes these adorable little noises every once in a while, pawing loosely at the sheets. I finish my food and curl in beside him. He quits grabbing the sheets and settles, his hand finding mine and pulling it to chest. He sleeps better with company, having somebody to hold makes him much more relaxed. I press myself more firmly against his back and nuzzle the nape of his neck, his curls tickling my cheek. I move so that I'm sitting up against the headboard, Mattie's arms around my waist. I watch cat videos on my phone and wish I could have a cat in the apartment. I wonder if Matt would want a cat, a dog, or nothing at all. I've never had a pet, but then again I've also never lived with somebody. I would have to take his wants and needs into account. Still, I smile at the thought of us with some pampered old cat. I can dream.

A few hours pass. Matt's awake and reading a book I've never heard of. He's cuddled next to me, brow knit with whatever's on the page. The room door buzzes like a keycard has been swiped. I assume it's housecleaning. Who else would have a key? But then, the familiar click of heels on hardwood approaches the bedroom until I can see Mary May standing in the doorway. She looks confused as she studies me and Mattie. He hasn't even noticed her yet, his head still on my shoulder.

"Aren't you cozy?" She says, unreadable as always.
"Oh! Mary May, I didn't even hear you come in. How are you?" Matt looks up.
"I'm good, thank you. How long has this been occurring?"
"How long's it been now, Sammy? Two months?"
"About that, yeah."
"I had no idea. Wait, are you keeping it private?" She at least has the decency to look embarrassed after barging into our hotel room unannounced.
"No, actually, I thought you already knew we were a couple." Matt says.
"Well, I'll be going then. Terribly sorry about this."
"Didn't you need something? I mean, you must have come here for a reason." I mutter, still a little scandalized.
"Just to see how you've settled into the room."
"Alright, see you later, Mary May."

Mattie just waves, nose already back in his book. I hold him a little closer. It's easy to forget how nerdy he is under that rockstar persona. Beneath all that leather and denim is a soft geek in *Star*

Trek-print fleece pants. It's probably time to bring him out of his book to eat dinner, but it can wait until after our food arrives. I ordered a few things from a Thai place that the internet says has the best chicken in California. The door buzzes again, but this time I'm ready. It's the delivery service, standing right outside the room. I pay the lady and she gives me a brown paper bag that smells divine. I take the food inside and find Matt already sitting at the table, set and ready. He must've put out plates and silverware.

"Did you set the table for us?"
"I don't know, must've been the table elves."
"Have you ever heard the old adage, *don't bite the hand that feeds you?* Well, I have the food."
"I'm sorry," He cowers away from me, and I worry that I've said something horribly wrong, "May I still have some?" *Holy shit, he thinks I'm going to starve him.*
"Yes, of course. Mattie, I'm sorry. I forgot how much the thought of hunger affects you. I would never do that to you. I'm so sorry, Birdie. I didn't mean to hurt you. Here," I hastily open the bag, "Take whatever you'd like. I didn't mean anything by what I said, I was just teasing you. I crossed a line and I'm so sorry."
"It's okay-"
"-no, it's not. I messed up."
"Yeah, but you apologized. I forgive you. It's gonna happen sometimes, where you or I do something that hits too close to home. You made a mistake. You handled it perfectly, though. It's okay."
"Thank you," I sigh, "This restaurant has nearly five stars on every site I saw. Try the chicken, the reviews said it was to die for."

The reviews are absolutely correct. I lean back and watch Matthew's contented expression as he finishes off the rest of the food. He makes that noise he always makes after a good meal. I feel terrible about what I said, even though I didn't know how it would affect him. He looks at me and purses his lips. I must look as guilty as I feel. He hauls himself up from the table and takes me hand. He brings me to the bedroom and lays down, patting the spot next to him.

"I'm sorry, Mattie," I whisper, sitting down, "I know that there was no way for me to know that what I said was going to hurt you, but I just feel terrible about it."
"Sammy, it's alright. I'm not mad at you. I know you're mad at yourself. I just need you to know that this isn't your fault. It was Nick that starved me. You've always, *always* given me food and taken care of me. It's not your fault that I still get scared of that, even though I have no reason to."
"I know you're not mad, but I hate the thought of hurting anyone. And I really don't want you to hurt anymore."
"I know you do. You're so caring, angel. It's one of the best things about you."

The end of the night sees us safe in bed, warm under the covers. I kiss his forehead and roll over so that we're chest to chest. My arm is around his back. I'm warm with him pressed up against me. It's plenty cozy under the duvet. I smile, smitten, and let him wrap himself around me. Mattie takes it upon himself to kiss me breathless before turning out the lights. I'm smiling up at him, lovesick and starstruck, as his cheeks dimple with joy. I reach out and poke his dimples, making him laugh. He's so handsome with his freckles and chubby cheeks. I'm laid out on my back with Mattie pressed up against my side. He twines our legs together and loops his arm around my chest. My eyes get heavy and I put my hand on the middle of Mattie's back. I fall asleep while he's still gently toying with my hair. In my semi-conscious state, I can feel Matt's hands fall still. His head nuzzles into my chest and I toss an arm over his shoulders. I relax and finally fall the rest of the way asleep.

Matthew

I wake up on Sam's chest. He looks so pretty when he's sleeping. I press my face into Sam's clavicle and start falling back to sleep. Soon, though, he's waking up and rolling over. I'm crushed underneath him. He quickly moves away and I kiss his forehead. I rub my thumb across his cheek bone. It's not particularly early in the morning when we climb out of bed to eat breakfast. We have to get up and go to the concert venue. It's an outdoor stadium that seats several thousand and is expected to be packed. We walk in through the backstage door. I do sound checks for more than three hours. A crew member is trying to pry Sam's old guitar away from him.

"You can have this one! It's so much nicer."
"No way. I've only ever played my guitar and I'm not stopping now."
"But it's trash-"
"How *dare* you!"

They give up on Sam's guitar. I have the microphone adjusted for my height (or lack thereof) and can sing without standing on tiptoe. I find Sam playing *his* guitar backstage, warming up with the riff from "Blackbird" by The Beatles. He's not paying any attention to me as I listen to him. I watch him smile and stare distractedly at the wall in front of him. He looks at me after the final chord. I tell him his guitar sounds fantastic. I give him a kiss on the cheek and wink at Gertrude, who has finally figured out that we're together.

It's not all that nerve wracking yet, but that's probably because the stadium is empty. I know it'll be full of fans soon. I'm excited to perform in front of this many people, even though the one person that needs to hear it won't be able to. She'll never hear the crowds, the music, the lyrics I've written. I hate doing this without her. I miss my mom so much. She believed in me and she'll never see that come to life. I hope she's watching me from wherever she is, listening to what I've written about her. I love her. I know the concert won't be the same without her, but I have to sing. I'll crank the volume and hope she hears me.

It's crowded. There are so many people and they're here to see me and my closest friends do exactly what we've wanted to do for years. I'm terrified of failing them. Not the fans, but my friends. Chris and Jamie were here when Mayhem was founded. Sam came to the rescue in the gig that ended up being our big break. I don't want to disappoint them. I sing for my life on that stage. I eventually start loosening up, telling little anecdotes between sets. People laugh when I talk about all the stupid things I always do. I know that these people are here for my music and my weird humor, but I somehow didn't think they'd like me. Even as the concert wears on, I'm still self conscious of my songs, my appearance. Especially my appearance. I love to defy conventional standards of beauty, don't get me wrong, but wearing tight jeans that are more holes than fabric? Normally, it's not an issue, but when this many people can see me... I start to wonder if I should have stuck to a hoodie and sweatpants. I could have passed it off as grunge. I don't know how this audience will react to me -a cute but well-into-chubby-territory *rockstar-* wearing something that I've been told time and time again "isn't for me."

I wish my mom was waiting backstage for me right now. She'd know what to say to me. Chris is starting the first song of our final set, so I guess I'll have to think about this later. The last chord rings out and we all walk backstage. I'm hit by how empty it is. Gertrude and Mary May are there, so are a handful of crew members, but other than that? It's vacant. There's a tour bus parked out back; we're all loaded in and given time to change from our stage outfits. I sit down in one of the seats and feel myself going numb. Sam slides in next to me. I barely notice. He says something that I don't hear. I start sobbing and clinging to Sam's t-shirt. He must've changed from his stage outfit like I did. Sam wraps his arms around me and cradles me until the ringing in my ears dies down.

"It was just *so much,*" I mumble into his chest, "So many people came to see me and-"
"Take your time, lovebird. Tell me whenever you're ready."
"-She wasn't one of them."
"Your mom?"
I nod and sniff.
"You made her proud, Mattie. She always said you'd make it here. I know that doesn't make it any easier for you."
"I just wish she could've heard me."

Sam stays quiet, just squeezing me tighter. I'm too tired to get up when the bus pulls up to our hotel. Sam gently helps me up and carries me to our hotel room. I fall into bed and tuck the blankets around myself. He comes in to find me, spooning up behind me and nuzzling the back of my neck. I relax in his arms a little, but stay too tense to sleep for at least an hour. Sam seems stressed as well. I don't know how long he stays up after I finally fall asleep.

Sam

I fall asleep against Matt's back. He's snoring when I wake up. I trace up his chest and feel him brace against me. He doesn't stir even though it's nearly noon. I wonder if he's feeling alright. Well, I know he's not feeling *great,* but sleeping this late seems a bit excessive for just "not great." Then again, when did we get back to the hotel last night? If I slept until noon, maybe there's no reason to be concerned. I yawn and head towards the shower. The hotel bathroom has a footed bathtub that I think Mattie would like. He loves bubble baths and those sparkly, fizzy bath bomb-things. I personally don't see the appeal, but that's alright. There's shower here which is much more my speed. I step in and let the warm water wake me slowly. It's a comfortable start to my day. I'm towelling off when Matt starts calling out for me.

"I'm in the bathroom." I say through the door.
"I- I'm having a- Sammy, please just come out here."
"On my way."

I put my pants on (backwards, but that doesn't matter) and stumble into the bedroom. He sounded so panicked when he spoke. I find Matthew sat upright in bed, scared stiff. He has his face in hands, his cheeks wet. I sit nervously on the side of the bed. I gently rest my hand on his shoulder. He looks at me with relief and falls into my chest. I hug him tightly as he rests his cheek on my shoulder, relaxing minutely. We stay like that for a few minutes.

"Thank you," He whispers, "I was having a panic attack, you know how it goes."

"You're welcome, and yeah. I know how it goes, Matt," I smile as he gets up, "It's lunch time, too. Do want to go out or order something? We could get room service."

"Let's go out. I need to get out of my head. A change of scenery might help."

"Okay."

There's a pasta place not far from the hotel. We get a seat in the corner, able to see the door, but not close to it. I hold Mattie into my side in that little corner booth and we order food. It seems like Mattie's feeling better. I still can't help but worry. He seems content to be eating a bowl of soup. I kiss Mattie's temple, trying to keep this good thing going. He's so tough, having just been through that concert last night, and now having to do another one tonight. I didn't know about his mom. Well, I knew that she died when he was in high school, but I had now idea how invested she'd been in the band. She would've been so proud of that concert, but she didn't get to see it.

Everything he's been through would've been awful on it's own, but to have all of that stacked on one person? He's so strong. Meanwhile, I'm still tired even though I slept so late. I guess it doesn't matter how late I slept if I went to bed at one o'clock in the morning. My sleep schedule is going to be a mess for quite a while. Well, it's only a small price to pay for living my dream.

"Are you okay?" Matthew says.

"Yeah, why?"

"You're staring off into space and you haven't even touched your food."

"My food's here?"

"Yes, Sammy. Are you sure you're feeling alright?"

"I'm really tired, but that's all," I yawn, "I need to sleep on a strict schedule or else I won't feel like I've slept at all."

"We should head back to the hotel after lunch. You could take a nap. It doesn't help with the scheduling aspect, but you might feel a little more rested."

"I could try that," I say, but then I think of something, "What would you be doing while I'm sleeping?"

"I'll be sleeping too. I don't think I slept well last night. The concert was stressful, and I don't usually sleep well when I'm stressed."

"Alright, nap it is then."

I finally start in on my soup (it's cold) and Matthew leans on my shoulder. It's nice for me to be held right now, but I'm nodding off. I'm comfy and tired and that is a dangerous combination. I yawn into a spoonful of soup. The waitress brings over our tab and Mattie pays before I can fight for the check. I don't particularly have to anymore, what with both of us in a famous band and all. I still try to pay though. It just seems like the right thing to do, splitting the check or alternating who pays with Matt.

It's time to head back to the hotel. I walk out of the restaurant with my arm around Mattie's shoulders. We sit on a bench in the shade, waiting for our Uber. It shows up and opens its doors; the driver gives us a funky look as we climb into the backseat.

"Aren't you in Mayhem?" They ask.

"Yeah. We don't have a car in Cali, though, and still need to get places."

There's no other conversation on the way to the hotel. It's awkward, but luckily our ride isn't far. We walk into the hotel lobby and wait for the elevator. The moment we get into the room, I fall face first into the bed. Matthew lays beside me, gracelessly shucking off his jeans and cuddling against my back. He makes himself comfortable, settling his soft frame behind me. I smile to myself as he holds me into his chest. I'm half asleep when Mattie asks me something.

"Do you think that I should cover up more? Like, wear the kind of stuff I've been told to?"

"Only if *you* want to change how you dress," The second part of what he said bothers me, "Has someone been giving you a hard time recently?"

"No, I just felt really emotionally naked on stage yesterday. I like wearing what I do, but I don't know if other people think I look... I don't know. Ugly?" He deflates on the last word, "I've been told a lot of shit in my lifetime. It lingers even when no one's saying it."

"I highly doubt that the people coming to our concerts think that about you. You're trending on instagram, for one, and for two, you are *gorgeous*. Truly, Birdie, you're handsome to the point that sometimes I'm overcome by it. That you, a talented and beautiful man like you, is with me. I can hardly believe it sometimes. I know that I don't give myself enough credit, but even if I tally the points from a more neutral perspective, you are still way out of my league. You are everything I've ever wanted and more."

"Thank you, Sammy. You're so kind to me," He stops and looks away, "Am I really trending?"

"Yeah, Mattie. Most of the comments are great. Wanna look?"

"I think so, yes."

We look for a while. There are a lot of nice comments, a few nasty ones, but that's life. Mattie seems happier after seeing that most people think he's good in some way or another. We lay back down and I start dozing off again. Mattie wraps around me, his hand laid across my chest. I hold his hand and fall asleep. It's the most relaxed I've been in a long time.

Matthew

I get some good sleep after talking to Sam. Sometimes I get insecure about the things I love most, probably *because* I care about them so much. I don't want to look bad on stage, but I've decided that looking like *me* isn't bad at all. I want to go on stage tonight as myself. I'm already feeling better about the rest of the tours.

Sam is still asleep in my arms. We need to get going -Mary May is waiting for sure- but I can't stand to wake him. I slip out of bed and put my jeans back on, deciding it'd be frowned upon to leave the hotel in my boxers. I find myself something to eat before we have to leave for the venue. There's some rustling from the bedroom, then Sam comes out with his hair askew and his clothes still rumbled from sleep. He glances at the clock and starts putting on his shoes.

"No need to hurry." I say.

He nods and keeps getting ready. I find a pair of sneakers and put them on. The tour bus is already outside when we get to the lobby. I take a seat next to Sam and rest my eyes for a minute. I cuddle into Sam's shoulder while he hums to himself. The drive goes too fast, and then I'm shoved into a dressing room backstage. Gertrude is waiting for me with a pair of black jean shorts and a pastel tie dye crop top. She drops them onto a nearby chair and tells me that she's been making a clothing line with Lucifer Jones, and she wants me to try these on.

"Wait, as in my friend Luci? In Ricky's band, Defy? Sure, I mean of course I'll wear this, it's cute as hell, but why me?"
"More guys should wear crop tops. It's freeing."
"You sound like me in high school." I mutter.
She laughs, but continues her statement, "You're a major social influence. If you wear something that isn't traditional to the role you've been given, it'll get noticed. People love how go against social norms in your appearance and such."
"Alright, gimme the crop top."

I actually quite like it. It shows off my stomach (that's something I never thought I'd say) and is much cooler for the Los Angeles heat. The shorts are nice too, a little tighter than I would usually wear, but all and all I look fantastic. I admire myself in the mirror for a good couple of minutes before walking into the main area backstage. Sam is there, guitar strapped over his shoulder. He sees me and brightens, a delighted grin spreading across his face. I saunter over and smile, getting up on my toes to kiss his cheek.

"I like the shirt," He says, "Pastels look incredible on you."
"Thanks, angel."

Mary May shouts that it's time for us to go on stage. I head out to cheers with Sam, Chris, and Jamie not far behind. I have more confidence this time, and I think the audience can hear it. I'm proud of myself, which is something I don't often say. I feel comfortable in my skin on stage and happy with what I'm doing. I have a life direction and the power to influence others to maybe be more comfortable with themselves. A few of my songs really pound that point home.

I feel like I've earned this. I deserve to be happy. I'm having the time of my life; I have everything I ever wanted as a kid. I didn't have much growing up, paycheck to paycheck kind of life, but I had enough then, too. I had food and safety and my friends and family back then. I lost all of that for a while. I think I'm just glad to have that back. It's not about having my "dream life," it's about having my life back. I had almost forgotten how to do what I want. That's over now. I have my life back, my dream job, and a partner that respects me. I am, for the first time in a long time, truly happy.

We keep touring, finishing our second night in LA and moving to Seattle, then Salt Lake City. We traverse the country and I keep getting better at living on tour. Sam's doing better, too. He's taking care of himself, sleeping better, eating without needing to be reminded, and actually *enjoying* himself, as near as I can tell.

We went to a restaurant Krista recommended in New York last week. It had a really romantic atmosphere and fantastic food. It was a real date, like an *outside the house* date. I loved the whole affair of it, getting dressed up and going out. Sam made a show of us being together, holding my hand across the table.

We've made it all the way back to Chicago. It's March now, but still cold. At least it's not snowing. This is our last concert of the tour. It's time to debut a few songs, keep things relevant. I'm a little nervous about how the songs are going to hit. It should be alright, though. Nothing major has changed, stylistically. I think the lyrics are meaningful, not just for me. I'm more concerned about the fact that my family will be in the crowd tonight. I can't let them down.

Sam is tuning his guitar (which he apparently named "Julia Child") and staring blankly at a wall. He always does that when tuning. He's so concentrated on listening that he nearly goes cross eyed. On one occasion, his left eye was looking straight ahead and his right was looking up. I have a fantastic picture of that. I walk right through his supposed field of vision and he doesn't notice. I then turn around and do it again. I don't realize that I'm pacing and mumbling to myself until Mary May tells me not to wear myself out. I stop and sit down. Sam, evidently finished tuning, comes to sit beside me. I rest against his shoulder to catch my breath.

"Is everything alright, Mattie-Bird? You're not usually this nervous before a performance."
"My dad's going to be here. I don't want to disappoint him."
"You won't. He'll be proud of you for doing what you love."
"I know, but what if I screw up? What if-"
"It'll be alright. You don't need to worry about this. I know that doesn't help much, but it's true."
"Thanks, Sam."

I tuck myself under his arm, hiding the best I can. Sam squeezes me gently, taking my hand in his. I hold him until it's likely past time for us to be out on stage. I watch the crowds shift and cheer as I step out. The world spins and my vision goes fuzzy at the edges, but I push on. I sing the usual sets that I've been singing all along. I tell my little anecdotes between sets, with Chris, Jamie, and/or Sam piping in with details. I relax as time goes on, but Sam seems more tense. His shoulders are up to his chin, his eyes wild. I spare a few glances to him, but there's nothing I can do during the concert, as much as that hurts.

The final set is new, even Chris, Jamie, and Sam have never heard me sing it. I wanted it to be a surprise, but seeing the state Sam's in at the moment, I'm starting to regret my decision. Still, I announce the last piece I'm to sing tonight, smiling softly at the audience.

"I have a new song for all of you tonight. It's going to be released for real soon, I think. No promises. The current title is *Saving Grace.* Might keep it, might not. Please don't hate it?"
"They're not gonna hate it, Matt." Chris scoffs.
"You haven't even heard the lyrics yet!"
"So?"
"So-! You are insufferable."

The song starts anyway. Jamie strums a muted chord with all the precision I've come to expect from him. The crowd is almost silent when I come in with the lyrics I've written and revised so many times.

You don't have to stop my dear
Just keep on driving down the road
Cuz it's never going to stop my dear
The damage is done

You should have never stopped my dear
Now you're stuck with my mood
Cuz I'm a good deed
And you won't go unpunished

So stop, stop, stop
Don't try to care about me

My dear, am I really not
A burden to you?
You must be my saving grace

Because you didn't have to stop my dear,
My angel driving down the road

So stop, stop, stop
Please stop to save me
So stop, stop, stop
Slow it down for me, oh

You didn't have to stop, stop, stop

The crowd is standing, cheering. I'm vaguely aware that I'm sobbing. I'm smiling, but tears are streaming down my cheeks. I look at Sam, who's shaking in place, and go to take his hand as we walk off stage. He smiles feebly at me. We're loaded into the tour bus and taken back to the record company. On the way there, I cuddle up against Sam's side. He doesn't move into my embrace like he usually does. I try nuzzling his shoulder, but he still doesn't move. He's stiff and tense, staring at the floor.

"What's the matter, Sammy?" I say, "You seem upset or stressed or something."
"My mom was in the front row. I don't know why, maybe she just likes the music, but I didn't like seeing her. I should really let it go now, though, shouldn't I?"
"Yeah, probably. We're going to the studio now, then home. We'll be back in the apartment tonight. You can just relax and sleep in a bed that isn't a weird hotel mattress. I'll be right here with you the whole time."

"Thank you, Mattie. That all sounds lovely. I'm looking forward to some time off."

Sam finally loosens up a bit and wraps his arms around me. I have to let go of him when we reach the studio, but for now I'm comfortable. We aren't at the studio long, just so a couple executives can give us a quick congratulations. Then, Mary May puts us all in an unmarked van with no windows. It feels surprisingly unlike kidnapping; trust me, I know. Mary May says it's so that we can get home without any tabloids or fans following us. I appreciate that immensely. Sam and I are dropped off at our apartment complex, but not without Chris asking why we haven't moved somewhere nicer.

"You can afford it," He says, "So why haven't you moved?"
"I like the kitchen." Sam says.
"Never even crossed my mind." I say.

I'm still overjoyed to have a safe home. The fact that it's a fairly cheap two bedroom, one bath apartment doesn't bother me in the least. Sam walks into the foyer first, greeting the landlord. She's handing someone a key and telling them not to lose it again. The elevator is out of order again. It's good to be home. The apartment is the same as we left it, except for a little more dust. Sam has barely closed the door by the time I've left a trail of clothes, grabbed a towel, and sunk into the bath.

"Matthew? Where'd you go? Wait, are you already taking a bath?"
He sounds smug through the door.
"Maybe."
"You are precious. Take your time, love."
"Thanks, angel."

I submerge myself in the tub, letting my face go under for a second. I get out when the water's cold and I'm missing Sam. He's asleep in a kitchen chair with the oven on and a timer due to go off in five minutes. I shake my head fondly, puttering around the apartment for a little more than four minutes before stopping the timer so it doesn't chime and wake Sam. I retrieve a tray of brownies (Sam's typical relaxation food) from the oven and turn it off. Then, I gently touch his shoulder to wake him up. He looks at me with half closed eyes.

"I got the brownies and turned off the oven. You should head to bed, Sammy. You'll be stiff if you sleep here all night."

He grunts in agreement and stumbles out of the kitchen, complaining that his leg is asleep.

"Well, don't sleep in chairs, then. You could've just gone to bed."
"I was staying up, waiting for you."
"Oh, sweetheart, you didn't have to do that. I take long baths, you know. I would've come to bed and cuddled up with you afterward."
"I'll remember that, thank you."

I lay in our bed for the first time since we went on tour. Sam has already collapsed next to me. He's sound asleep with his arms around my chest. It's easy for me to rest here. I didn't realize how tired I was until I laid down. It'll be nice to get some good sleep.

I wake up to find Sam watching TV next to me. I must've nestled into his side in the night, my head on his chest. His arm is slung over my shoulders, giving me a squeeze before moving his hand to my hair. I sigh and melt into his touch. I missed waking up to lazy mornings like this. I yawn and roll over, leaning against the pillows and Sam's shoulder. He's watching some reality TV show. I kiss his jaw and drape my arm over him. He pulls me closer, hand sliding down to the small of my back.

"Good morning, my angel."
"G'afternoon, songbird."
"It's not that late, is it?"
"It's twelve thirty."
"I didn't keep you waiting, did I?"
"I just woke up ten minutes ago," He covers a yawn, "So do we eat breakfast or lunch?"
"Or brownies?"
"Sure, why not?"

He wraps his arms around me, then pulls me up to go to the kitchen. I sit in a chair and consider asking Sam whether he wants to talk about seeing his mom. I decide to wait until after "lunch," give him some time away from the incident. Sam places a plate of brownies in front of me, sitting across the table. He kisses my hand. I smile smittenly at him. It's definitely not the right time to ask him about the incident. He talks about how happy is to be home. I smile and nod, telling him even the broken elevator was great. He snorts and agrees.

"Y'know," He says, "I think my mom wants to apologize. For everything. I don't know what to do about it, though. I want to talk to her, I think. Tell her that I understand she was in pain and trying her best. I just don't want her to think what she did was okay."
"Maybe call her and tell her that. Or ask her out to coffee or something if you'd rather speak face to face."

"I might ask her to go to that cafe with the good hot cocoa. And...
would you come with me?"

"If that is what you want, of course."

"Please come." Sam sighs and reaches for his phone. He dials his
mother's number and waits as it rings.

"Samuel?" She says, voice distorted through the phone's speaker,
"Why are you calling?"

"You were at the final Mayhem concert. Why?"

"I wanted to see you. You didn't need to see me, I just wanted to
see what you've done to make yourself happy. I'm sorry, Samuel. I
failed you, I know that. I wanted you and Krista to have a better
life but I was so scared. I didn't know how to leave."

I squirm uncomfortably. I was ready to give Sam my blind support,
but I know how hard it can be to leave, and that's without having
to get a divorce and having a custody battle. I have to feel for her.

"I know. Let's meet at a coffee shop and talk face to face."

"Alright. What time?"

Sam

I'm seated across from my mother. Matthew is next to me, his
hand on my thigh. I can barely sit still. I have a cup of chai tea
that's too hot, and Matthew is leaning on my shoulder.

"I was scared of him." She says.

"I know." I say.

"That doesn't make up for what you and Krista went through. He
tore up the family and... I didn't have enough money or courage to
divorce him. Make him leave. I was scared he'd kill me if I tried.

Then what would happen to you kids? I still could've done better, there must've been something-"

"No. Don't beat yourself up for being afraid. You could have done better now because *you* are doing better. I'm not going to lie, I hated you when Sam told me about what he went through. What happened wasn't okay, don't take this as condonation, but I know how terrifying abuse can be. It is his fault, not yours." Matthew murmurs, voice deadly.

"He would've *killed* you?" I whisper, "I am so sorry I held you responsible. You did your best, given the circumstances."

"I wish it would have been better." She hangs her head.

We leave the cafe and for the first time in probably twenty years, I hug my mom. She's crying on my shoulder. Matthew comes up behind me and wraps around both of us. He says something about pulling the car around and I nod. He comes back and puts the car in park. I jerk away from my mother, not used to her showing me affection. I slide into the car, feeling too much to feel anything at all. Matthew starts to drive away and the scenery blurs out the windows. He looks at me at every stoplight, brow knit with worry. I smile at him, but it's forced and I'm sure he knows.

"I'm proud of you. She was- That wasn't what you were expecting, was it?"

"No, it wasn't. You know, I wish she had it easier, and not just because it would've my life better. She must've suffered, I mean, you've been through that and you didn't even have kids-" *I want to sink through the floor of the car. That came out so wrong.*

"I don't have kids, no. I can't even imagine how stressful that would've been. She had to protect more than herself," His gaze flicks to my horrified face, "Quit looking like that. I'm not offended, Sam. I know what you meant. It's two different situations. I went through some of what she did, but not all of it, and vice versa."

"But I phrased it terribly. I didn't mean to belittle you."
"And you didn't, Sammy. Let's head home; it's lunch time. We can cook together again, if you'd like."
"Sounds great."

Matthew plants himself on the counter as always. I fill a pot with water and put in some dry pasta. I have a saucepan burbling with stewed tomatoes and spices. I hold a spoonful of sauce to Mattie's lips and he happily slurps it. He leans back on the counter with a contented hum. I hide a smile as Mattie rocks back and forth on the countertop. He's precious, truly, and I love him dearly. As I strain the pasta and ladle sauce over it, Matt wraps his arms around my waist and rests his head on my shoulder. We take a seat at the kitchen table. I'm exhausted from today. Hopefully some comfort food will make me feel a little better. Matthew is watching me intently, like he's trying to decipher life's greatest secrets. I give him another feeble smile.

"You don't have to do that, you know." He says.
"Do what?"
"Smile when you're miserable. You don't have to force yourself to look happy."

I nod and turn back to my food. He's right, but I still feel like I'm disappointing him if I'm not as peppy as usual. I pick at my food more than I eat it, too lost in thought to care. Matt decides that I'm not going to spiral today, though. He grabs my plate and takes it to the living room. Then he takes me by the collar and all but drags me to the couch.

"Sit. Eat. You *will* take care of yourself today. I know this has been hard on you but I will not let you fall into another rabbithole. You don't have to claw your way out of those alone, Sammy. I will help you. So I am going to get you a glass of water and you are going to care about yourself as much as you do others. I know it's tough. I'll be right back, okay?"

"Thank you, Birdie." I don't smile. It feels good.

He comes back with water and box of store bought cupcakes. (You know, the ones with the little swirl on top?) I flop over onto his shoulder as he hands me the water. I ask if he could tell me more little things about him I don't know yet. He smiles broadly and launches into a story about his college lab partner, who apparently hated him.

"I don't blame her," He says, "I hardly ever had the work done because of Nick and-"

"When did you go to college?" *I thought Nick was a more recent development.*

"I started when I was 20. I took a couple years off to travel with Ricky and the guys. Started dating Nick my second year, and it took awhile for things to get bad. This poor lab partner had to deal with me senior year and... you know the rest."

"Yeah. Alright, now why is this a happy story? I want to feel better."

"Because," He chuckles, "She so clearly knew something was wrong in my life that she wrote two copies of the lab reports, changed the wording, and made sure I passed that class. I got a B. She was such a hardass to everyone else, too. I was shocked she was doing this for me. She loathed me for making her do so much work, but she could have let me fail. I told her that once and she said she couldn't live with herself if she did that. That she had to help me 'get out of there' somehow. If getting me to graduation so I can make money on my own, if that's something she can do, she was going to do it."

"She helped you get your degree."

"Yeah. We'd known each other beforehand so she knew I wasn't just slacking. I still wonder where she is now. I mean, I've seen her name in research articles before, but how is she? Is she happy? She's so fucking successful, but that doesn't mean she's happy."

"Have you ever contacted her, after everything?"

"Yeah, we text all the time. I just wonder if her life is complete, if she has everything she wants. Is she seeing anyone, does she want to be?"

"Seems like she's got things figured out."

"It does, but," He sighs, "What if she's just as miserable as I was? What if she's staying at work all day 'cause she doesn't want to go home? Sorry, you wanted something uplifting and this isn't it."

"That's alright. I think you're worried about nothing, Mattie. There's always a chance that those are someone's motives, but I don't think you've seen any proof, have you?"

"No, I haven't."

"That's good. Everyone on earth has something in their lives they aren't content with, whether it's big and scary or that their favorite butler is on maternity leave. I think she'll be fine."

"I know she will. Thank you, Sammy."

Mattie leans against my side and unwraps a brownie-cake-thing. He hands it to me and I eye it dubiously. No food should have a freshness date several years into the future. It isn't right. I eat it anyway and it isn't bad, despite the fear it instills in the hearts of men. Mattie's already scarfed down two. I nuzzle the top of his head. He looks at me and smiles, the slightest hint of chocolate on his lips. I lean down and cradle his cheek, kissing him sweetly. He melts into me, arms slung around my shoulders. I lift him up and onto my lap. He breaks the kiss and rests his head on my chest. I lean back into the couch as Matt folds himself into me. He's warm and solid against me, chest rising and falling with his breath. I wrap an arm around him as he shuffles to get more comfortable. I kiss his forehead and turn on the TV. We watch a renovation show and talk some more. I tell him about my roommates in college and their parties. I tended to shut them down and/or sleep in the library. The librarians liked me. He laughs and says I would've hated his crowd on fridays.

"The rest of the week we'd probably get along fine, but friday was party day."
"You've never struck me as the party type."
"I'm not, but Ricky is. I just tagged along. Some of the places I went were real hole-in-the-wall celebrity joints, too, so that was fun."

I hold him a little closer. He relaxes in my arms and closes his eyes, murmuring something about taking a minute's rest. I nod and stroke his hair. I can barely stay awake myself. Soon, his head lolls against my shoulder. I gently scoop him up and carry him towards our room. He looks blearily at me as I lay beside him. I tuck the blankets around us and tangle myself with him. He nuzzles into my neck and wraps his arms around my shoulders. I kiss his cheek and fall asleep in his arms.

Matthew

Sam is wrapped around me when I wake. He's awake enough to rub circles on my sides, but his eyes are still closed. I stretch and smush my face into the dip of his shoulder. He drapes his arm across the small of my back and pulls me on top of his chest. I grope around for his other hand, lacing our fingers. The blankets are strewn around us, resting at my hips. Sam reaches for them, pulling them up until they meet my shoulders. He settles his arm back around me with a gentle *pat-pat* on my side. I blush and press my face harder against him. I'm still not used to anyone liking my softness. It's overwhelming but wonderful to have Sam hold me like this. He has no idea how much it means to me. He lightly touches my back, moving up and down my curves. I absolutely melt into his hands, his gentle ministrations. He presses firmly against my shoulders, tension in my muscles falling away. I make a small noise that is the human equivalent of purring. Sam chuckles and rubs my back, hand sliding lower down my spine. I close my eyes and rest my cheek on his chest.

I don't know when I fell back to sleep, but I wake to find I've drooled on Sam shirt. It's gross for me and must be even worse for Sam. I sit up and look away, apologizing for the disgusting stain. He laughs and says it's fine, that he's glad I slept well. I smile gratefully then smittenly at him as he tugs the shirt off and throws it vaguely at the hamper. He puts on a clean, dry shirt. It's old and faded, unraveling at the seams. It's also my favorite shirt of his to steal. Well, not *steal,* but borrow with the possibility of never returning the thing. I don't think Sam minds. He smothers me in gentle affection and chocolate and knitted blankets whenever I wear something of his. I asked him why he does that, once. I was a bit worried that it was some kind of a possessive trait, but I was wrong. He said it's because when I take something of his for comfort or enjoyment, it makes him happy. He likes that I associate *him* with comfort and safety. I was hit with so much love when he said that, that it threatened to spill out from everywhere. So, yeah, I don't think Sam minds when I take his shirts. (And he is right about why I take them. I hole up on the couch wearing a worn out tee shirt when he's out doing something. I like the comfort.)

With Sam redressed, I follow him into the kitchen. He left his phone there when I dragged him off for some self care. When he turns it on, he has seven missed calls from Krista. His face twists up as he calls her back. He drums his fingers on the counter, waiting for her to answer.

"Why the fuck did you speak to her?" Sam recoils from his phone at Krista's shouting.

"Because she came to my concert and I wanted to know why. She didn't expect me to see her but I did." He says and puts the phone on speaker.

"Well, she just called me and told me about the divorce and whatever she went through. I'm sure it sucked for her, but I've been working forty hour weeks since I was an actual child. I don't know what to think when she does shit like this. I'm sure she means well, but I just want her out of my life. She can divorce him, good for her, but I don't want her calling me. If you want her back, go right ahead and let her break your heart again but don't have the time for that horseshit."

"I want to give her a chance."

"You do that. When the other shoe drops, don't come crying to me unless you're looking for an 'I told you so.'"

"Alright, I will," He sighs, "I know you hate her, Krista, but let me try. I'm not doing it for her; I'm doing it for me. Let me have this."

"Fine. You can try, but don't let her hurt you, Sam." Her voice breaks at the end of her words.

"I won't. Thanks for looking out for me, Kris."

Sam hangs up. I look at him worriedly. He scrubs a hand down his face and shakes his head. I hug him around the waist, pulling him close. He doesn't relax right away, but I squeeze him tighter. He shuffles closer to me after a few seconds, sinking into the embrace.

I run my hands along his shoulders and guide him to the sofa. He sits down and leans into my side, turning the TV on for some background noise. He turns and tips my chin up. I love it when he does that. He presses his lips to space between my brows. I lean into him slightly, hand gravitating to his chest. He smiles softly at me then leans down for a tender kiss. I press myself into his chest. He makes the softest noise I've ever heard and winds his fingers through my hair. I move away from him, just to drink in the besotted look on his face. I kiss him again, letting myself feel his chest and just hold him. He lifts me up and into his lap, resting his fingers on my hips. I curl my arms around him, hands lingering at the hem of his shirt. He's giving teasing touches to my stomach and thighs. His fingertips sink into my sides. I settle myself more firmly on his lap and slide my hands under his shirt. His hands wander across my tummy and up to my shoulders. I tilt my head to get closer to him. Sam pulls away from me, lips kissed red. I smile at him, give him a peck on the cheek.

"Do you wanna keep going?" He whispers, breath hot on my face.
"Yeah, I do. I think I want to take this to the bedroom. No promises on how far I'll want to take it after that, though."
"Okay, Birdie."

I stand and stumble into the bedroom, twined with Sam. He takes my hand as he props me up on the pillows. I sigh and throw my leg around his waist. He lays out across my chest, seated between my knees. I reach out to tangle and tug and hold, moving in slow tandem with Sam. He's all over me, cautious as he lifts the hem of my shirt. I nod and tell him it's alright. He's placing feather kisses on my stomach, nuzzling at the freckles and stretchmarks there. I sigh in enjoyment. He's careful with me, but doesn't treat me like I'm fragile. It makes me feel appreciated. I pull him back up towards my face. I kiss him rougher than I usually would, but today is a day for firsts. He's holding my hip, squeezing harder than I'd like. I squirm away from him.

"Hey, angel, I know you like the hips but ease up, okay? You're not going to get all of me in one hand."
"Sorry, sugar. Did I hurt you?"
"A little. It's alright, though, you didn't mean to."
"Okay. Can I kiss you again?" *He's doing better at not over apologizing.*
"I'd like that."

Sam leans forward and catches my lips. I hold him and trace the muscles in his back. His heart's beating so hard I can feel it straight through him. I tuck my face into his neck, smiling against his skin. We're so close that I can barely tell where he ends and I begin. That's not a bad thing, not right now. I like being melded together like this. I feel incredible, my body's being worshipped and my *everything's* being praised. He's on top of me, over me, covering me and shielding me. It doesn't feel overwhelming. For once in my life, this feels good. Sam's kissing and touching and-

I push Sam off of me hurriedly. I don't know why. He's looking at me worriedly. I shift back, only to find that I've already slammed myself against the headboard.

"Mattie?" I blink and glance at him, "Hey, honey. How are you feeling? Do you need a glass of water or anything?"
"No, I'm alright. Well, not alright, but I don't need anything. I don't know what happened."
"That's fine, Mattie. I actually have a theory about what might've happened. I... bit you? That sounds gross, sorry. I was getting a little overzealous, I guess, and I probably nipped. Again, sounds gross, but I think it happened."

"Don't worry about it sounding gross. I like that you're honest with me. Also, that would make sense with what I did. Nick used to-" I stop myself. I don't want to live under his thumb, "I don't do well with teeth. Everything else was great, Sammy, but no teeth."
"Got it. I'll be more careful. Do you want to stop for tonight?"
"Yeah, I do."

I do not apologize, even though I want to. I have nothing to be sorry for. Sam cuddles against my side, head on my shoulder. I grab my phone from the nightstand and pull up a video of turtles eating watermelon. It's relaxing in an odd way. I lean into Sam and tilt my phone so he can watch. The video is on autoplay so we end up down a YouTube rabbithole. Currently, a man is playing accordian for a herd of cows on screen. I pause the video and shut off my phone. It's getting to be time for dinner. I peel away from Sam and tell him I'll order something to eat. It's been a long day; we deserve it.

We eat fried chicken in bed. It seemed like a good idea at the time. I am now hauling sheets downstairs to our apartment building's laundry room. Sam said he would bring them down in the morning, but I didn't want grease stains festering overnight. So, I start walking down the final set of stairs and into the basement. I'm carrying more sheets than I probably should. I can't see over them, so I adjust my grip. Sadly, that makes me trip over a loose end and tumble down the stairs. Now, I'm laid out on the laundry room floor, tangled in sheets, dignity in shambles. I didn't get hurt, thankfully, but I have to free myself from my accidental straight jacket.

Apparently, this ordeal has taken long enough that Sam got worried. He's standing behind me, trying very hard not to laugh.

He helps to untangle me and tosses the sheets in the wash. He asks what happened and I say,

"We are never eating chicken in bed again."

Which isn't an answer, but he laughs and agrees, wrapping his arm around my shoulders. I smile a little, relieved that he's willing to hold me even after seeing that. I still get so nervous about keeping up some impossible appearance. I don't have to do that anymore, nor do I try, but I still worry about it. I lean into Sam, who is staring impatiently at the elevator. It chimes and we step in, holding the railings for dear life as it rattles and bumps and stops at random. The elevators here are a death trap. We make it safely back to the apartment. Sam puts clean, non-chicken stained sheets on the bed as I putter around and try to look useful. I flop backwards onto the bed and roll around. Sam comes over and baps me with a pillow.

"You untucked the bottom sheet. Get up so we can fix it." He smiles at me.
"Alright, but can we watch a movie in bed after?"
"Of course."

Sam fixes the bed and lays down. I curl up next to him and rest my head on his shoulder. He turns on the TV and finds something to decent watch. I have no interest in actually *watching* the movie, I just want to cuddle my angel. It's nice and warm under the covers, and they don't even smell like chicken. I press myself flush against Sam's side and wrap my arms and a leg around him. He sighs contentedly and holds me around the middle. I finally look at what movie we're "watching" and I'm surprised.

"I thought you hated horror movies." I say.

"Eh, I haven't watched one in a long time. I might be over it."

He is not over it. He has his hands over his eyes and is still flinching. I offered to find a different movie, but he's determined to get through this one. I hold him close and comb my hands through his hair. He opens his eyes and *squeaks,* promptly shoving his face into my chest. I consider changing the channel, but Sam's made it clear that he wants to get past this fear, so I opt to hug him instead. He clings to my shirt and slowly lifts his head up. It's not good timing; the creature is on screen and terrorizing some newlyweds. Sam throws himself away from the TV, burying his face in my stomach this time. I can feel him panting with how scared he is. It's time to pull the plug on this.

"Why don't we watch this some other time? It's nine o'clock and you don't need to be kept awake by this." I change the channel to the Food Network.
"Okay. Thank you, Mattie." His voice is muffled against my shirt.
"You're welcome, darling," I rub his shoulder, "I turned off the movie, so you can move if you'd like."
"Can I stay here for a little while? You're comfy."
"Sure, Sammy. Stay as long as you'd like."

He falls asleep there. I smile fondly at him and turn off the TV. I have to roll over to turn out the lights, but he doesn't stir. I drift off shortly after him, holding him loosely. I'm not asleep for long, woken by Sam's tossing and turning. I wait for him to wake up on his own. He does so with a gasp, flailing and thrashing into a sitting position. I turn on the light and reach out to Sam. His eyes are wide but relieved as he leans into my arms. I wrap around him and rub his shoulders until his breathing steadies. He pulls away and murmurs at about not watching scary movies before bed anymore. I nod and beckon for him to lay next to me. He does, snuggling against my back and slinging an arm over my middle. I reach for his hand and lift his knuckles up to my lips. He melts and rests his hand against my tummy once I'm done kissing it. We sleep easy after that.

Sam

I should get up. It's morning and I'm hungry, but Matthew's sleeping sideways across my chest. I don't want to disturb him. I sigh and lift him off of me. He opens his eyes a little, smiling at me before falling back against the pillows. I feel around for the door, not turning on any lights yet. I safely make my way into the kitchen and cook an omelette for myself. I'll make one for Matt when he wakes up. I've never been able to relax in the morning like this before. It feels fantastic to just cook some breakfast and crawl back into bed. I can sit on the couch and cuddle my boyfriend all day. It's strange. I'm not used to sleeping in and snuggling. I love it, don't get me wrong, but I'm still fidgety. I can't sit still; I feel like I need to be working.

Matthew comes pattering into the kitchen, stretching his arms over his head. I get a glimpse of his soft tummy as his shirt rides up. I avert my gaze in favor of cooking another omelette. I don't want to stare, even if Mattie says it's okay. It feels rude and I don't deserve it in the first place.

"Sammy, I can feel you overthinking. I saw you look at me. I know I've told you this before, and I know you don't believe me, but I want you to look at me. You make this face like I'm the eighth wonder of the world. Besides, I just like it when you look at me. It makes me feel good."

"I know, but I feel like I don't deserve you."

"Really? Sweetheart, you deserve the world. Is it something I did?"

"No! No, of course not. I want to look and admire and hold you but- I just don't want to screw things up."

"You wouldn't screw things up. You don't need to deny yourself pleasure and indulgence. I'm telling you it's okay, that I want this."

"Alright, thank you. I'm still working on letting myself have nice things."

"I know. Also, that egg is done."

I turn back to the pan and quickly flip the omelette onto a plate. Mattie takes it without complaint, even though it's a little burnt. I sit down with him at the table. We don't talk anymore, giving me time to think. I need to cut myself some slack because I do deserve nice things. Some of the things I deny myself aren't even indulgences. I don't always eat or sleep when focused on something. I force myself to finish my work (even if it's nothing important) regardless of what it does to me. I hate what I do to myself, but I do it anyway. Maybe I should work on myself, now that I have the time. I sigh and take an aggravated bite of egg. Matt glances up at me, tilting his head to the side. I meet his eyes and shrug.

"Just thinking about how bad I am at self care." I say.

"You can get better. Practice."

He makes it sound so easy. I reach for his hand and give it a brief squeeze before slipping off to wash the breakfast dishes. Matt shoos me away, saying that I cooked, so I should get to rest. He's right, but I still don't want to stop working. It's all I've ever been good for. I compromise with myself and only dry the dishes while Matt washes them. I can get better. Matt wraps his arms around my waist and pulls me to the couch. I nuzzle into his shoulder before draping myself across his lap. He smiles and pets my hair. I'm cradled by the soft crease between his hip and stomach. I fall to the side and allow myself to relax. Matt asks if there's anything I want to do today and I suggest going to a movie.

"In the theater?" He says, sounding surprised.
"Sure. There are like seven action movies out right now."
"Alright, sounds good. I'll wear sweatpants and smuggle in some candy."
"That right there is why I love you."

He grins and pats my head. I grab my phone to find some tickets online, never moving from Mattie's lap. We head out around lunchtime, knowing that lunch will be candy and popcorn today. It's a nice treat, especially for Mattie. He absolutely loves sweets. I don't care for them as much, but I like them.

The theater is dark and cozy. I move the armrest out from between us and tuck Matt under my arm. He wiggles a little, gets comfy. The previews are rolling as he drags candy out of his pockets. I yawn, the darkness of the theater putting me to sleep. A Junior Mint is shoved into my mouth. I laugh and nearly choke on it. Mattie snickers and pats my shoulder. He leans into me and shoves a handful of popcorn into his mouth. The movie starts and I watch Mattie's fascinated expression. It's so cute, how he twitches at all the action. I hold him to my side and kiss the top of his head. He sighs contentedly, resting his head on my chest. He seems pleased with everything happening around him. My focus alternates between caressing whatever bit of Mattie I can reach and actually watching the movie. The movie is good, though it didn't pay particular attention to physics. Cuddling Matt makes it much better. I kiss his forehead, earning a warm smile. He snuggles up against me until he's nearly in my lap. I steal another Junior Mint and get comfortable in Mattie's arms. He hums happily and nudges his face into my neck. I doubt he can see the screen from there, but he seems pleased.

By the time the movie ends, Mattie's half asleep on my shoulder. I twirl his hair until he lifts head. He stretches and stumbles down the shadowed aisle. I follow, equally uncoordinated. My legs are stiff from sitting so long. Matt tosses an empty Ziploc bag in the trash. I blink at the harsh light of the hallway outside the theater. Mattie's still wrapped around my waist, his shoulder pressed flush against my side. It's thrilling but foreign to go out on dates where I enjoy myself this much. He makes me happy and we go places we *both* like. I've never had a partner that doesn't walk all over me. I usually just let them take what they want, even though I know it's wrong. Like with Jess, I knew she was manipulative, but I didn't want to be alone. I was alone so often that I would do almost anything to have some company. I don't have to do that anymore. I just have to be myself, be respectful. I'm in the healthiest relationship of my life and I couldn't be happier. It doesn't feel real. I'm still looking at the love of my life and waiting for him to walk away. I know he wouldn't, not right now, but I'm suffocating in my own fear.

I don't remember falling, but now I'm sitting on a sticky bench, Mattie hovering me. My vision is blurry and spotted, then dark. I come to a second later, Matt holding my head so it doesn't hit the wall behind me. I shiver and watch my chest heave for breath.

"I'm right here, angel. Breathe with me. You're safe." He whispers and shelters me.
"I'm sorry." I whimper.
"Nothing to be sorry about, Sam. Let's go home."

I manage to calm down a little in the car. Mattie has a symphonic orchestra CD playing. I sniffle miserably. *What is wrong with me?* All this for something that isn't going to happen. I start crying again, hiding beneath my sleeves. I'm ashamed of always being so afraid. I know it's not my fault, but I feel broken. I climb out of the car and go upstairs to find our old couch, numb and exhausted. I collapse onto it, Mattie following me worriedly. I fold into a ball and make myself as small as possible. I close my eyes and let myself sob. Matt drapes a blanket over me and plops down beside me. I don't want him to see me like this. He wraps his arms around me and holds me. I try to shove tears back into my eyes, but end up wiping them on a tissue handed to me. I sniffle and rest my head on Mattie's chest. He strokes my hair and pats the top of my head.

"You're alright, my dear. I got you, I'll take care of you." He cooes reassurances that I do not deserve.
"I'm sorry." I say again, then again and again until my throat burns.
"Sammy, honey, what brought this on?" He says softly, "Maybe talking about it would make you feel better."
"I've never been happy before and now that I am, I'm scared I'm going to lose everything. My life was desolate before I met you and the band. I can't go back there, Mattie. I can't lose this." I gesture vaguely to the apartment.
"You're not going to lose me, Sam. I know that's not the only thing you're worrying about, but if it helps, I'm not going anywhere. I love you, angel. Everyone we've met with the band cares about you. You're incredible; you don't need to worry about losing your new life. It's not leaving anytime soon. Here, why don't you teach me how to make macarons?"
"Alright, but those take awhile." *And the suggestion came out of nowhere.*
"That's the point, Sam. It'll take your mind off things."

I smile and follow him into the kitchen. He's so considerate. I find the things needed for macarons and pat Mattie's knee. He's sitting up on the counter, watching attentively. I hand him a jar of nutella and a piping bag. I tell him to load the bag, pointing vaguely with a wooden spoon. He nods and starts scooping nutella, definitely sneaking some for himself. I whip egg whites until they form a meringue. Then, I slowly fold in flour, sugar, and cocoa powder until the macaron cookies are ready to be baked. Matt has started eating the nutella with a spoon. That's a difference between us: he'll eat half the batter before it's baked, while I like the delayed gratification of waiting for things to cook and cool. Matt puts the jar down and slides the tray of cookies in to bake. I set a timer and lead the way to the couch. Matt sits and leans on my shoulder, warm and full of chocolate. I wrap an arm around him and thank him for suggesting we do this. He brushes it off, telling me that it's no trouble to help me take better care of myself. I hold him closer. The timer chimes and I spring up to grab the tray from the oven. Matt tries to snatch one, but I bat his hands away.

"They need to cool," I say, "Then we can ice them and have actual macarons. That's what the bag full of nutella is for."
"Fine, I'll wait."

We watch a few minutes of some sitcom, (they all blend together), then I go to ice the macarons. Matt insists on being the one to sandwich the two halves of cookie together. I have no objections to that. After all the cookies are assembled, I make a little toast. Not the food, but a glasses-clink-together-and-everyone-says-cheers toast. Except, I don't clink glasses with Mattie. Instead, I bump my macaron against his and mumble "cheers." He smiles and giggles with genuine glee. He doesn't laugh at me, but he's amused and fond and *I am so in love with him.*

"Cheers, Sammy," He smiles, "God, you're so sweet. I love you."
"I love you, too."

We munch and snuggle on the couch for a while. Mattie's curled up under a blanket, his head on my shoulder. I drape my arm around him, tugging him in closer. He hums and melts into my side. I never want to move, not when I'm so warm in a way I've never been before. I won't lose this new life, I know that now, but I don't think I could bear losing him, either. I'm in so deep, so scared to lose him. It's normal to want to keep your loved ones close, but I don't want to make it seem like I wouldn't let him go if he wanted to leave. It would hurt, but I would never force him to stick around. Relationships like ours need both people's full commitment. I sigh and lean on him. I'll hold him close for as long as I can.

Matthew

Sam still worries himself sick. He's doing so much better, going to therapy and all that, but he bottles everything he thinks isn't important. I think it's pretty damn important if it stresses him out this badly. I wish there was some magic cure for him, something I could do to make him feel better. Obviously, there isn't. I would have gotten it for him already if there was. I hope he talks more about what bothers him. It would help him, I think. I know how hard it is to talk, but I hope he tries. Well, he is trying. He's trying so hard to get better. I can't ask anything else of him. I just wish he could find something that works better for him. I remember his therapist said something about seeing a psychiatrist, but Sam didn't want to do that. I thought it'd be a good idea, but I didn't want to push him. I might push him a little bit more now. Antianxiety meds work great for some people; they can make therapy easier. Besides, it wouldn't hurt to see a psychiatrist, would it? It's not like he would have to take their advice, but he could get a second opinion. I really think this might help him. There's no miracle cure, but maybe a different approach could help.

"So, what do you think, Sammy? A psychiatrist might be able to help you."
"I don't know. I would be willing to make an appointment, but I don't want to go on medication. I'll only do it if the doctor thinks it'll practically cure me."
"Alright. Let's find the name that the therapist gave you."

The doctor has time to get him in the next morning, and Sam insists that I go with him. I wholeheartedly agree, willing to do almost anything to get him in the office. He looks extremely uncomfortable in the waiting room, to the point that I almost ask if he wants to go home. I stop myself. This is to get treatment for his anxiety. I can't let him back out now, even though it hurts. He leans on my shoulder and I give his hand a gentle squeeze. The receptionist calls us back to the doctor. Sam is shaking slightly, and I'm starting to regret bringing him here. Maybe I made a mistake. Maybe this was too much for him. Maybe-

"Hello, I'm Dr. Martha Brown," A young lady with gorgeous, curly hair says. I'm jealous.
"Hi, I'm Sam and this," He points vaguely in my direction, "Is my partner Matthew." *Already past the "boyfriend" stage! Wahoo!*
"Okay, Matthew, will you be staying for the appointment?"
"Yeah, I'm moral support."
"Alrighty then. Let's get started."

Dr. Brown lets out on onslaught of questions. They aren't difficult, but there are so many. Sam is twitching again, looking around the room with fearful eyes. I place my hand on his knee. He relaxes a tiny bit and keeps answering. The doctor nods thoughtfully at him. Eventually, she says that Sam has a panic disorder and generalized anxiety disorder. He stiffens at the diagnosis, looking at frantically between me and the doctor.

"Having a panic disorder is not the end of the world, Sam. You can receive therapy and medication if you so choose. It says on your chart that you've been in therapy for a few months, is that right?"
"Yeah, it is."
"Okay, so here's what I think you should do. I suggest that you stay in therapy and take the medication I am prescribing."
"Does it have side effects? I really don't like meds, I don't trust 'em."
"That's alright, Sam. These might make you either nauseous or hungry, but those are the main side effects. They seem to mostly affect appetite. You should be fine."
"Okay. I'll try it."

I'm shocked. He must be getting desperate to even consider medication. I hope it helps him. I squeeze his knee under the table. He lays his hand over mine and grants me a smile. The doctor writes a prescription and hands it to Sam, telling him to take it to the pharmacy. I hug him the moment we leave the clinic. He falls into my arms and tucks his face into my shoulder. I kiss his hair and hold him close. We walk to the car and I drive to the pharmacy. Sam drops off the prescription and I snoop around for the molasses candy he likes. I buy some just as Sam saunters up to the counter. He wraps his arm around my shoulders. I lean into his embrace and walk out of the store. He smiles as he peeks in the bag I'm holding.

"You bought these for me?"
"Yeah," I say, pressing closer to him, "What you did today took a lot of courage and I wanted to get you a treat."
"Thanks, Mattie-Bird."

He holds my hand over the gear shift before tearing into his candy. I feel warm all over seeing him like this. He's getting help and I am so fucking proud of him. I decide that I'm going to spoil him today, not the other way around. When we get home, Sam sits comfortably on the sofa, more relaxed than I've seen him in months. I wonder if just seeing somebody and knowing help is out there made him feel a bit better. He wiggles in place and tugs a blanket over himself. We keep the apartment cold because blankets are good. I sigh fondly and ruffle his hair.

"I'm going to change into something more comfortable. No innuendo, though, I'm just tired of jeans." I say.
"M'kay, lovebird. Come sit awhile when you're ready."

I do, curling in next to him and cozying up in the blanket. Sam wraps himself around me, leggy octopus man he is, and I settle into him. He starts telling me a story from when he was a kid, how he and Jackson wandered off to an alleyway and right into a street fight. He chuckles because apparently, Jackson got them lost a few blocks from their school and they still couldn't get home.

"So we had to call Krista," He smiles, "And tell her we got lost and meandered into danger. I was maybe ten, at the most. So Krista stole Dad's car and picked us up. She somehow knew how to drive, which was concerning because she was in middle school, but we got home fine. She was so mad, though. *Out of all the places to get lost, Sam!"* He does a scary-good impression of her.

"You didn't get hurt, though?"

"No, we were fine. I was more scared of what Krista was going to say than the fight itself."

"Pfft. She is a spitfire, isn't she."

"You didn't even phrase that as a question."

"I didn't need to."

He laughs and rests his cheek on my head. I ask him what he wants for dinner, and he says he doesn't care. This leads to a fifteen minute conversation of *well, I don't care what we eat, what would you like? I don't know.* Eventually, I grab one of many takeout menus that hold residence on our coffee table. We're having Italian. Sam's phone chimes right after he hangs up with the restaurant. His prescription is ready at the pharmacy. He says he'll go get the food and his meds in one trip. I nod and kiss his cheek. I don't want him to leave, but this is important. He goes, and I set about finding plates and silverware. I also grab a bottle of wine and glasses, completing the table. Sam comes in, arms full of food, and I rush over to help him out. I place the bags on the counter, Sam close behind me. He's reading the directions on his medication. I loop an arm around his waist and he leans into me.

"Just one glass of wine for me," He says, "I'm supposed to 'limit alcohol consumption.'"

"Alright, just one."

We sit to eat and I wiggle a bit in place at how good the food tastes. I haven't had lasagna from here since before the tour! That is way too long. Sam is smiling at me from across the table. I smile back, sticking my leg out and hooking his ankle. He looks so comfortable and I couldn't ask for anything more. I love him so much. I finish my food with a sigh and take my dishes to the sink. Sam hugs me from behind a moment later, hands resting on my stomach. I've come to love it when he does that. I look at him over my shoulder and feel him hold me tighter. He kisses my head and drifts off to grab a towel. We sit down and cuddle up on the sofa once the dishes are done. I lean my head onto his chest and listen to his heartbeat. Sam holds me, his thumb stroking my cheek. We stay there in silence, finding no reason to talk. I pull myself closer to him, into his lap, until there is barely a breath between us. I settle there, eyes closing and world slowing. I doze off, but have to wake for Sam get up and take his medication. I wander to the bedroom and fall (face-first) back to sleep. I am vaguely aware of the bed dipping when Sam climbs in next to me, when he tucks himself into my shoulder, but I'm still safe and warm so I don't truly wake until the next morning.

Sam

It takes two weeks for my body to adjust to the medication. I spend the first week eating everything in sight and the second unbearably nauseous. Today, it seems like my stomach has settled. I'd gotten so used to panicking that *normal* feels weird. I walk around the apartment, looking for Mattie. He stormed out earlier this morning without even eating breakfast. I'm worried about him. Maybe I should look for clues about why he left, but I don't want to snoop. I do it anyway. There's red ink on the calendar in Matt's scrawly handwriting. *3/21: mom.* That's is. Just "mom." I don't know what it means and he's not picking up his phone- wait. His mom died in the spring. What if today is the anniversary of her death? Where is he? Is he alright? I sigh and pull at my hair, a bad habit I've yet to kick. My phone rings and I scramble for it.

"Hello?"

"Hey, Sam."

"Mattie! Oh thank God you're okay. I didn't know where you went and you were so upset-"

"Yeah, no, I know. I'm under the 12th street bridge. Can- can you come pick me up? I walked here and it's cold."

"I'm on my way, Birdie. Go in a store or cafe, maybe, to warm up."

"Good idea, I love you."

"I know, dear, I love you too."

I drive too fast to get to him. He texts me the name of the store he's in and I park without paying the meter. I scoop him into the car and drive off, already looking for a spot to pull over. I find a 7-11 and pull into the parking lot. I glance over at Mattie, only to see him crying. He's sobbing, really, a snot-dripping kind of cry that is breaking me into pieces. I lean over the console to hug him and clings to me like velcro. I hold him for a solid few minutes, until his shaking relents. He pulls away from me and I get a good look at his face. He's a wreck; his eyes are bloodshot and sunken, his cheeks stained with drying tears. I drive him home and usher him to the couch, rolling him in a blanket then pattering off to boil water for tea.

"You don't need to be alone today," I whisper, "I'm here if you need me."

"Thank you."

I bring him chamomile tea and some pastries I made yesterday. He grabs my wrist as I start to walk away and in the smallest voice he says, "don't leave me." I sit beside him and wrap around his shoulders, tracing the spot on his back that never fails to calm him. He sighs miserably but melts into me nonetheless. I cradle him and pick up a muffin, trying to get him to eat something. He huffs and turns away, burying himself further into my chest. I drop the issue for now, even though I *know* he's hungry. I can't let him go hungry.

"Do you need to talk?"
"She died ten years ago today and she had been doing so well. She had been remission a month before she died and then she got sick. She was so sick and it went so fast. She was fine, she was *fine-*" He breaks off and nuzzles into my collar, "I miss her so goddamn much, Sammy. She never got to see me do anything *worth seeing,* she never got to meet you, and now it's too late. I thought she'd pull through. She'd done it before, but-"

He stops to take a heaving breath. I don't know how to help him. He'd been so ostracized from everything because of Nick that he fell out of touch with his family. Maybe that's making this hurt that much worse.

"I wish I could tell her about everything, see her at the holidays, just call her on the phone."
"I know you do," I murmur, "I can't even imagine. What would make you feel better, lovebird?"
"Give me the muffin. I should eat something."

I grab the discarded muffin from the coffee table and press it to his lips. Matt rolls his eyes but takes a bite. I smile, relieved, and feed him the rest of the muffin. He sighs and nuzzles into my palm when he's finished. *It's an oddly intimate gesture*, I think, as I'm kissing his forehead. He holds my hand and places it on his chest. He's warm as always, his heart beating under my fingers. I hug him into me, pulling a blanket over us. He reaches for the remote and turns on the TV. He finds a feel good movie and settles his back against my chest. I wrap my arms around his waist, wanting to give him some security. I grab the rest of the pastries and hand them to him. He eats them and wiggles a little to get comfortable. I pat his side gently. He smiles and watches the movie. It's as nice as it can be, considering the day today. He starts to doze off in my lap and I hold him closer so he won't fall. I turn the volume down on the movie so can rest if he wants.

"I was alone last year," He says softly, "I'm not alone anymore. Thank you for that, Sammy."
"You're welcome, Mattie."
"I'm so happy to be with you now, darling. You are a part of my home, my family, the very core of what I hold dear. I am safe. I can let go of all the pain I've clung to."
"Yeah, you can. I'm glad to be held in such high regard, songbird."
"You deserve it, angel."

I hug him tighter. He exhales and leans into my arms. I lift him up and turn him to face me. He rests his face on my shoulder and coils his arms around my shoulders. I trace the curves of his hips and up to his shoulder blades. I hum and press kisses to his hair. I feel him smile against my neck. I ask him what else would help him and he says he wants to go to an arcade. I agree wholeheartedly; I've always wanted to see the arcade Mattie went to as a kid. We head out and Mattie says the place looks the same as it did ten years ago. I toss an arm over his shoulders, though it's quickly thrown off as he runs to a pinball machine.

"No! My highscore's gone." He's climbed halfway on top of the machine.
"The odds of it lasting ten years aren't good."
"I know, but I wanted it to last forever."

I hide a laugh and wander around a bit. The floor has that ugly bowling alley carpeting and neon lights are emanating from so many games. I wonder if this is what it feels like to have a stroke. The music is loud but decent, some kind of 80s mix. I find my way back to Mattie. He's bouncing next to Dance Dance Revolution. I am pulled onto the platform and before I really know what's happening, the screen in front of me lights up with little arrows that I have to hit.

"Mattie, I can't dance, you know that!"
"That's fine, just have fun with it!"

And I do. Matt is shockingly good at DDR. It's impressive in a nerdy kind of way, spending the afternoon at a coin operated arcade kind of way. He flips his bangs out of his eyes as he steps off the platform. I spot a few crane games, the ones you could find in a grocery store. There's a cat plushie in one of them and I want it. I know that five year olds do this kind of thing, but I don't care. If I want to try to grab something from a rigged game, I will. So I put a quarter in the slot and move the joystick until the claw is over the cat. It actually does grab the cat, but drops it soon after. This means war. I put in another quarter, then another. I end up spending $4 on the stupid thing, but I got it. I run over to Mattie to show him my bounty only to find that he has twelve little toys already.

"How did you get all those?" I say, jaw on the floor, "It took me sixteen tries to get this one!"
"I bought them with tickets from the other games. Those claw things are impossible. I'm amazed you got anything."
"Huh. Maybe I should have tried that."
"Yeah, maybe." He laughs.

We walk over to the arcade's bar. It has pizza and it's well past lunch time. I tear into it without really cutting a slice. Mattie does the same, ending up with half a pizza in his hands. He murmurs some kind of thanks for coming here with him. I tell him I had fun. I leave "I would do anything for you, anything to make you happy" unsaid. He already knows.

We leave the arcade with arms full of useless prizes. I will likely keep them forever. Matt sits in the passenger's seat and covers himself in stuffed animals. I take a picture of him and turn phone so he can see it. He laughs from somewhere no sorrow touches. He asks if I could post the picture online. I smile and nod, posting it right then and there. The drive home is relaxing, even if I did have a few plushies fall on me after a hard left turn. I carry some of the loot upstairs to our apartment and help Matt *name all of them.* I suppose it makes sense, with today being so full of nostalgia.

By nightfall, I'm nestled in bed with Mattie, a box of chocolates, and thirteen little plushies. I fall asleep to the hum of the TV and sugary kisses. It's so cozy and achingly soft. I sink into the pillows and a warm embrace. I know when morning comes I'll have to get up and leave our nest, but for now I will soak up every second I have. I will let myself have nice things. I deserve this.

Epilogue

Matthew

I realize something when I'm snuggled in Sam's arms. I have a family. I have a home. I have love beyond what I could've imagined. I still need to heal, yes, but I am alive despite thinking I wouldn't be. I press my lips to Sam's cheek and rest against him, letting my eyes fall closed. I have overcome so much to be here. I thought my life was over after my mom died. I thought my life was over because of Nick. I have survived more than I thought I could, and I am happy now, curled against Sam's side. I wouldn't have met him if my life had gone how I planned. Everything works out in the end, I guess. I'll get up in the morning to a home full of heart. I'll eat three full meals, cuddle with Sam, and live better than I ever dreamed. I have no real complaints about my life, which is strange to some people. I've said in interviews and social media that the overwhelming majority of my life has been good. No one seems to believe me and I don't exactly blame them. I've been through a lot, but I have a good life now. I always have. As I drift off to sleep for the night, I stare at the ceiling and give a silent thanks to my mom.To have a life like this, someone must be looking out for me.

---

3 years later

"Oh, Sammy look! Her name is Snail."

Sam turns to face me. I'm holding an old, scruffy-looking cat. She's well cared for, but her fur is in a constant state of disarray, according to the volunteer I've been talking to. The cat tilts her head and meows at Sam. He walks over and scratches her behind the ears.

"I love her," He says, still petting her, "Is she adoptable yet?"
"Yes," The volunteer says hurriedly, "She's been in the shelter since she was a kitten. All her siblings got adopted. She's five years old."
"We have to take her home, Sam."

"Absolutely. She is magnificent. Yes, yes you are. You're a gorgeous little baby, yeah."

We welcome a new family member into our house. We moved out of the apartment shortly after getting engaged. Sam proposed to me in the living room, too nervous to wait until we got to the restaurant where he was planning to do it. I said yes (obviously) and we still went to the restaurant. Sam proposed again at the restaurant so that maybe we could get some free celebratory food. I got a molten lava cake. Our new house is small but not cramped. It's a two story with a studio area upstairs. There's a fireplace that I love and a garden that Sam grows herbs and vegetables in.

Sam carries the cat inside. We've scattered some cat toys and scratching posts around. There's a cat bed at the foot of our bed. Snail ignores all of this and sits on the sofa. She stretches and lays on her side. I sit down next to her. Sam sets about finding some cat food. He was in titter about how skinny the cat is the entire drive home from the shelter. I think that's just how cats look, but hey. Anyone living with Sam is required to pack on the pounds. (Yes, this requirement applies to me.) Snail takes a few steps before plopping down on my lap. I smile at her and rub her chin.

I have a family and I'm making one of my own. I love that concept. *I'm engaged to the love of my life and we have a furry daughter named Snail.* There is nothing better than that. Well, except maybe for when Sam and I actually get married. I twist the ring on my finger. I'm thrilled to see what each day brings. I will not waste the life I thought I'd lost, not when I have so much left to give.